TF176574

D0492970

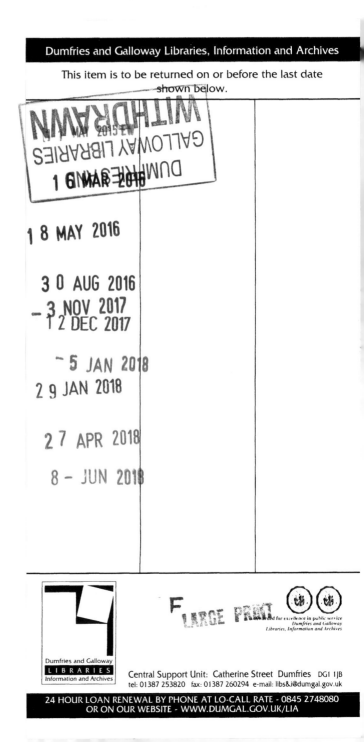

DEAD ERNEST

Nobody expected Ernest to die, least of all Ernest...

The death of her husband after sixty years of miserable, abusive marriage leaves Annie Bentley trying to understand her feelings. Soon afterwards, two uninvited and, at first, unwelcome visitors come into Annie's life: her teenage granddaughter Ophelia, and Andrew, a local vicar who is struggling with his own unhappy marriage. As the story of Annie's life unfolds and she learns to face her demons, Ophelia and Andrew also find some answers about themselves. Finally, Annie and Ophelia fly to Austria to scatter Ernest's ashes – but will this allow Annie to come to terms with her past?

DEAD ERNEST

DEAD ERNEST

by

Frances Garrood

Magna Large Print Books
Long Preston, North Yorkshire,
BD23 4ND, England.

British Library Cataloguing in Publication Data.

Garrood, Frances
    Dead Ernest.

    A catalogue record of this book is
    available from the British Library

    ISBN   978-0-7505-2830-6

First published in Great Britain in 2007 by
Macmillan New Writing, an imprint of Macmillan Publishers Ltd

Cover illustration © Andrew Holt by arrangement with
Britain On View

Published in Large Print 2008 by arrangement with
Pan Macmillan Publishers Ltd

Magna Large Print is an imprint of Library Magna Books Ltd.

Printed and bound in Great Britain by
T.J. (International) Ltd., Cornwall, PL28 8RW

In memory of John Garrood, and for our four wonderful children, Toby, Daisy, Barney and Joe. And for John Stott, who rescued us.

Prologue

BENTLEY Ernest. Husband of Annie and mother of William (Billy) passed away suddenly on January 2nd 2004 aged 83. Funeral January 10th at 12.30 p.m. at Great Mindon Crematorium. Family flowers only.

'What about *beloved?* Something liked that?' Billy asked, scrutinising Annie's crabbed handwriting.

'Beloved? Beloved what?'

'You know. Beloved husband, much-loved father. That sort of thing.'

'Did you love your father, Billy?'

'Of course. Well, I suppose so. Yes, of course I did.'

'Well then. We can put much-loved father.'

'And husband? What about husband?'

'No,' said Annie. 'Not beloved husband. Not any sort of husband.'

'But Mum!' Billy looked hurt, as though even now he were taking his father's part. 'You must. What will people think?'

'It doesn't matter what people think,' said Annie firmly. 'I *know.*'

CHAPTER ONE

Dead Ernest

No one had expected Ernest to die, least of all Ernest. He prided himself on coming from tough, Yorkshire stock, and had often told Annie that he would easily outlive her. So when he had his heart attack, Annie's feelings were at first of surprise rather than anything else.

'Are you sure?' she asked the policewoman, who was making tea in the kitchen. (How odd that it was always the police who were sent to break bad news; almost as though dying in the street were an offence against the law). 'Are you sure he's dead?'

'Quite sure. I'm so sorry, dear.' The policewoman handed her the tea (much too sweet, and not hot enough) and put an arm around her shoulders. 'It must be a terrible shock. Is there anyone you'd like us to contact?'

'Billy. My son Billy. You'll need to contact him.'

Because of course Billy must be told. Strangely, Annie had rather wanted to keep the news to herself for a while; to taste it and think about it on her own before sharing it with anyone else. But Billy would think it odd if she didn't tell him at once, and besides, there would be things that would need doing. Annie had only the vaguest idea of what those things were, but she was sure Billy would know how to deal with them. Billy

11

was good at that sort of thing.

'How do you know it was a heart attack?' Annie asked. 'How can they tell?'

'Well, they can't tell. Not for certain. But that's what it looks like. There'll have to be a post-mortem, of course.'

'Ernest wouldn't like that,' Annie said, remembering Ernest's dislike of being touched and even greater dislike of anyone seeing him in a position of disadvantage. A post-mortem, she could see, was going to place him in a position of considerable disadvantage.

'It has to be done, dear. It's the law. Because he didn't die in hospital.' The policewoman poured herself a cup of tea, although Annie hadn't invited her to have one. Death, it would seem, muddled up all the rules of normal behaviour.

Ernest would have hated dying in the street like that, with everyone watching. Dying in hospital would have been acceptable, with dignity and nurses and clean sheets. But then Annie might have had to sit with him while he was doing it, and she wasn't sure she could have managed that. Perhaps, after all, it was a blessing that he had died in the street.

'Where was he?' she asked. 'Where did Ernest die?'

'Outside the fish and chip shop.'

'Outside the fish and chip shop,' Annie repeated, surprised. It seemed such an odd place to die. She wondered what he had been doing there. The fish and chip shop was the wrong end of town for the barber's, which was where Ernest was supposed to be, and he'd only just had his lunch, so he couldn't have been hungry. But now she would never know. Nobody would ever know what Ernest was doing before he died outside the fish and chip shop.

Annie was aware of the policewoman watching her, waiting to see how she would behave. 'What do people usually do?' she asked, suddenly interested.

'Do?' The policewoman looked bemused.

'Yes. When someone dies. You must see a lot of them. When you tell them, what do they do?'

'Everyone's different of course,' said the policewoman carefully. 'They cry, of course, and some people even scream. And sometimes they're just shocked and quiet. Trying to understand what's happened.'

'And what am I?'

'What are you?' The policewoman's teacup paused, trembling, halfway to her lips.

'Yes. How would you say I was taking it?'

'I would say,' the teacup returned firmly to its saucer, 'I would say that you were being very brave. Perhaps it hasn't quite sunk in yet,' she added gently. 'It's a terrible shock for you.'

Was it? Was it really a terrible shock? A surprise, certainly, but a shock? Annie wished the policewoman would go away and let her think. She needed time to sort herself out; to get to grips with what had happened. Ernest was dead, and she didn't feel anything much at all. Not sad, not happy, not anything. Was she normal? Was it okay to feel like this?

'Ernest is dead.' She tried the words to see what they felt like. 'Ernest – is – dead. It sounds so

13

strange.' She paused. 'He had this little joke he used to tell: "Once upon a time there were two worms fighting in dead Ernest." I never thought it was funny, and Billy didn't like it, but it always made Ernest laugh.'

The policewoman smiled.

'Did he have a sense of humour then, your Ernest?'

'Oh, I wouldn't say that. Ernest only had the two jokes, and I've forgotten the other one.'

'Would you like another cup of tea?' the policewoman asked.

'No thank you. I think I'd like you to go now,' Annie said.

'But we can't leave you here on your own. Not at a time like this. Is there a neighbour who might sit with you? Just until your son gets here.'

Annie thought of her neighbours. Of odd, secretive Mr Adams, a tiny man of indeterminate age who lived alone and who hoarded things. Annie had only once been inside his house and had been left with an impression of disturbing smells and what appeared to be wall-to-wall jumble and bric-a-brac. The piles were neat and appeared to be in some kind of order, but the impression was not welcoming. On the other side lived a young couple, with a frog-faced toddler who screamed a lot. Annie certainly didn't want to involve them, and she quite definitely didn't need the toddler.

'I don't really have much to do with the neighbours.' She stood up. 'I want to be by myself now. I don't need anyone else.'

After the policewoman had gone, Annie locked

14

and bolted the door. Then, because it was getting dark, she drew the curtains and turned on the gas fire. Ernest would be home any time now, and wanting his tea. Ernest was very particular about his tea. He always had it at six o'clock on the dot, the same time as he used to have his meal when he got home from work. Ernest liked routine and order, and because it was easier to do what Ernest wanted, Annie had always gone along with it. Yes. She must get Ernest's tea ready. A nice piece of fish (it was Friday) and some mashed potatoes and cabbage. Annie thought it was odd to have cabbage with fish, but Ernest had read a book about green vegetables being particularly good for you, and recently he had insisted on having them with everything.

But Ernest is dead, she realised again. *Ernest is dead.* He isn't coming home for his tea. The green-vegetable book came too late to save him. He won't be coming home at all; not ever. His heavy tread on the gravel (a slight limp because of his bad hip), his key in the door, his voice calling her name as he hung up his coat and cap. None of these things would ever happen again. The coat and the cap were – where? At the hospital, presumably. And Ernest himself where exactly was he? Lying somewhere cold waiting for the post-mortem. Annie shivered. At least she wouldn't have to go and identify him. Billy would see to that. She couldn't understand why anyone had to go and identify Ernest, when he'd been carrying his pension book.

CHAPTER TWO

Annie

Travelling in the black limousine, Annie felt an unaccustomed and not unpleasant sensation of importance. For only the third time in her life, she found herself the centre of attention (the first being her wedding day, and the second the day she give birth to Billy), and it was with some difficulty that she managed not to look as though she were enjoying the ride. The mortal remains of Ernest were in the hearse in front, his coffin accompanied by a wreath from Annie and a bouquet from Billy and his wife.

'He always did have to be first,' Annie said suddenly, remembering the way Ernest would precede her through doorways, or take the biggest slice of cake.

'What was that, Mum?' Billy asked.

'Your father. He was always in front.'

'But of course he's in front. It's his funeral! What did you expect?'

'Don't upset her, Billy.' Billy's wife Sheila leant across and put a hand on Annie's arm. 'This must be very difficult for her.'

'I'm not upsetting her, am I Mum? You're okay, aren't you?'

'Yes, thank you. I'm – coping.'

Coping. Well, that was the word, wasn't it?

She'd heard it a lot in the past few days. How are you coping? (to her); how's your mother coping? (to Billy). And she was coping. She was coping quite well.

Outside, the familiar street looked much as usual, and Annie stifled an impulse to do a Queen Mother wave as people paused to watch the funeral cortege pass by. *Dignified*, she said to herself. That's what this was. Dignified. This car (were the seats real leather? Annie sniffed, but couldn't tell), the shiny black and chrome of the hearse, everyone looking so smart. Ernest would have approved. The thick red neck of the driver reminded her of Ernest's, and for a fleeting second, she wondered what she would do if he were to turn round and actually prove to be Ernest. It was with a little shock that she realised that she wouldn't be pleased. Not pleased at all. For the first time in over sixty years, Annie had nothing to fear from Ernest. She had forgotten what it was to feel safe.

The service at the crematorium was short and businesslike. There were prayers and a hymn ('The Lord's My Shepherd', accompanied by a blue-rinsed lady at the electronic organ); a priest Annie had never met said a few words which seemed to have very little to do with Ernest; then there was the bit about the Resurrection and the Life, and Ernest departed on cue in a swish of silk curtain. He would have liked that; the punctuality and the precision would have appealed to his sense of order. But then that was probably why he had chosen to be cremated.

So that's it, Annie thought, surprised. It's all

over. Eighty-three years of life swept neatly away, to be collected later in a small container. Ernest's ashes. Annie contemplated the prospect with distaste.

Afterwards, at the reception ('Not reception, Mother. This isn't a wedding,' Billy had chided her), someone asked her what she was going to 'do' with Ernest.

'Do?' Annie was puzzled. 'Do with Ernest?'

'Yes. His ashes.' The woman smiled sympathetically. (Who was she? Annie wondered. There seemed to be so many people she didn't recognise). 'Did he want to be – scattered somewhere special?'

Annie smiled at the bizarre idea of scattering Ernest somewhere special, and the woman frowned. Immediately, Annie erased her smile, and put on a more suitable expression. 'Nowhere special,' she said, fingering her teacup. 'There wasn't anywhere – special.'

'My husband wanted to be scattered in the Lake District.' The woman offered the information as though it were a small gift which might ease Annie's pain.

'Ernest hated water.'

'Oh.' The woman looked disappointed.

'We'll find somewhere,' said Annie, taking pity on her. 'We'll find somewhere nice. Don't you worry.'

'You've got some lovely cards.' The woman tried again. 'They must be a great comfort to you.'

Annie considered the condolence cards festooning the mantelpiece and the sideboard: pictures of flowers and crosses and hymn-books, most of

18

them from people she hardly knew, many of them assuring Annie of the sender's 'thoughts and prayers at this difficult time'. Annie was puzzled by the thoughts and prayers. She knew for a fact that some of the senders never darkened the door of a church and didn't appear to believe in anything much. Did death make people more prayerful? Or was it merely an assumption that her loss would turn Annie to prayer?

'It was nice to get the post,' she confessed. 'I don't usually get much post. I've enjoyed opening all the envelopes.'

This was true enough. In the long interval between Ernest's death and his funeral, opening the post had been an unexpected diversion. Some of the cards and letters were from people Annie hadn't even heard of (Ernest's colleagues from the bank, possibly, or those shadowy figures with whom he used to sit on his committees), and she had enjoyed arranging the cards in the living-room. It had made the house look almost festive.

'I had a lot of cards when my Charlie died,' the woman said. 'I've kept them all.'

But Annie was losing interest. She had no wish to hear about this stranger's bereavement, and she could see that very little encouragement would be needed to elicit a full account. However she might feel about Ernest's death (and if she was honest, she still wasn't at all sure), today was her day. She didn't wish anyone to hijack or even share her new status of widow.

'Excuse me,' she said, standing up. 'I think I'd like a sausage roll.'

Afterwards, when everyone had gone home,

Billy persuaded Annie to take a large glass of sherry and go and have a lie down. Contemplating the big double bed (Ernest's pyjamas – striped, Marks & Spencer's, Large – were still neatly folded under his pillow, as though they alone expected him to return), Annie moved her pillows into the middle. She had kept to her own side since Ernest's death, but now she didn't see why she shouldn't take possession of the whole bed. After all, it wouldn't do to let one side of the mattress wear out before the other, would it?

Lying back against the pillows, Annie sipped her sherry and contemplated her new position. Yes. It felt quite comfortable. After a while, she pulled Ernest's pyjamas out from under his pillow and dropped them onto the floor by the bed. She wished very much that she had brought the sherry bottle upstairs with her.

CHAPTER THREE

Andrew

'I'm worried about my mother.' The man – big, florid, with the well-fed, upholstered look that goes with material success – stood on the vicarage doorstep. 'I thought perhaps you might help.'

Andrew surveyed him with mild surprise. He had never seen this man before, and had no idea who his mother was. It was supposed to be his day off and he had been about to have his lunch (cold ham and salad, for Janet was out at one of her meetings), and he was slightly irritated at the interruption. But he put on what Janet used to call his vicarage smile, and opened the door wider.

'Perhaps you'd better come in and we can discuss ... your mother.' He led the way into his study and swept a pile of books off one of the chairs, releasing a cloud of dust. 'Do take a seat.'

The stranger took off his heavy tweed coat and settled himself in the chair. He looked as though he intended to stay for some time. Andrew thought wistfully of the ham and salad, and the peace of a solitary lunch in the kitchen with the newspaper and the crossword. Janet always talked at mealtimes, and disapproved of reading at the table.

'Your mother,' he said now. 'You wanted to talk about your mother.'

'Yes.' With some difficulty Billy withdrew his gaze from the chaos of books and papers, the ancient tabby cat asleep on the desk (was the creature stuffed? It looked as though it had been there for years), the dying plant on the bookcase, the general air of decay. 'My mother.' He folded his large hands in his lap and looked down at them. 'My father died a few weeks ago, and I'm afraid she's having difficulty in coming to terms with what's happened.'

'And you think I can help?' The salad would be getting limp in the warm kitchen. Andrew wished he had had time to put it back in its plastic bag.

'I really don't know.' Billy sighed. 'I've tried the doctor, but he says she's fine. And the health visitor says it's not really her problem.'

21

And so it's mine, Andrew thought. My problem. This man and his mother are about to become my responsibility. I could say no, of course (unless she's a churchgoer), but I shan't. I never say no. It's the only thing that makes me feel better about myself and my job, not saying no.

'So what makes you think your mother isn't coping?' Andrew put on what he knew was his interested, listening face and tried to concentrate on what his visitor was saying. Nowadays, with so many problems of his own, he was finding it increasingly difficult to concentrate on those of others, and today he found, to his shame, that his thoughts kept drifting back to a particular cross-word clue and the problem of dried-out ham and wilting lettuce.

'Well, she's not grieving properly. Not showing any feelings. And she's acting very strangely. I think she needs to talk to someone; someone professional, like yourself.'

'But what about you?' Andrew dragged his thoughts back from the kitchen. 'Wouldn't you be the best person to talk to her? After all, you know her best, and of course you knew your father. You would probably understand far better than I could.'

'But I don't. I don't understand.' Billy got up from his chair and started pacing about the room, circumnavigating the piles of books and waking the cat, which yawned prodigiously and opened a tawny eye (so it *was* alive). 'I don't understand how she can be like this. Not crying, not sad, not lonely, not worried. Not anything. She's behaving as though nothing's happened. Sometimes she even forgets he's dead, and cooks him a meal. Last week I called in and she was putting out his arthritis tablets for the morning. I told her she ought to hand them in to the chemist; that it wasn't safe having tablets about the house. But she told me not to be so silly, and of course she must keep Dad's tablets, and what was it to me anyway. She was quite nasty about it.'

Looking at the irritable red face of his visitor, Andrew could imagine wanting to be quite nasty to someone like that, and began to feel some sympathy for this man's mother. 'Does she know you've come to see me?' he asked.

'No, of course not. She wouldn't like it at all. But I thought – well, I thought that perhaps if you were to call in, saying you'd heard that she'd been bereaved. Something like that. Then she might talk to you. She's never been much of a church-goer, but she respects the clergy. She might listen to you, anyway.'

'And why are you so anxious for your mother to – well, to grieve? Perhaps she's grieving in her own way. It sounds to me as though she's coping rather well.' Andrew was becoming interested in spite of himself.

'Oh, she's coping. For the moment.' Billy paused in mid-stride. 'But can't you see? If she doesn't let it all out there'll be trouble later. Sixty years of marriage – that's a long time. She can't just pretend it's not happened. Everyone knows that when it comes to bereavement, everything's got to come out sooner or later. Well, so far nothing at all's come out. She's bottling it all up, and that's bound to lead to trouble. Depression,

23

or maybe even a nervous breakdown. And she'll have to be looked after, and I simply haven't got the time, what with the business to run. Not,' he added quickly, 'that I don't want to care for her. I – we – we'll always be there for her, if necessary.'

I bet you will, thought Andrew, provided this poor woman doesn't overstep the mark or make uncomfortable demands or – heaven forbid – become an embarrassment. 'And you – do you have a family?' he asked.

'I've a wife and daughter. But Sheila and Mother have never really got on, so it's a bit difficult.'

'I see.' Andrew reached out a hand and stroked the thin body of the cat, which stretched out purring, its tail making feathery patterns on the dusty desk. 'And do you live near?'

'Oh no. That's part of the problem. It's a two hour drive. In fact,' Billy looked at his watch, 'it's time I was going. I've got to pop in on Mother, and then hit the motorway before the afternoon rush.' He buttoned his coat. 'So can I leave it with you? You'll go and see her?' He handed Andrew a piece of paper with a name and address on it. 'She's only a couple of miles away in the village. And perhaps you'll keep me informed of her progress?' He took a business card from his wallet.

Andrew looked at his visitor with barely-concealed dislike.

'I'll go and see her,' he agreed, taking the paper. 'But I shan't be needing this.' He handed back the business card. 'You must understand that anything that passes between your mother and me will be in the strictest confidence.'

'But I'll need to know–'

24

'If you need to know anything, I'm sure your mother will tell you herself,' Andrew said smoothly, leading the way to the front door. 'If I see her she will be, as it were, my client. Anything she says will be between the two of us. I'm sure you'll understand.'

Round one to me, thought Andrew with satisfaction, as the sleek company car swept away down the road. He would go and visit this old lady – in fact, he was quite curious to see what she was like – and offer what help he could, and he would enjoy keeping her secrets (if indeed she chose to share them with him) from her fat pompous son. In the meanwhile, the lettuce was hardly limp at all, and Janet wouldn't be back for another hour yet. The morning had not been without its compensations.

CHAPTER FOUR

Andrew

'Did Billy send you?' Annie peered through the narrow opening allowed by the safety chain on the front door, but what little she could see of her visitor (a wavy figure wearing something long, together with what looked like a dog collar) was badly out of focus. She was wearing her reading glasses, and walking round the house in them always gave her the not unpleasant sensation of swimming under water.

'Does anyone need to have sent me?'

Annie thought about this.

'No. But if someone hasn't sent you, how do you know about me?'

'Know about you?'

'Yes. About me. And Ernest. Someone's told you about Ernest, haven't they?'

'Well, let's just say I heard about him. And I'm so very sorry.'

'That's all right,' said Annie graciously. Then, after a pause, 'I'm afraid I can't see you properly. I'm wearing the wrong glasses.'

'Well, if you go and find the right glasses, you'll see that I'm the vicar. Quite harmless.' Andrew gave a little laugh. 'And then perhaps I could come in for a minute?'

By the time Annie had found the right glasses and given her seal of approval to the dog collar (although, as she pointed out, the collar could quite easily be a fake) Andrew had been standing on the doorstep for nearly ten minutes, and was becoming impatient.

'I'm afraid I shan't be able to stay long,' he said, as he followed her into her small living-room.

'Well, it's not as though I invited you,' Annie replied. 'You can go any time you like. I'm not stopping you.'

'No. Of course you're not. I'm sorry.'

'That's all right, then.'

They stood for a minute regarding each other. Andrew saw a dumpy, grey little woman with an ordinary face and fluffy pink slippers. Annie saw a tall, wispy-looking man of indeterminate age with pale sad eyes and a worn raincoat. Neither

26

of them much liked what they saw.

'How are you coping?' Andrew asked now, lowering himself into a small armchair (he avoided the larger wing-armchair; something told him that it had belonged to the deceased, and must therefore be treated with due respect).

'I'm all right,' Annie said. 'You're like everyone else,' she added, disappointed. 'You all ask the same things. Am I coping; am I all right? Ernest's the one who's not all right. He's the one who's dead, isn't he? He died outside the fish and chip shop. And we'd only just had our lunch. What do you suppose he was doing there?'

Andrew said he had no idea what Ernest could have been doing outside the fish and chip shop, and there followed an awkward pause. I ought to know what to say, Andrew thought. I've done bereavement courses and bereavement counselling. I *know* about bereavement. But somehow he felt out of his depth with this odd little woman. He was beginning to see what her son meant.

'Billy did send you, didn't he?' Annie said, as though reading his thoughts.

'Well, yes. He asked me to come. He's worried about you.'

Annie gave a little snort.

'Billy's not worried about me. All Billy ever worries about is Billy. He wants me to say things and feel things the way he thinks I ought to, and I'm not going to do any feeling just to please Billy.'

'And what is it that you feel?' Andrew asked. 'You must be feeling something.'

For the hundredth time Annie asked herself the same question, and for the hundredth time she

27

came up with the same unsatisfactory answer.

'I don't know,' she admitted. 'I feel – nothing. Billy says I'm in denial, but I'm not. I may forget sometimes – you do at my age – but I'm not denying anything. I know Ernest's dead. I get him out every day and look at him, and he's dead all right. But I feel nothing at all.'

'You get Ernest out?'

'Yes. His ashes. They're in a pot in the larder. I thought they'd be in a Grecian sort of urn, but they're just in a pot; a plain brown pot. More like a sweet jar, really. Would you like to see them?'

Andrew had no particular desire to see the remains of Ernest, but felt that it would be churlish to say no. 'Yes. Of course I would. If – well, that is if you don't mind.'

'You're the only one I've shown him to,' Annie said, when she returned a few moments later with the container of ashes. 'And I'm only showing you because you're the vicar, and you'll understand. Billy wanted to see them but I said no. They're private. They belong to me. I can do what I like with them.'

'And what are you going to do with them?' Andrew asked, as Annie removed the lid of the pot.

'I've not decided yet.' Together they contemplated the coarse grey ash. 'He looks very peaceful, doesn't he?' Annie suddenly giggled. 'I suppose I shouldn't have said that, should I? But it seems so funny having Ernest in a little pot like this. He was thirteen stone, you know. Hard to believe, isn't it?'

'I suppose it must be.'

'I took him to Tesco's the other day. He used to hate Tesco's. He always preferred Sainsbury's. Said it had much more class, and that they do the best sausages. But Tesco's is so much nearer, and I can take the bus.'

'You took this – you took Ernest on the bus? Wasn't it – he – rather heavy?'

'He was a bit heavy, but I didn't have to carry him far. I had him in my shopping bag of course, so no one else could see him. I did tell the lady next to me, but I think she was a bit upset. Nothing to be scared of, though, is there? Just a pot of ashes. She didn't want to see him. She said better not to take the lid off in the bus. She said anything could happen.'

'Yes.' Andrew wondered what direction this curious conversation was going to take next. 'Have you – have you taken him anywhere else?'

'No. But I move him about a bit. I put him under the bed last night, just to see what it felt like, but I decided he was better in the larder. Billy wouldn't think of looking there.'

'I'm sure he wouldn't. I wonder – I mean, would you like to have the ashes interred? In the churchyard? You could visit them there, like a grave. Have a little headstone with his name on. It would be somewhere to put flowers. Somewhere to go.'

'Ernest wasn't a churchgoer. He didn't like flowers much, come to that. He always said they gave him hay fever, though I can't say I ever noticed. I think it was just his excuse for never buying me any. No. I think I'll keep him here for the moment. Until I decide.'

'You do what you feel is best. There's no hurry,' Andrew said.

'Yes. Ernest isn't going anywhere, is he?'

Andrew wondered if this was another of Annie's rather inappropriate little jokes, but her expression was serious, almost wistful. She looks lost, he thought suddenly. She's floundering around with her pot of ashes and her memories, whatever they may be, and no one understands. How can they, when she doesn't even know how she feels herself? It was with some surprise that he realised that he really would like to do something for her; that he would like not only to understand, but also to help. Funny, eccentric little Annie Bentley had touched him in a way he hadn't expected.

'May I call on you again?' he asked gently. 'I'd like to see you again, if you don't mind.'

Annie thought for a moment, cradling the container of ashes in her arms.

'Yes. You can come again. If you want to,' she said. 'I think I'd like you to come again.'

CHAPTER FIVE

Ophelia

'It's time you visited your grandmother.' Billy's voice on the telephone was unexpected and not particularly welcome.

Ophelia sighed. *Your grandmother.* People only

seemed to belong to her when there was some sort of problem. If her parents had had a row, it would be 'your mother' or 'your father'; and now, it would appear, her grandmother was, in some mysterious way, about to become hers too.

'Why? I mean, why now? I should think at the moment I'm the last person Gran needs.'

'You're family. She needs her family at this difficult time. We're all she's got. I'm very busy at the moment, and I've been to see her several times in the past few weeks. You could go down for a weekend. It's not a lot to ask.'

'A *weekend?*' Ophelia was appalled. In the whole of her life, she had never spent a night under the roof of her grandparents' gloomy terraced house. Family visits had usually consisted of lunch (almost invariably steak-and-kidney pie and cabbage, followed by one of Annie's huge tasteless blancmanges), and departure as soon afterwards as was possible within the bounds of politeness. 'You want me to stay with Gran for a whole weekend? Gran never has visitors overnight. She probably hasn't even got anywhere for anyone else to sleep.'

'Of course she has. She's got two spare bedrooms. I'm sure one of them can be made comfortable for just a couple of nights. Come on, Ophelia. Surely you owe her just two nights.'

'*Owe* her?'

'Yes. Owe her. What with missing the funeral, and–'

'But I was away! I didn't even know Grandad had died! News like that doesn't exactly make the headlines in Tunisia.'

31

'Really, Ophelia–'

'Okay, okay. I'm sorry. And I'm sorry I wasn't around when – when you and Mum might have needed me. But now – well, what can I do now? You say Gran seems fine.'

'But that's just the point. She's not really facing up to what's happened, and I think perhaps she needs to talk. She won't say anything to me, and the priest I asked to go and see her was a bit – secretive. An odd fellow. Wish I hadn't bothered him, now. Anyway, I thought she might talk to you. To another woman.'

So now, thought Ophelia, I'm a woman. For years, her father had insisted on treating her like a foolish child, but now, when it suited him, her adulthood was finally acknowledged, and she was considered sufficiently grownup to take over some sort of responsibility for her grandmother.

'Okay. I'll go. But only for two days. I don't think Gran will want me for any longer than that, and to be honest, I don't see what good I can do. We've never been exactly close.'

But after she had put the phone down, Ophelia had to concede that perhaps just this once her father had a point. She hadn't seen Annie since her bereavement, and maybe she did owe her something. Annie had always been kind to her, if not overtly affectionate, and while Ophelia had few illusions about the state of her grandparents' marriage, the loss of a partner after so many years must leave a gap. The loss of someone like Ernest, she could see, would leave a considerable gap.

Although she didn't know her grandmother well, Ophelia had, in a strange way, always felt a kind of affinity with her. Even as a small child, she had recognised that Annie was up against the same kinds of pressures as herself. She could see that Annie wasn't at all what Ernest wanted in a wife. She could be scatty and disorganised, given to bouts of dreaminess and mild eccentricity, all of which, it was quite obvious, offended Ernest's tidy mind.

And if Annie was a disappointment to Ernest, Ophelia was most certainly a disappointment to her parents. For a start, there was her name. Who could live up to a name like Ophelia? She was quite perceptive enough to know that in choosing it (her father, not the most romantic of men, nevertheless had a strong and inexplicable affection for Hamlet), her parents had dreamed of a quite different daughter from the one she was destined to become. From their hints and criticisms over the years, Ophelia had gathered that she was intended to blossom into a young woman who was not only beautiful, willowy, feminine, but also clever, accomplished and successful. To this end, a great deal of trouble, not to mention money, had been lavished upon her appearance and education. Photographs of the infant Ophelia showed a plump baby, pink and frilled and beribboned, her hair (what there was of it) teased up into an enormous bow. Later photographs showed a solemn child ('Sulky,' said Billy. 'You never would smile for the camera.') uncomfortably over-dressed and over-brushed, posed and awkward, polished shoes and staring white socks standing to attention beneath layers of petticoats and frills.

In addition to a series of expensive boarding-schools, there had been ballet lessons and piano lessons; swimming lessons and tennis coaching; and on one terrifying and never-to-be repeated occasion, Orienteering (Billy believed that this last would bring out Ophelia's latent leadership qualities; sadly, it transpired that she had none).

But to no avail. In a triumph of genetics over parental ambition, Ophelia proved to have inherited her mother's modest intellect and lack of athletic prowess, together with her father's well-rounded figure and sturdy legs; and while her parents, in increasing desperation, had continued to throw money at the problem, by the time their daughter reached eighteen, even they had to admit defeat. Ophelia knew that her parents loved her in their way, but she didn't feel they loved her for herself, and so the disappointment was mutual and, for Ophelia at least, not a little damaging.

Now, at nineteen, Ophelia lived in a small bed-sit and worked in a nursing home as a care assistant. Her mother had tried to sound encouraging about her choice of occupation ('It sounds very worthwhile, dear.') but Billy had been furious.

'I didn't give you an expensive education just so that you could spend your life wiping bottoms!'

'I quite like wiping bottoms,' Ophelia had replied. 'After all, someone has to do it, and it's the owners of the bottoms that matter.'

And it was true. Wiping bottoms was fine once you got used to it, and besides, that was only a small part of her job. Ophelia liked the old people in her care; they had led interesting lives, and above all, they needed her. Ophelia had never in her life felt needed, and it was a new and rather pleasurable experience. Some of the residents would smile when they saw her arriving in the mornings; ask when she was coming back if she was leaving for her day off; offer her elderly chocolates or dried-out fruit off their bedside lockers. No one expected her to be a success or look glamorous (it would have been hard for anyone to look attractive in that unappealing sack-like uniform). Ophelia was accepted for what she was, and while she wasn't exactly happy, she had at least found a measure of contentment, and for that she was grateful.

'You could train to be a proper nurse,' Billy had said, in a last-ditch attempt to persuade his daughter into some sort of recognised, respectable career. 'Get some letters after your name.'

Ophelia thought of application forms and interviews, of lectures and exams and the very real possibility of failure at the end of it all, and declined. She had done exams; she had also done failure. She wasn't going to risk repeating the experience.

Now, Ophelia thought of her grandmother on her own in that dreary house, without the threatening, critical presence of Ernest, and for the first time tried to imagine what it was like for her. Unlike her father, she could well imagine that Annie might not grieve for Ernest in the conventional way (whatever that was), but her life was bound to have changed dramatically, and Ophelia's curiosity was aroused. She thought of Ernest's big wing-backed Parker Knoll chair;

35

Ernest's huge wellington boots by the back door; Ernest's chickens (Ernest had always kept chickens, and no one else was allowed to go near them. As a small child, Ophelia had been spanked for feeding them peanuts and crisps); Ernest's allotment (potatoes, carrots and greens, but no salad vegetables. Ernest had abhorred salads); the ancient packs of cards with which Ernest had played his endless games of patience (a strange game for such an impatient man, Ophelia had always thought). What had happened to them all?

Ophelia sighed again. She had a feeling she was soon to find out.

CHAPTER SIX

Andrew

'It's the chickens! Oh, the chickens!' Annie's face, shocked and ashen, hovered behind the security chain across her front doorway. 'Oh dear, oh dear!'

'Have I come at a bad time?' Andrew immediately realised that under the circumstances, this was a particularly stupid question, but Annie's distress had taken him by surprise.

'No. Come in! Come in at once! You've got to help me! I don't know what to do!'

'Well, can you unfasten the door?'

Annie scrabbled feebly at the chain, her scrabblings punctuated by little gasps of anxiety, and finally managed to get the door open.

'Now, what's the problem?' Andrew asked, wiping his feet carefully on the doormat.

'The chickens!' Annie repeated, wringing her hands.

'What chickens?'

'Ernest's chickens. Rhode Island somethings. Ernest was very fond of them. And now they're all dead!'

'But how? I mean, what happened to them? Was it a fox?'

'No. No fox. It was me. I killed them. I – I forgot to feed them.'

'Ah.' Andrew was beginning to understand. 'How long were they without food?'

'Weeks,' said Annie. 'I haven't fed them since Ernest died. He always did it himself. He wouldn't let anyone else near them. I forgot all about them. And then I went down to the bottom of the garden and there they were. They look terrible.'

Andrew could imagine that chickens which had been starved to death over a period of weeks might indeed look terrible.

'Would you like to come and see them?'

'Well, I'd rather not,' Andrew said. 'After all, if they're dead, there's nothing much I can do for them, is there?' Ernest's ashes he could cope with. Ernest's dead chickens Andrew felt he could do without.

But Annie appeared not to have heard him.

'They're this way,' she said, visibly cheered by his presence, as she led the way through the house and down the garden path. 'They all had names, you know. You wouldn't think that Ernest

37

would be the sort of person to give chickens names, would you?'

Andrew, who felt that he was beginning to know Ernest quite well, agreed that you wouldn't.

They made their way though a rickety gate in the hedge which divided the small back garden, and found the half-dozen pathetic little bundles of feathers scattered haphazardly about the bare earth of the chicken run. Together, they stood regarding the scene of devastation.

'What do you think we should do?' Annie asked.

'Well, they'll have to be removed, of course,' Andrew said, with the sinking realisation that the task of disposing of the corpses was almost certainly going to fall to him.

'We could bury them,' Annie suggested. 'Or,' she added, thinking of Ernest and what he would have liked, 'we could burn them.'

'I don't think that would be a very good idea,' said Andrew, who had neither the time nor the inclination to start making bonfires. He had allowed half an hour for this visit, and if you took into account the length of time it had taken Annie to answer the door, he had already been with her for twenty minutes. 'We'll bury them. It shouldn't take long.'

But anyone who has ever had to dig a hole big enough to accommodate the remains of six chickens in rock-hard ground in the middle of February could have told Andrew that his approach to the task was somewhat over-optimistic, and, with Annie making encouraging noises from the relative warmth of the garden shed, it took nearly an hour for the job to be completed.

'There!' said Andrew at last, treading down the last of the soil and acknowledging that he had greatly underestimated the work involved in grave-digging. 'That's done.'

'Should we – should we mark it in some way?' said Annie, who was still somewhat preoccupied with ritual and funerals.

'I don't think so,' said Andrew quickly, for he had three more visits and a confirmation class to squeeze into the rest of his day, and was already running late. 'After all,' he added more gently, 'they were Ernest's chickens, and he was the one who would have wanted to remember them. It's probably best just to leave them like this.'

'Then we'll have a cup of tea, shall we?'

'That would be nice. Just a quick one.'

As Andrew stood in Annie's kitchen watching her fill the kettle at the sink, pour milk into a jug, and assemble blue and white cups and saucers, it occurred to him that he still didn't really know any more about her than he had at the end of his last visit. He had come hoping to draw her out; to get her to talk. And all he and done was spend an uncomfortable afternoon burying chickens.

'How – how are you then?' he asked casually, as Annie passed him his cup.

Annie looked at him warily. 'What do you mean, how am I?'

'Well, how've you been managing recently? How are you feeling?'

Annie stirred her tea. 'I wish Billy hadn't sent you,' she said suddenly. 'It would be better if you'd come without Billy having sent you.'

'Billy didn't send me,' Andrew said. 'He asked

me to visit you. And,' he added, guessing where this was leading, 'what you say is strictly between the two of us. I shan't tell him anything of what we talk about.'

'You won't? Not even about the chickens?'

'Especially not about the chickens.'

Annie smiled, and it occurred to Andrew that it was the first time he had seen her smile. He leaned forward and patted her hand.

'You can trust me, you know.'

'That's all right, then.' Annie paused, sipping her tea. 'Ophelia might be coming to stay,' she said suddenly.

'Ophelia?'

'My granddaughter. Billy's daughter. She's coming to spy on me.'

'Oh, I'm sure she's not.'

'Yes, she is. She's never been to stay before, and then she rings up, bold as you like, and says can she come and stay for the weekend. What d'you think about that? I've managed to put her off for a few weeks, but I can't do it forever. And I haven't even got any bedclothes for the spare bed. I expect she's used to sleeping under one of those thick fluffy things, and I haven't got one of those, either.'

'You mean a duvet?'

'That's the one. Nasty hot things. Ernest and I had to sleep under one once in this bed and breakfast place. It kept sliding off, and I woke up to see Ernest's feet sticking up at the bottom of the bed. He had very big feet, did Ernest. Size thirteen. They gave me the fright of my life, I can tell you.'

'What's she like, your granddaughter?' Andrew asked, anxious to get away from the subject of Ernest's feet.

'I don't see her that often,' Annie said. 'She's all right, I suppose. Not pretty, and she's inherited Billy's figure. Not clever, either, or that's what Billy says. But she's nice enough. To be honest, I don't really feel I know her that well.'

Andrew privately thought that for a young girl to be the same sort of shape as Billy as well as being his daughter must be an unfortunate start in life, but at least the girl was making an effort, and that had to be applauded.

'It will be company for you, anyway,' he said. 'Someone to talk to.'

'Someone to talk to!' Suddenly Annie was shouting. 'Someone to talk to about Ernest dying! That's what everyone wants, isn't it? That's what Billy wants. It's what you want.'

'Not necessarily–'

'Yes it is! But why should I want to talk about Ernest? Ernest is dead. He died outside the fish and chip shop. Why did he have to die there?' She was banging about the kitchen now, clearing away the teacups. 'He'd had his lunch, hadn't he? What was he doing outside the fish and chip shop? You tell me that, if you can. I gave him a nice lunch of sardines. What was he *doing?*' Annie paused, red-faced, clutching the teapot to her chest.

'I don't know,' Andrew admitted. 'But it's okay to feel angry, you know. In fact, it's quite normal. Lots of people feel angry when someone they're close to dies. It's quite natural.' Just for a moment, he felt he was on home ground. Annie

41

was going through one of the recognised stages of bereavement, and Andrew knew all about those. Maybe at last he was getting somewhere. Perhaps he would be able to help after all.

'But don't you see?' shouted Annie, exasperated. 'I wasn't close to Ernest! No one was ever close to Ernest! Well, perhaps Billy was a bit, but not me and not anyone else, either. It's you I'm angry with. You and Billy and everyone. All asking questions and wanting to know how I feel. No one ever used to ask how I felt when Ernest was alive. That was when I needed asking. Not now. Not any more.'

'I'm sorry,' Andrew said, feeling that once again he was getting out of his depth.

'I don't want sorry!' Annie cried. 'Everyone's sorry now, when it's too late! No one was sorry then. Not when I needed them. No one understood. Not even Billy. He saw the marks. He should have known. But he never said, and Ernest wouldn't let me tell anyone.'

'Are you saying – are you telling me that Ernest hurt you?' In spite of himself, Andrew was shocked.

'Not often. Not so much recently. He wasn't so strong recently, what with the arthritis.' Annie put down the teapot. Her anger seemed to have evaporated as quickly as it had been aroused, and she looked tired and drained. 'But he's always had a nasty temper, and if things weren't right – if I didn't do things the way he wanted – then he'd get angry and sometimes he'd hit me.'

'And you never told anyone?'

'Who was there to tell? Billy wouldn't have

been any good. He'd never hear a word against Ernest. And there wasn't anyone else. Ernest said I wasn't to tell anyone and that no one would believe me anyway, and I expect he was right. People – other people – thought a lot of Ernest. He was on committees and things. Not the sort of person you'd expect to hit his wife. Not that sort of person at all.'

'So now you feel he's – got away with it.' At last Andrew was beginning to have a glimmer of understanding.

Annie considered for a moment.

'I suppose that could be it. Now no one will ever know what happened, will they?'

'Not if you don't choose to tell them.'

'But I've told you. I shouldn't have told you.' Annie plucked anxiously at her cardigan. 'Not now he's dead.'

'But that's exactly why you can tell me. It's safe to tell me now. Perhaps you need to tell someone what happened. It's a big secret to keep to yourself, isn't it?'

'A big secret,' Annie echoed. 'Not a very nice secret, though.'

'A horrible secret,' Andrew agreed.

'But there's a lot more. A lot more that Ernest wouldn't want me to tell anyone.' Annie paused. 'Could I tell you all that as well, even though I promised not to?'

'I suppose it depends what it is. Would it harm anyone? That's what you need to ask yourself.'

'It would harm Ernest. That's what he always said. He said it would harm me, too, but I didn't mind as much as he did. "What would people think, if they knew?" he used to say. He minded very much what people thought. Because of the committees and things.'

'Well, it can't harm him now, can it? And if it makes you feel better to tell someone, then I don't see that it would matter that much. But only you can decide.'

'Only I can decide,' Annie repeated, and it occurred to Andrew that she had probably been allowed to make very few decisions in the course of her marriage. Ernest would have seen to that. 'It's got sex in it,' she added unexpectedly.

'What has?'

'The secret.'

'That's all right. Lots of secrets seem to be about sex. You'd be surprised.'

'All right then. I'll have to see.'

'Think about it. In the meantime, it's time I got going.' Looking at his watch, Andrew saw that he was now running horribly late. His remaining visits would have to be postponed, and even then, he would be in danger of being late for confirmation class. He stood up.

'Shall I come back?' he asked. 'Would you like me to come again?'

'I think you'd better.' While her expression was serious, there was a note in Annie's voice which was almost teasing. 'After all, you've only heard the beginning, haven't you?'

CHAPTER SEVEN

Andrew

Nowadays, Andrew rarely thought about sex. There had been a time when, in common with most young men (or so he imagined), he had thought of little else, but that time was long past. It must be a couple of years – maybe even more – since he and Janet had made love, and now it seemed no more than a distant memory. She had never been keen, although she had always made herself available (that was how Andrew thought of it) when required, and finally, thus starved of encouragement, any desire he might have felt for her had shrivelled and died. He could see that she was still a nice-looking woman, but he no longer wanted that kind of intimacy with her. Years of one-sided sexual activity had made him feel somehow vulnerable and at a disadvantage, and he was at enough of a disadvantage in his marriage as it was. Eventually, he had moved his things into the spare bedroom, pleading insomnia, and Janet had let him go without comment. Their sex life had died, its death unmourned and unacknowledged.

At first, Andrew had blamed himself. Janet had never enjoyed sex, but maybe there was something more he could have done. She had been a virgin when they married, her Christianity and her virginity packaged together and presented to him like a dowry, and while he himself had had one or two groping sexual encounters, he had hardly been experienced himself. He had – naively, he now realised – imagined that married love would be something special; that the fact that their sexual congress had been sanctioned by the church would make it easy and natural, as well as enjoyable. But the solid, lumpish, dutiful form of Janet waiting for him between the sheets on their wedding night had put paid to that. Whereas before, she had appeared to be affectionate and responsive, now she seemed braced, as though for some form of combat. In vain had Andrew murmured endearments, kissed her and caressed her, but all to no avail. Janet and her honeymoon nightdress (white broderie anglais – she had pulled it up over her hips to aid his progress) awaited his attentions with stoicism but no enthusiasm. I am here, she seemed to say; take me; do what you have to do. But don't expect me to get involved.

Afterwards, as they lay awkwardly together while Andrew tried to think of a suitable way of disposing of the wedding-night condom (no instructions on the packet for that), he tried to talk to the still silent Janet.

'Was that all right? I'm sorry if – if I wasn't very good.'

'It was fine. Just fine.' She pecked him on the cheek and turned onto her side. 'Let's go to sleep now. Goodnight.'

Later, Andrew realised how foolish he had been to hope for anything more. His marriage hadn't

46

been exactly a love match, and a church ceremony, however splendid, could hardly have been blamed for failing to transform it into one. He had been a busy young parish priest, living on his own and greatly in need of companionship. Single women of the right age were in short supply, and in any case, Andrew wasn't much good at socialising. Janet, his senior by some five years and experienced in the ways of the church (she was the daughter of a minor bishop) seemed a good if not perfect choice as a partner. It had been as simple as that.

And for a while, it had worked. Andrew immersed himself in his work, and Janet threw herself into her new role with, quite literally, a missionary zeal. While Andrew took church services, prepared sermons, and busied himself with the visiting, baptising, marrying and burying of his flock as required, Janet ran things. She ran the flower rota and the church bookstall and the crèche; she organised the annual church fête (a formidable operation involving some twenty stalls and a great deal of rather unchristian rivalry and backbiting, as well as the raising of astonishing sums for church funds) and played the organ (badly) when the organist was away. She rang round PCC members with news of cancelled meetings or revised agendas, and she put together the parish magazine. She was, everyone agreed, a wonder of energy and resourcefulness.

Sometimes when they passed each other in the course of their duties, Andrew would put out a hand or attempt to give Janet a hug, but she moved quickly away with a little laugh.

'No time for that, now, Andrew. Jobs to be done!' And she would bustle off to arrange yet another meeting or make more phone calls.

What Andrew missed most, when he allowed himself to think about it, was the physical contact; the feeling of another human body close to his own. Although Janet had never been demonstrative, he had found some comfort in the warmth of her presence in the bed beside him and, in the earlier days, the feeling of her hand in his. If he discounted the people whose hands he had to shake and the infrequent attentions of his barber and dentist, no one touched Andrew at all. Occasionally he would take the hand of a grieving parishioner, or pat a head or a shoulder, but no one actually touched him. Sometimes, baptising a baby, feeling the warm, soft little body in his arms, he would have a sudden urge to gather it up close to his face; to smell the baby skin, feel its cheek against his, kiss the downy top of its head. In other cultures, this might be acceptable, but while popes and politicians could kiss babies, ministers of the Anglican church were not encouraged to do so, and so he refrained. The cat, Andrew's companion from his bachelor days, was the only living being who had, as it were, open access to his body, and being a cat, took full advantage of its privileges, jumping onto his lap or winding itself round his neck whenever the opportunity arose. Andrew could well understand why the old and the lonely took solace in the company of pets. Janet disliked cats, claiming to be allergic to them, but Andrew suspected that it was more likely that she was inconvenienced by unsightly cat hairs on the furniture of the house which she kept in a state of show-home cleanliness. Only Andrew's office was spared her attentions, and it was here that the cat, Tobias, lived out his old age among the dust and the books and the saggy, comfortable cushions on the ancient sofa.

Once, Andrew had dreamed of a house full of noise and laughter and children; most of all, children. But Janet didn't want a family; she said that Andrew had a vocation, and that her own calling was to assist him in it. Andrew knew that this was only part of the truth. The reality was that there was no room in her life for the inconvenience and untidiness involved in the bringing up of children. Janet had fined down in the years following their marriage, and her neat figure was not to be sullied by the bearing and suckling of babies. Her waist would remain trim; her stomach flat; her breasts firm. Andrew guessed that Janet was proud of her body, and when he glimpsed it, which was increasingly rarely, he could see that her pride was justified. But he would much have preferred her to have allowed herself to sag and droop a little with the battle-scars of motherhood. For him, that would have made her more truly a woman.

Of course, they should have discussed the matter of children before they married, he realised that now. But at the time, he had simply assumed that Janet would want a family. It had never occurred to him that twelve years down the line, he would find himself a helpless prisoner in a loveless, childless marriage.

Was Janet happy? It was hard to tell. Once, only

49

once, he had asked her, and had been surprised when her eyes had filled with sudden tears.

'Happy? What is happy?' Quickly, she had whisked the tears away. 'I do what I have to do. I feel – I hope – I'm useful. Happiness is something I try not to think about.'

'But us. What about us?' Andrew had persisted. 'Ours is hardly a fairy-tale marriage, is it? I can't believe it's given you everything you want, has it?'

'I never expected to have everything I wanted,' Janet said. 'I have – enough.'

'I'm sure you don't love me any more. In fact I know you don't. But do you like me at all? Do you like – our life together?'

'Does it matter? I help you in your work, don't I? I support you as much as I can. If I have nothing else to offer, then I'm sorry. Maybe that's just the way I am.'

'And that's enough? That's really enough for you, is it?'

Was there a slight hesitation? The merest pause before Janet replied? For a moment, she had looked as though she might say more, but instead she simply gave Andrew a small, tight smile.

'It's enough. Of course it's enough. We do what we have to do, you and I. I don't believe in all this – looking into relationships. All this navel-gazing. You take what you've got, and you make the best of it. That's how I try to live my life, and I'm sure you do the same. There's no other choice. Besides, we don't argue, do we? We don't fight like so many other couples. I can't remember when we last had a disagreement.'

No, thought Andrew. We are beyond arguing.

We neither of us care enough any more to argue.

These thoughts passed through Andrew's head as he drove home from Annie's house, and later on as he arranged chairs in his study for the confirmation candidates. Annie's marriage had obviously been far from happy, but had it been so much worse than his own? Physical violence was terrible, especially when the victim was frail and a woman, but there had been occasions when he had felt that he would almost have preferred Janet to throw things at him or even hit him; anything rather than her seeming indifference. She might not mean it – in fact he was sure that she didn't – but sometimes her behaviour felt almost like a form of abuse.

But it's my fault too, he thought, making a feeble attempt to tidy his desk. It takes two to make a mess like this. Gently, he picked up the cat and tipped it out of the open window into the garden, where it slithered into the bushes, snarling ill-temperedly. Janet said he shouldn't allow the cat in the room during confirmation class. She said it was a distraction.

Janet again. *Janet*. In a rare moment of fury, Andrew picked up the overflowing wastepaper basket and hurled the contents into the flower bed beneath the study window. He would have to clear it all up again in the morning, but just for the moment it made him feel better.

CHAPTER EIGHT

Ophelia

Contrary to the belief of her parents and of her friends, Ophelia was not a virgin. On the part of her friends, this was an assumption. They all discussed their conquests and sexual activities openly and in detail, and because Ophelia didn't join in these discussions, it was assumed that she had nothing to add to them. She would listen in some bemusement to the lengthy and, to her, rather boring accounts of who did what with whom, where, and how many times. And while she was entertained by the antics some people appeared not only to perform, but also to talk about afterwards, she herself kept quiet. It was safer that way, she decided. Apart from the fact that she had no desire to discuss any activities of her own, she had no wish to become the subject of gossip. Such friends as she had weren't close friends, and they certainly were not to be trusted.

Sometimes someone would ask her what she had 'been up to', but Ophelia found that she could quickly turn the conversation away from herself. One of the things she had learnt early on in life was that people were on the whole much more interested in talking about themselves than asking about her, and when it came to sex, she was grateful for their lack of interest.

Her parents were another matter. Some months ago, her mother had asked her outright whether she had ever slept with anybody,

'Because if you haven't, we need to talk. And if you have, I suppose we still need to talk.' Sheila had laughed, apparently pleased with her own openness; her willingness to accept whatever Ophelia might or might not have done. 'It's all right, darling,' she added, perhaps anticipating that some reassurance might be necessary. 'You can tell me.'

'There's nothing to tell,' Ophelia had said, wondering which planet her mother inhabited if she really thought it necessary to have a birds-and-bees discussion with her nineteen-year-old daughter.

'You mean – you mean you haven't?'

'I mean I'd rather not talk about it.'

'But darling, there's nothing to be ashamed of.'

'Why should I be ashamed?'

'If you haven't – if you don't – well, you know.'

'If I'm still a virgin, you mean?'

'Well, yes. I mean, lots of girls your age like to wait a bit. Wait for the right person, or at least for someone special.'

'Do they?' Ophelia very much doubted whether her mother had even the vaguest notion of what girls of her age did or didn't like. From her friends' conversations she couldn't recall that any-one had seemed particularly interested in waiting for anything, never mind for someone special to come along and relieve them of their virginity.

'Oh, come on, Ophelia! Don't be so coy! You can talk to me, you know you can.'

'Can I?' For a moment, Ophelia was curious. She had never felt able to talk to her mother about anything that really mattered, and she was intrigued that Sheila had managed to convince herself otherwise. In the course of her childhood, Ophelia had at various times been teased and bullied at school, witnessed minor acts of shoplifting by her classmates, and once, alarmingly, been touched by a male teacher in what could only have been called a thoroughly inappropriate manner. At the time, she had felt unable to tell her parents about these things. She knew that she could never be the daughter that Sheila and Billy had hoped for; the least she could do was to refrain from causing them any additional worry by burdening them with her problems.

'Well, of course you can talk to me. After all, I am your mother. I – I might be able to help.'

Ophelia thought about her sexual experiences, and laughed. There were no circumstances under which her mother would have been able to be of any assistance whatsoever.

'What are you laughing at?' Sheila sounded hurt. 'I'm only trying to help.'

'I know you are, Mum. And I'm not laughing at you. It's just that there's nothing to tell, really there isn't. My life is pretty uneventful.'

'Well, if you're sure.'

'I'm sure.'

Afterwards, Ophelia found herself feeling quite sorry for her mother. Sheila was no doubt looking forward to a nice, confidential girly chat. But it was too late for that now. The foundations for such confidences should have been laid years ago, when Ophelia needed them; not now, when her mother appeared to.

In fact, if you discounted the recent Tunisian experience (drunken fumblings in smoky bars with virtual strangers) Ophelia had only had sex twice, and neither occasion had really been worth writing home about. The first time had been more or less by mistake (the mistake being Ophelia's), in the front seat of a Ford Fiesta. The boy in question was not someone to whom Ophelia was particularly attracted. She didn't even like him very much. He was giving her a lift home from a party, and when they stopped in a lay-by, Ophelia naively assumed there was something wrong with the car. It wasn't until her companion lunged across and put his hand down the front of her blouse that she realised her mistake. By the time her knickers had arrived round her ankles, and what she thought was the gear-stick thrusting eagerly into her thigh turned out to be something quite other, there appeared to be no going back. At least the gear-stick sported a condom, and for that Ophelia supposed she should be grateful.

Of course, she could have fought him off, but she was very drunk at the time, and suddenly overcome with a sort of gung-ho bravado. Her virginity was there for the taking; she had never valued it much anyway.

Afterwards, in the cold light of day, she had felt ashamed and disappointed. Ashamed that she should have been so easily seduced, and disappointed in what had been altogether a rather messy, ugly experience. For while she had had no high expectations (given the circumstances, she could hardly have had any expectations at all), she had nonetheless thought that sex – even sex with someone as unexciting as that – might have a little more to it than that cramped, sticky tangling of clothes and hair and limbs. It was some time before she could, as it were, look a Ford Fiesta in the face again, although afterwards she did wonder how on earth her seduction had been accomplished in so small a space. In her more optimistic moments, she wondered whether she could have imagined the whole episode, but its legacy of physical discomfort the following day had left her in little doubt.

Ophelia's second experience of sexual intercourse nearly a year later got off to a much more promising start. She was – at least she told herself she was – in love with Simon. They had been going out together for several weeks, and she felt ready to make love. Simon, who had been ready for some time ('For goodness' *sake*, Ophelia! What's the big deal?'), was becoming impatient, and besides, it was high time the ghost of the Ford Fiesta was, in every sense, finally laid. Simon would awaken her body as it was meant to be awakened, and her womanhood would blossom as nature intended. Simon was usually banished to the sofa when he stayed the night; tonight she would invite him into her bed.

Poor Ophelia. Despite all the trouble she had gone to – the candlelit meal, the flowers, the freshly-laundered sheets – the night was a disaster. Simon's idea of foreplay was to pour himself a stiff whisky to take to bed (the whisky being his only contribution to the evening. Ophelia disliked spirits), and the actual lovemaking (if you could call it that) was over in a matter of minutes. On one level, Ophelia was terribly hurt that the sexual act evidently meant so little to Simon; on another, she was furious that she had wasted so much time and trouble creating what she had hoped would be an appropriate ambience for their first proper sexual encounter. She had spent hours preparing the dinner, and the champagne (real champagne; not just sparkling wine) had cost much more than she could afford. And all so that she could end up lying awake and furious while Simon, sound asleep beside her, breathed gentle whisky fumes into her ear.

In the morning, Simon had declined the bacon and eggs Ophelia had bought for his breakfast, and made what could only be described as a quick getaway, accompanied by the vague promise to 'be in touch some time'. Even Ophelia knew what that meant, and after he had gone she wept tears of disappointment and humiliation into her pillow, and later on, into the remains of the candlelit dinner, as she cleared away last night's debris. What had she done wrong? she wondered, licking duck pâté off the end of her finger. What was the matter with her? Was it her lack of expertise? Her naiveté? Or, worst of all, was it her body?

Ophelia had gone back into the bedroom and examined herself in the mirror. Certainly, her tear-stained face wasn't looking its best, and it had always been on the round side, but she had good skin and her eyes were quite a nice shade of grey. She let her dressing-gown fall to the floor and regarded her naked body critically. If she pulled in her tummy and held her shoulders back, she didn't look too bad, although she wished for the hundredth time that she had inherited her mother's hour-glass figure. Her breasts were firm, if a bit on the large side, her hips broad (but unfortunately not broad enough to make her waist appear small), her legs... But no, there was nothing that could usefully be said to recommend her legs. Hers was quite a good childbearing body, she concluded sadly, but probably not sufficiently seductive to attract a man who would care for her enough to want to put the child there in the first place. Not a bad body for a one-night stand, but finding someone who would want to wake up beside it every morning and love it enough to forgive it for its inevitable deterioration in its declining years was going to prove tricky.

And yet why was she blaming herself? Hadn't Simon failed her every bit as much as she appeared to have failed him? Come to think of it, he wasn't that good-looking himself, and while Ophelia had been reluctant to acknowledge it at the time, he had looked pretty ridiculous last night, standing by the bed in nothing but his socks.

She had pulled her dressing-gown on again, and stripped the bed, hurling sheets and pillowcases in a heap on the floor, removing every scrap of evidence of the night's activities. She took the sweater Simon had left behind (she noted with satisfaction that it looked new and expensive) and threw it in the dustbin, and as a final gesture, she took his empty whisky glass and flung it against the wall, where it shattered into a hundred bright splinters. Ophelia smiled. She had never liked those glasses, and besides, what kind of parent gives a teenage daughter cut-glass tumblers for Christmas?

Ophelia wondered whether she should give up on men altogether. All the men she had been out with had ended up rejecting her, and she had already suffered enough rejection in her life to know that repeat performances would only further damage her fragile self-esteem. Maybe she would be better going it alone, at least for the time being. She had her friends, her colleagues at work, and the old people in her care. They at least seemed happy with the way she was, and didn't appear to care about the quality of her intellect or the shape of her body. All Ophelia had ever wanted out of life was for someone to love and accept her for herself. Was that so much to ask? Her parents hadn't managed it, and now it looked as though any men friends she might have were going to be equally hard to please.

Finally, when she had satisfied herself that no trace of Simon remained in the flat, she had flung open the window and leant out over the sill between the billowing curtains into the grey, rainy morning. She felt suddenly and inexplicably cheerful. Ridding her flat of Simon had made her feel purged and, in a strange way, empowered. She gazed out over the wet roofs and the glistening roads towards a misty horizon of high-rise flats and factory chimneys. Somewhere out there, there just might after all be someone who would love her just the way she was.

Ophelia was prepared to wait.

CHAPTER NINE

Annie

If it hadn't been for the drink, Annie would probably not, as it were, have lost Ernest for the second time.

In the weeks following his death, Annie had discovered the pleasures of alcohol. Like most people, she had had the occasional drink, and had enjoyed the small glass of sherry Ernest used to pour for her before Sunday lunch. Ernest himself had favoured beer, and a regular nightcap of the whisky he kept in a locked cupboard. But he had never offered either to Annie, and something told her that any request on her part would be met with displeasure. Annie encountered enough of Ernest's ill-temper in the normal course of things without wishing to risk further outbursts, so she went along with what he appeared to think best for her.

But the funeral set Annie thinking about that bottle of sherry.

She had never in her life drunk alcohol on her own, but she could see that that was the way it would probably have to be if she were ever to drink again. And in an attempt to replicate the pleasant sensation of euphoria following her unaccustomedly large post-funeral sherry, she once again got out the sherry bottle.

At first, she restricted herself to one glass, which she had last thing at night to help her sleep. Annie had never had any problem sleeping, but it was to help him sleep (or so he said) that Ernest had drunk his nightly tots of whisky, and as it appeared that in order to drink alcohol one had to have a good reason, Annie decided this was as good as any.

But a single bottle of sherry doesn't last long, and soon Annie found herself adding sherry to her weekly shopping list. At first she felt self-conscious passing through the supermarket checkout with the sherry bottle standing brazenly to attention among her obviously shopping-for-one purchases, but as no one seemed to notice, she became bolder, and even on occasion bought two bottles at a time.

It wasn't until several weeks later that she remembered Ernest's whisky.

She had run out of sherry and was trying to make do with a (rather unsatisfactory) cup of tea, when her eyes fell on Ernest's cupboard. She knew where the key was – it was on the bunch which had been returned to her with his other possessions after his death – but so far, something had prevented her from using it. Some of Ernest's authority still lingered about the house like a malevolent mist, threatening her from odd corners and warning her against overstepping some undefined mark, and so Annie had been reluctant to tackle that cupboard. But Ernest was dead, wasn't he? His will had clearly stated that everything was now hers, and that included the cupboard. And, of course, its contents.

Annie was surprised to find not one but three bottles of whisky, together with two bottles of wine, a small quantity of brandy and sundry papers and other oddments. Guiltily, she removed one of the bottles of whisky and poured herself a sherry-glassful.

The whisky hit the back of her throat like a ball of fire, and it was some time before she had recovered sufficiently to risk another, smaller, taste. But it wasn't long before she had gone from wondering what on earth Ernest could have seen in this violent, even dangerous, drink, to understanding exactly what he had seen in it.

'Oh, my darling Clementine,' warbled Annie merrily, pouring herself another glassful and thinking, through a fog of uncaring, that it was a long time since she had felt so cheerful. How could Ernest have been so dour and joyless when he had a cupboard full of this magic fluid?

The hangover the following morning was something Annie was to remember for some time. With dry mouth and throbbing head, she tottered unsteadily around her still-revolving bedroom, trying to find her clothes (she appeared to have slept in some of them) and her glasses, which had disappeared completely. Of course, she had known there were such things as hangovers, but she had had no idea they felt like this. How had she managed to get upstairs, she wondered, discovering her knickers hanging over the banisters, and, more importantly, how long was this –this *condition* – going to last?

In the event, it lasted nearly two days, and while Annie did eventually return to the whisky bottle, she did so with more respect. But as so often happens, respect dwindled upon closer acquaintance, and by the time Ernest had been dead three months, his widow was well on the way to becoming an alcoholic.

Thus it was that Annie found herself one afternoon at the local police station.

'I've lost my husband,' she confided to the young policeman at the desk.

'Oh dear. I am sorry.' The policeman looked concerned.

'Yes. It is a nuisance,' Annie said, wondering if there was a chair she could sit on.

'A nuisance? Well, I should think it's a bit more than that. But are you sure you've come to the right place?'

'Oh yes. Quite sure. You see, I left him on the bus.'

'I see,' said the policeman, who didn't see at all but was relieved that at least he didn't have a bereavement on his hands. He took out a pen and notebook.

'And can your husband not find his own way home?'

'No. Not now.'

'Confused, is he?'

'Not exactly. Is there somewhere I could sit down?'

'Yes, of course.' The policeman led Annie into a bare interview room and sat down opposite her. 'Now, which bus was it?'

'The 3.15 to Little Mindon.'

The policeman wrote carefully in his notebook. 'And what was your husband wearing?'

'Oh, he wasn't wearing anything.'

'Let me get this straight, madam.' The policeman laid down his pen. 'You left your husband naked on the Little Mindon bus?'

'He wasn't naked,' Annie explained, leaning forward confidentially. 'You see, he's dead.'

'Dead,' said the policeman, who was fairly new to the job and still shockable.

'Yes. I was taking him to bingo. Ernest hated bingo. He wouldn't have gone if he'd been alive.'

'No. I daresay he wouldn't.' The policeman wondered whether he ought to get help. This was outside his normal experience. 'So how come nobody noticed? I mean, a dead man on a bus isn't exactly commonplace, is it?' He thought he detected alcohol on Annie's breath, which might explain her predicament. Perhaps she was confused. It was quite possible that there wasn't a husband at all, never mind a dead one.

'He was in a Tesco bag,' Annie explained. 'Well, in an urn, actually. Ernest in an urn. Uuurnest!' She giggled. 'It was just his ashes,' she added, patting the policeman's hand. 'Nothing to worry about.'

'Just his ashes,' said the policeman, relieved. Ashes in a plastic bag shouldn't pose too much of a problem, but there was still the question of what to do with this woman, who was clearly in no state to go home on her own. 'Is there anyone I can contact for you?'

Annie thought for a moment.

'There's the vicar, but I can't remember his name.'

A vicar, even to the solidly atheist policeman,

sounded just the person, and he energetically began the task of tracing him. Half an hour and several phone calls later, he had located Andrew, who had explained the situation and was on his way to collect Annie. He had also contacted the bus company, who had promised to search for Ernest as soon as the bus returned to the depot.

'What were you thinking of?' asked Andrew crossly, over the cup of strong instant coffee he had made back at Annie's house (Annie certainly needed it, and after this afternoon's performance Andrew felt he needed it too). 'And how long have you been drinking like this?'

'Not long.' Annie took a sip of her coffee and grimaced. 'I don't usually drink coffee this strong,' she added.

'Well, you do today,' Andrew said. 'It might knock some sense into you.' It was his day off, and Janet was away visiting an aunt. He had been looking forward to having the house to himself for the afternoon; to reading his library book (a jolly romp of a novel, reassuringly secular in nature), finishing the crossword, and pottering in his greenhouse. He was therefore not in the best of moods. 'If things are this bad, why on earth didn't you phone me?' he asked more gently. 'I'll always come round if you need some company.'

'I didn't think I did need any company.' Annie's voice was bleak. 'But things get on top of me sometimes, and a drink helps.'

Andrew, who knew only too well about the helpful nature of drink (he had a modest supply in his own study), softened.

'I think,' he said, 'it's time we had that talk. Tell

65

me about Ernest. About your marriage. Tell me how it all started.'

'How it all started,' mused Annie. 'Well, it was during the war, wasn't it? The war was on, and that took over everything. You wouldn't understand,' she added. 'You're too young.'

'Try me,' Andrew said. 'I'd like to understand. Just give me the chance.'

Annie closed her eyes, trying to conjure up a past she hadn't thought of in years.

'I was quite pretty,' she said, remembering almost with surprise the fair-haired, long-limbed girl who was her child-self. 'A bit of a dream-boat, you might say. Not stupid, though. Even my father said I wasn't stupid.' She smiled. 'That was some praise, coming from my father, I can tell you. Some praise.'

CHAPTER TEN

Annie's Story

'You're not stupid, our Annie,' her father said, not for the first time. 'Even you can see we can't go on like this. Those damn land girls don't know a cow's backside from a pig's face. You'll have to stay home and help.'

It was the spring of 1940 and, as everyone kept reminding each other, there was a war on. Annie, who was bright, and had hoped to further her chances in the job market by achieving at least some basic qualifications, was not best pleased, but there was little she could do about it. She was fifteen years old, as her father pointed out, and her two older brothers were away fighting for their country. The least she could do was to take their place and pull her weight at home.

Annie did not enjoy her war. The work was hard, the two land girls of whom she was put in charge moody and recalcitrant, and there was no social life to speak of. The farm was isolated, buses were infrequent, and there was no telephone. They had access to more fresh food than most people, it is true, but Annie would willingly have foregone the luxury of eggs and onions for a new frock and a night at the pictures. The flowering of her womanhood (with her strawberry-blonde hair and milky freckled skin, Annie was not without vanity) was wasted on the farm animals, and there was only poor simple Derek, who sometimes helped with the milking, to make eyes at her. Derek hadn't been the same since he fell into the canal at the age of nine, and therefore didn't count. It seemed a very long time since everyone had been cheerfully assuring each other that the war would be over by Christmas. Of course the war was never going to be over by Christmas. Annie, who was a realist, could have told them that. She felt sure that she would be an old old woman by the time the war was over. And then who would want her?

So the years and the seasons rolled by, with their rituals of sowing and haymaking and harvest, of milking and mucking-out and feeding, of scorching summers and icy wet winters. Annie patched and re-patched her leaking wellingtons (wellingtons were in short supply) and stuffed newspapers round her feet before she went about her tasks. Her father became increasingly short-tempered and her mother, hitherto a cool, practical woman, grew haggard and exhausted, fretting constantly about the safety of her sons, troubled with recurring nightmares of boys on bicycles with yellow envelopes bearing bad tidings from the Front. Doris, one of the land girls, became pregnant. How? Annie wondered. How on earth did anyone manage to get pregnant with no apparent assistance from a member of the opposite sex? The finger of suspicion hovered uncertainly over poor Derek, but there was no proof, and Doris, defiant and unashamed, refused to talk. Of course, she had to go.

And so they struggled on, one pair of hands short (although, as Annie's mother pointed out, that particular pair had been better at filing its own nails than doing much in the way of work). Annie, however, was surprised to find that she missed Doris. She might have been difficult, and she was certainly lazy, but she had had a wicked sense of humour, and Annie had grown fond of her. Goodness knows, there had been little enough fun on the farm, but while Doris was around she had contrived to make life a little less humdrum than it would otherwise have been. Now, with Mavis, the remaining land girl, in a more or less permanent sulk because of what she saw as a workload increased through no fault of her own, there was no opportunity for a giggle or a gossip. Annie sometimes didn't smile, let alone laugh, from one day's end to another. There was nothing to laugh *about*.

She first met Ernest in the early spring of 1943. 'There's a dance on in the village hall, our Annie,' her father said. 'You ought to go. Mavis, too. Do you both good. You're becoming a right pair of miseries. I'll drop you off in the car, though you'll have to find your own way back.'

Annie was not one to let a rare opportunity such as this pass her by. It was unlikely that another offer of a lift would come her way for some time; this one, she knew, was only thanks to a recent illicit deal on her father's part involving extra petrol in exchange for a side of bacon. The village was several miles away, and at the end of an exhausting day she rarely felt like making the journey on foot. She went off to tell Mavis the good news before her father could change his mind.

Mavis perked up amazingly at the prospect of a night out, and the two girls set to tackling the problem of what they should wear. The only possibility for Annie was her old Sunday best. Since Sundays came and went unobserved these days (there was simply too much to do) it would at least be a change from gum boots and trousers. The dress would need to be let down, for Annie had grown, but with a wash and a press and her mother's butterfly brooch it would look festive enough. For her part, Mavis, who turned out to have talents for which there had been little call on the farm, shut herself away with the old Singer sewing machine and emerged in triumph some time later clad in a skimpy little frock made from blackout sateen.

'What do you think?' she asked, giving a twirl in front of the mirror in Annie's room.

'Isn't it a bit short?' Annie tweaked at the stiff black skirt, trying to keep the envy out of her voice.

''Course it's short,' Mavis laughed. 'My legs are my best feature. Oh!' She gave a sudden groan. 'I haven't any nylons. We've got to have nylons!'

Annie, who had never in her life possessed such a luxury, didn't see the problem. Apart from the cold – and they were used to that – bare legs would be fine. No one would notice. But Mavis was having none of it.

'Cocoa. That's what we need. You mix it with water and paint it on. And black pencil for the seams. I read it in a magazine.'

So it was that on the night of the dance Annie and Mavis dressed themselves up and teetered forth unsteadily on their unaccustomed high heels, their lips a matching brilliant vermilion (they only possessed the one lipstick between them) and their legs an interesting shade of blotchy fawn, a slightly drunken black line meandering up each one.

'Not bad if you don't look too close,' observed Mavis cheerfully, straining to see the results over her shoulder. 'Not bad at all.'

The village hall was dim and noisy, the music being provided by scratched records played on an ancient gramophone.

'Not my idea of a dance,' sniffed Mavis, who had been a city girl in her former existence, and was used to better things. 'Not even a live band!'

70

Annie, who was five years her junior but often felt herself to be at least ten years wiser, forbore to remind her that the players of band music had mostly been called up. But Mavis was soon distracted.

'Boys!' she breathed, detecting shadowy male figures through the haze of cigarette smoke. 'Uniform, too.' And she was off, leaving Annie standing awkward and alone by the door.

But not, as it turned out, unnoticed.

'May I have the pleasure?'

Ernest was somewhat formally dressed in a suit and tie, his shoes highly polished, his moustache neatly trimmed. He didn't exactly cut a romantic figure, and like Mavis, Annie would much have preferred a uniform, but a partner, any partner, was a passport to respectability at a dance, and Annie gladly accepted.

As they made their inexpert way round the dance floor (neither, it seemed, had had much practice in such matters) Ernest told her that he worked for a bank. He was obviously anxious for her to know that while he had volunteered for the army, the fact that one of his legs was markedly shorter than the other had made him unfit for active service. Annie, trying not to giggle, was disappointed, of course, but Ernest couldn't help it. And he looked quite smart in his suit, which made him look older than he was, and almost distinguished.

'May I see you again?' Ernest asked towards the end of the evening, after several more dances.

Annie thought for a moment. She was not attracted to Ernest, and wasn't even sure that she

71

liked him all that much. His air of studied respectability and his lack of humour made him heavy going, and if she was honest, she found him rather boring. On the other hand, he had nice eyes, and a boyfriend was a boyfriend. Annie had never had one, and Ernest was certainly better than no boyfriend at all.

'Yes. All right. Thank you.'

They arranged to meet the following week. Ernest had access to a friend's car, and more importantly, petrol. He would pick her up.

'A boyfriend and a car!' Mavis was much impressed. For her part, she had managed to pick up a soldier, but he had no transport and his leave was nearly over, so their chances of meeting again were slim. 'You are lucky!'

But as the weeks went by, Annie began to wish she hadn't met Ernest at all. Their weekly outings (for a walk or perhaps a drink) were unimaginative, and their conversations (mainly centring round Ernest's job and Ernest's life so far) unbelievably dull. She disliked his kisses, which were wet and loose, and tickly on account of the moustache, and was becoming nervous at what was obviously his increasing attachment to herself. On the other hand, as Mavis pointed out, respectable young men were thin on the ground with a war on. Annie should count herself lucky and stop complaining.

But in the end, events were to take a turn which would remove any decision from Annie's hands and change the direction of her life in a way she could never have imagined.

CHAPTER ELEVEN

Andrew

'Where've you been?' Janet sounded exasperated. 'I've been trying your mobile, but then found it on the hall table. What's the point in having it if you don't carry it with you?'

'It's my day off.' Andrew took off his coat and went to put the kettle on. 'It's nice to be out of touch occasionally. Besides, this was an emergency. I didn't even think to take it with me.'

'What kind of emergency?'

'Annie Bentley.' Andrew put a tea bag in a mug and fetched milk from the fridge. 'She was in – a bit of trouble.'

'What sort of trouble?'

'It's a long story. She got a bit tiddly, and left her husband's ashes on the bus.'

'She *what?*'

'She seems to have taken to drinking, and I suppose it makes her do silly things. The police phoned me to collect her. She hasn't anyone else.'

Janet, who rarely did silly things, had little patience with those who did.

'She ought to be – put somewhere. Someone in her condition needs proper care.'

'No. She doesn't,' Andrew said. 'She just needs time and a bit of understanding. She's quite capable of looking after herself most of the time.

She just has these lapses.'

'Well, it seems to me that these lapses, as you call them, are becoming a nuisance. And besides, why are you getting yourself involved? She isn't even a churchgoer.'

'I am getting involved,' said Andrew carefully, 'because I care about her. It's my day off. On my day off I can do what I like. I work for my parishioners six days a week. If I choose to spend part of the seventh day with Annie Bentley, what is it to anyone else?'

'If you've got time to spare on your day off, then you could be doing something about that leak in the porch,' said Janet, banging pans about on the cooker (always a bad sign). 'Not running round at the beck and call of some old woman who's losing her wits.'

'Annie is not, as you put it, some old woman.' Andrew raised his voice. 'She is someone I've grown fond of, and who I think I can help. You know nothing about her. You haven't even met her, for goodness' sake!'

'Are you a shouting at me?' Janet's voice was icy.

'Yes. I rather think that I am.'

'Well, it's a good thing Josephine's not here to hear you, that's all I can say!' (Josephine was the secretary who sometimes helped Andrew out with his paper work. She was elderly and very deaf, and her services were entirely voluntary.)

'As I think I've already said, it's my day off. Josephine rarely comes on my day off. What would be the point? Besides,' Andrew added, with the dangerous sensation that he was about to overstep a mark which he had been hovering

74

near to for some time, 'I don't bloody care what Josephine thinks, or come to that, what anyone else thinks. Okay?'

'How dare you swear at me!'

'Quite easily, actually. In fact, I'm surprised I haven't done it before. I shall be in my study if anyone wants me.'

Our first row, Andrew thought to himself a few minutes later, safely closeted in his study with his mug of tea and the newspaper. Well, perhaps not a real row, but it had had the potential to become one. He had often been tempted to shout at Janet, but had been aware that he would gain little satisfaction from something which was almost inevitably going to be one-sided. Janet's cold contempt had shown this to be indeed the fact. She wasn't interested in why he was angry; she wasn't at all interested in Annie, who to her was just a nuisance. What had mattered to her was that Andrew had raised his voice; he had actually sworn at her. Her self-control in the face of his undoubted rudeness would keep her in Brownie points for some time.

As he toyed unsuccessfully with the crossword, Andrew's thoughts went back to what had been altogether a rather extraordinary afternoon. There had been the incident of Ernest's ashes and the bus, of course, but then there had been Annie's story. He had found it strangely compelling, and after a while had seen not the small rather dishevelled figure telling it, but the young Annie who had worked out her war on the family farm. Annie had shown him a faded photograph of herself as a girl, and Andrew had been im-

75

pressed. The girl Annie had been leaning against a gate, laughing into the camera. Boyish in her shirt and trousers, her fair hair blown about her face, she had looked very young and undeniably pretty.

Andrew wouldn't have recognised her, and the thought, although hardly a surprising one, made him feel oddly sad. This Annie – the new, young Annie – was someone he would never know. He could hear about her and he could become involved in her story, and yet he would never really know her. The years which lay ahead and which he had already gathered were to hold much unhappiness, were as yet unknown to the girl in the photograph.

After her tale had come to an abrupt end ('I can't tell you the next bit yet. I'm not ready,' Annie had said firmly), Andrew had helped her tidy away the coffee cups.

'Ophelia's coming soon. I keep trying to put her off, but I know she'll come sooner or later. I expect Billy's behind it. He's always bossing people about.' Annie paused. 'The house is in a bit of a state, isn't it?'

Andrew, who rarely noticed such things, looked around him. The house had an air of dusty neglect probably unknown in Ernest's time. The small rooms looked cluttered and uncared-for, and Annie herself was wearing a skirt and cardigan which even he could see could do with a wash.

'I've let myself go, haven't I?' Annie said, as though reading his thoughts.

'You've probably been feeling low,' Andrew

said, avoiding the question. 'But if you could cut down a little on the drink, I'm sure you can soon have the place shipshape. Or maybe Ophelia could help you?'

'Oh, no,' said Annie, shocked. 'I couldn't possibly do that. She might tell Billy, and then goodness knows what would happen. I suppose I'd better throw away the whisky, hadn't I?' she added rather bleakly.

'Why not allow yourself just a small one at bedtime?' Andrew suggested. 'No need to throw it away.'

'Would you like one? Shall we have one now?' There was a twinkle in Annie's eye.

Andrew thought of Janet's reaction if he were to arrive home smelling of drink, and laughed.

'No. I'd better not. I must be going. But I'll come and see you again soon, if that's all right?'

Now, however, gazing out of his study window (the lawn needed mowing), Andrew decided that a drink was just what he needed, although he rarely had one this early in the evening. And if Janet found out, then so be it; after what had just happened, he had very little to lose. He unlocked his desk cupboard and brought out a bottle and a rather grubby glass. I'm no better than Annie, he said to himself, holding the glass up to the light, frowning at the traces of amber fluid and the smeary fingerprints.

He poured himself a generous measure.

CHAPTER TWELVE

Ophelia

At the precise moment that a bemused bus driver was discovering the mortal remains of Ernest on the back seat of his bus, Ophelia was being summoned to the matron's office.

'It's not that you're not good enough at your work, Ophelia,' said the matron, opening a file with Ophelia's name on it. 'You're hard-working, and the old people seem fond of you.'

'But?' said Ophelia helpfully, with the familiar feeling that she was about to clock up yet another failure.

'But?'

'Yes. *But.* I've done something wrong, haven't I?'

'You mean you don't know? After this morning, you really don't know what you've done?'

Ophelia gazed out of the window. Tiny fluffy clouds dotted the milky blue sky of a glorious May morning. It was a day to be happy, not a day to be carpeted by this conscientious but humourless woman, whose mission in life, it seemed to Ophelia, was to make her life and the lives of everyone else around her as joyless as possible.

'No. I don't know,' she replied with perfect honesty. 'I've no idea what I've done.'

The matron sighed.

'Edie O'Brien. Does that mean anything to you?'

'Oh yes. Of course.'

Edie had escaped that morning wearing nothing but her nightdress and slippers (she had refused to get dressed). This happened fairly regularly, for despite strong locks and as much vigilance as was possible, Edie seemed to have a sixth sense where unguarded exits were concerned. Usually, she got no further than the garden, so no one was unduly alarmed, and Ophelia had been given the job of looking for her.

Today, this had proved more difficult than usual, because for once Edie had managed to bypass the grounds, negotiate a complicated gate and get out into the street. As Ophelia scurried after her in what she hoped was the right direction, she wondered how it could be that someone as frail and confused as Edie, not to say as unsuitably clad, could disappear so thoroughly in so short a time. But disappear she certainly had.

The road was busy with traffic, and this was an especial hazard, for Edie spent her time drifting in and out of a pre-war time-warp, where cars were fewer and slower. She thus had little awareness of the dangers posed to her, and was quite likely to launch herself across the road and under the first vehicle which came along.

After fifteen frantic minutes, Ophelia had finally ran her to ground sitting on a bench eating an orange.

'Oh Edie! There you are!' Ophelia sat down beside her. 'Where did you get that orange?'

'Found it, didn't I?' said Edie, sucking contentedly, juice dribbling down her chin. 'Don't get many of these, what with the rationing. Nice here in the sun, isn't it?'

'We've got to go back now,' said Ophelia, mopping up orange juice with her handkerchief. 'Matron will be worried.'

'Bugger matron,' said Edie cheerfully, and then, suddenly returning to the twenty-first century, 'let's go for a nice cup of coffee, shall we?'

Ophelia hesitated. She ought to get back. People would start to worry. On the other hand, the idea of taking Edie, nightdress, slippers and all, out for coffee suddenly appealed. She had some change in her pocket, and it would be a treat for Edie, who received few visitors, and rarely recognised those she had.

'Come on, then,' she said. 'But we've got to be quick.'

They found a quiet cafe, and Ophelia chose a corner table where she hoped they wouldn't be noticed. After all, Edie's nightdress might at a pinch be taken for a summer frock, and the slippers would be concealed under the table. Edie herself, who had returned to the days of rationing, was overjoyed to see all the sugar, and having added a generous quantity to her coffee tried to persuade Ophelia to fill her pockets.

'You don't know when you'll get the chance again, girl,' she whispered. 'The Germans will have all our sugar off us if we're not careful.'

'Edie, we've got to go,' Ophelia said, when the coffee was finished and Edie was spooning the sugary dregs into her mouth. 'They'll be waiting for us.'

'Oh, them,' said Edie with contempt. 'They can wait.'

Ophelia looked helplessly round. Edie could be very abusive when crossed, and had even been known to throw a punch, so she could hardly ask for help to get her on her feet. She could phone the home and ask for assistance, but she didn't especially want to draw attention to this little expedition.

'Come on, Edie,' she begged. 'Please? Just for me?'

'For you?' Edie snorted, munching on her sugar. 'Don't even know who you are. Why should I be doing you favours?'

The situation could have continued for some time, but fortunately, the distant siren of a fire engine came to Ophelia's rescue.

'Air raid!' she said, with sudden inspiration and vague memories of a history lesson involving life during the Blitz. 'Quick, Edie! We've got to find shelter!'

Fortunately, Edie had spent much of the war in London, and knew all about air raids. Hand in hand, they hurried out on to the pavement and set off back down the road, Edie stumbling and cursing, both of them by now attracting some very odd looks. A police car stopped, and the driver, sensing a problem, offered his assistance.

'We're fine,' Ophelia said. 'Just getting ourselves to the air-raid shelter.'

'Bloody Germans,' said Edie.

'Would you like a lift? I'm going that way myself.' The policeman winked at Ophelia.

'That would be lovely. You'd like a ride in a car,

wouldn't you, Edie?'

'Don't get many cars like this, do you?' said Edie, graciously allowing herself to be manoeuvred into the back of the police car. 'Just wait till mother sees me!'

Fortunately, nobody saw them, and when they arrived back at the home ('Very posh for a shelter. I'll come here again,' remarked Edie) it would appear that no one had missed them, either. Thankfully, Ophelia settled Edie back in her chair, went back to her work and thought no more about it.

But now, this.

'So you do remember?' said the matron, sensing victory.

'Well, I remember going to find Edie this morning, but I brought her back safely,' Ophelia said.

'And what exactly were you and Edie doing all that time?' The matron's pen tapped irritably on the desk. 'Well, I'll save you the trouble, Ophelia. You were seen together in a rather scruffy cafe. Someone was public-spirited enough to telephone me this afternoon. It would seem that you took a vulnerable old lady out for coffee, without permission, and in her nightdress!'

From the matron's tone of voice, Ophelia might as well have strangled the vulnerable old lady with her own dressing-gown cord.

'It was Edie's suggestion.' But even as the words left Ophelia's mouth, she knew that she had condemned herself.

'Edie's suggestion! Well now, what a brilliant idea, Ophelia. And why don't we all follow Edie's suggestions, or come to that, her shining example? Why don't we take off our clothes and run around naked? Or use obscene language and throw Horlicks at the night staff? Since when have we followed Edie's example?'

'I thought it would be nice for her,' said Ophelia. 'The old people never get out; never do anything normal.'

'And what exactly do you mean by that? Would you care to explain yourself?'

Ophelia thought of the narrow, ordered existence of the residents. Some, like Edie, barely noticed their surroundings, but there were others who did and whose still-active minds were stifled through lack of stimulation and interest. She thought of the circle of armchairs round the television, which was always on, and which nobody watched. She thought of the colourless flavourless food and the endless cups of stewed tea; the dreary daily round of dressing, eating, being taken to the lavatory and kept clean; the sheer uselessness of the existences of people who had once had their part to play but had now been made redundant by an ungrateful society. The high spot of the week might be a game of bingo, and how humiliating that must be for a man or woman whose idea of a night out had once been an evening at the theatre, a concert or a game of bridge. And yet if people didn't take part, they were blamed for not being sporting; for not wanting to *join in*.

And then there were the recorder recitals by the Brownies, who came in order to get earn their musicians' badge (no badges for the residents who had to listen), and at Christmas the carol singing, the gifts of soap or chocolate from the worthy ladies from age-related charities, and the dull, mechanical sound of the handbell ringers. There was no escape from any of these treats. All had to be endured. It could have been because she herself had suffered from being crammed into a variety of moulds into which she wouldn't or couldn't fit; or perhaps because she had taken the trouble to get to know the residents properly. Whatever it was, Ophelia had come to feel passionately about the way they were compelled to lead their lives.

'We don't treat them as people,' she said now. 'They might as well be animals in a zoo. Aren't they worth a bit more than that?'

'Are you telling me my job, Ophelia? Do you think you could run this place on the budget we are given better than I do?'

Ophelia hesitated. She knew she should back down and save the day (and possibly her job). Taking on the matron was something which few did and even fewer survived. And yet what had she to lose? The job was hardly irreplaceable, and wasn't it time someone made a stand? It probably wouldn't make any difference, but it just might make the matron think a bit, and she felt she owed something to Edie and all the others. She would still be able to visit them. Not even the matron could prevent her from doing that.

'Yes. I think I probably could.'

There was a long pause. A few drops of rain spattered against the window (not such a lovely day after all) and the sounds of shuffling footsteps and the scraping of chairs heralded the start of supper.

The matron stood up.

'I can't sack you, Ophelia, although I'd like to. To my mind, putting Edie at risk and your gross insolence would more than justify your dismissal. But the procedure is, as you know, three formal warnings. You can consider this to be the first. You will of course receive it in writing. From now on, I would advise you to watch your step.'

'Don't bother,' said Ophelia, surprising even herself. 'I'll save you the trouble and sack myself. I'll work my notice, of course, but after that, you'll no longer be troubled by me.'

'In that case there will be no need for you to work your notice,' said the matron, standing up and closing Ophelia's file. 'I think we can just about manage without you, Ophelia. You will of course receive a month's pay in lieu, but I think that under the circumstances you will understand that you can hardly expect a reference.'

'Bugger the reference,' said Ophelia, taking a leaf out of Edie's book and feeling strangely liberated. 'Bugger the lot of you.' And she left the room, closing the door carefully behind her.

CHAPTER THIRTEEN

Annie's Story

'You'd like me to continue, wouldn't you?' Annie said.

She and Andrew were sitting drinking tea. Ernest's ashes, which Andrew had just collected from the bus depot, were safely back in their place beside the pickled onions in the larder.

'If you're ready, yes, I would. I think it might help you, and besides, I'm, well I'm–'

'Curious?' Annie suggested.

'Yes, if you put it like that, I suppose I am.'

'Well,' Annie put down her cup, 'I don't know where to start. You see, this is the difficult bit.'

Andrew nodded.

'I told you Ernest was getting keen, didn't I?'

'Yes. You did.'

'I didn't want to marry him. I really didn't. But you see in the end I had no choice.'

Ernest had decided to propose; Annie guessed that. They might only have been seeing each other for a few months, but she could see the signs. He would start to speak and then suddenly change the subject. He would blush and become confused, and then make some remark about the war or the weather. If Annie had loved him, she would have made things easier for him, but she didn't love him. If Ernest wanted to ask her to marry him, then she certainly wasn't going to assist him in his efforts to propose to her.

In the end, perhaps aware of Annie's lack of enthusiasm, Ernest approached her father.

'Ernest wants to marry you, our Annie. What do you think about that?' her father said, after Ernest's visit.

'I don't want to marry him, Dad. I don't love him.'

'He's a nice enough lad and he's got a steady job. You could do a lot worse. And he seems to be

86

'pretty keen on you.'

'Does he? He's never said anything,' said Annie guilelessly.

'Maybe you didn't give him the encouragement. Anyway, he says he'll wait as long as it takes. He'll not take no for an answer.'

'Well, he may have to,' Annie said. 'I'm not marrying anyone I don't love.'

'Then maybe you'll not marry at all. You can't afford to be too choosy, our Annie. Where are you going to meet anyone better? You'll not get another offer as good as this.'

But Annie had no intention of marrying Ernest. He was all right for the time being; for a walk or a drive or the very occasional treat of a night at the pictures. She could even put up with the wet kisses and the moustache. But not for life. Annie had set her sights a lot higher.

Long afterwards, Annie wondered that she could have been so high-handed. She should have let Ernest go, releasing him to find a girl who would love him, and she should have had the patience to wait for a man whom she herself might love. But the enslaving of Ernest had given her a pleasing sense of power, and she was in no particular hurry to relinquish it.

That harvest seemed more hot and more exhausting than any Annie had known. Long days out in the baking fields were followed by all-too-short nights, frequently disturbed by a combination of heat and mosquitoes. Sometimes Annie was so tired that she fell asleep as she was, and would wake to find that she was still wearing the previous day's grubby shirt and trousers, her head still itching with yesterday's dust.

In the midst of all this, Ernest remained attentive and occasionally even sympathetic, and since their outings together constituted the only breaks Annie ever had (her father sparing her from her duties presumably in the hope that these expeditions might further Ernest's cause), she found herself actually looking forward to them. It was a treat to be able to bathe and put on a frock and have a change of scene and company, and Ernest's accounts of his work at the bank, dull as they were, at least made a change from discussions about corn yields and the all-important question of whether the weather would break before the rest of the harvest was brought in.

By now, the shortage of petrol was such that the majority of drivers had been compelled to take their cars off the roads, but here again Ernest had the support of Annie's father, for while much of the time he was reduced to using a bicycle, he was allowed sufficient petrol from the farm's supplies to enable him to take Annie for the occasional drive. In those difficult days, this was luxury indeed.

Ernest rarely drank alcohol. If they went to the pub together, he might have half a pint of beer, but more usually he would drink lemonade. So Annie was surprised when he turned up to fetch her one evening in an unusually good humour and smelling strongly of spirits.

'Shall we go for a drink?' he asked her, as they drove off down the farm track.

Annie wondered whether she should mention the fact that Ernest had apparently already done just that, and maybe it wasn't such a good idea to add to the quantity he had already had. She hesitated.

'Oh, come on, Annie. I've got some celebrating to do. The least you can do is come and celebrate with me.'

'Celebrating?'

'The chief clerk has left the department, and his job is almost certainly mine.'

'Congratulations.'

'Congratulations? Is that all you can say?' The car swerved dangerously near the ditch, and Annie held on to her seat. 'It's wonderful news, and you should be pleased for me.'

'Of course I'm pleased for you.'

'Well then. We're going to celebrate.'

Annie too was unaccustomed to alcohol, and after three glasses of cider, which had always seemed to her to be one of the more innocent alcoholic drinks, she was inclined to take a much more favourable view of the world in general and Ernest in particular. As for Ernest himself, it only took a couple more drinks to render him un-characteristically uninhibited and affectionate.

'Lovely Annie.' The moustache tickling Annie's ear felt almost pleasant. 'Lovely lovely Annie.'

Annie bridled and simpered, and ignored the hand which was straying upwards from her knee. Maybe life wasn't so bad after all, and in the for-giving light of early evening, Ernest was looking almost handsome.

The journey home in the dusk was slow and precarious. The car meandered all over the road as though it had a will of its own, while Ernest's free hand had somehow reached the top of Annie's thigh.

'Shall we go for a little walk?' Ernest said, as he parked outside the farm gate and opened the door for Annie to get out. 'Just a little walk in the country?'

Annie resisted the temptation to remind him that most of her life was spent as it were walking in the country, and found herself agreeing. It was a lovely evening, the air blessedly cool and the lemony light of the setting sun throwing long shadows behind them. Arm in arm they walked unsteadily back down the lane and through the recently-shorn cornfields.

'Very prickly,' remarked Ernest, as he picked his way through the stubble.

This struck Annie as terribly funny, and she burst into a fit of giggles.

'Prickly tickly stubble,' said Ernest, pleased with the effect he was having. 'Prickly tickly Annie. Pretty prickly tickly Annie.'

'Silly Ernest.' Annie giggled again.

'Shall we sit down?' Ernest spread his coat on the grass under the hedge and pulled Annie down beside him. 'Pretty tickly Annie,' he repeated, fumbling with the buttons of Annie's dress. 'Pretty girl.'

Afterwards, Annie was to ask herself over and over again why she hadn't stopped Ernest while there was still time. Tipsy as she was, she wasn't particularly tempted to cooperate in her seduction. It would have been quite easy to get up and go home, for Ernest was in no state to prevent her. But her judgment was clouded, and a small part of her felt that she owed Ernest something after all he had done for her. And where was the harm? She was even a bit curious, and it would certainly be some time before she had another opportunity like this.

Annie knew little about sex, and it had never occurred to her that it was meant to be pleasurable, but now, with her head pushed back into the stubble, sharp corn stalks pricking the backs of her calves and Ernest rootling about somewhere in between, she wondered why anyone ever bothered to do this strange and extraordinarily rude thing. Ernest had stopped murmuring his little endearments, and appeared to be concentrating on the job in hand, while somewhere outside it all, as though removed from the whole business, all Annie could think of was that if only she had known what was going to happen, she would have put on a more respectable pair of knickers.

The pain, when it came, was sharp and unpleasant, but the lingering effects of the cider were sufficient to dull Annie's sensibilities, and she bore her ordeal with stoicism. Ernest, meanwhile, seemed to be finding the whole thing terribly hard work, and there was a great deal of puffing and panting as he pumped energetically up and down over her recumbent body. Annie watched the first pale outline of the moon appearing and disappearing rhythmically beyond Ernest's shoulder, and wondered whether he had done this before. She also hoped very much that he would finish soon.

Afterwards, Ernest rolled off her and stumbled to his feet, turning away to do up his trousers.

Any hint of the humour and affection which had preceded their lovemaking – if indeed that was what this was – appeared to have evaporated, and he seemed anxious to be on his way.

They returned to the car in silence, Annie hopping and stumbling after Ernest's hurrying figure (no complaints of prickly stubble now), carrying her shoes in her hand.

'What's wrong? What's the matter, Ernest?' she asked when she finally caught up with him.

'You don't know?' Ernest turned to face her, and while it was by now too dark to see his face, Annie knew that he was angry.

'No,' she said, with absolute truth. 'I don't know. I thought – that – was what you wanted.'

'What *you* wanted, you mean.'

'What *I* wanted?' Annie was stunned. Did Ernest really think that what had just happened had been an enjoyable experience for her?

'That's what I said.' Ernest opened the car door and retrieved the starting handle. 'What you wanted. We shouldn't – you shouldn't – well, it's too late to talk about that now. I just never thought you were that sort of girl. You've surprised me, Annie. You really have. In fact I think I'd better be going. You can find your way back from here can't you? You've only got to cross the yard.' Rather unsteadily, he began to crank up the engine.

'Yes,' Annie whispered, tears springing to her eyes. The effects of the cider had worn off, and she felt sore and humiliated and ashamed. All she wanted now was to get home, have a thorough wash and regain the security of her own bedroom.

She bent down to put on her shoes, wondering why it should matter if Ernest was displeased. After all, as she had told her father, she didn't really care for him, so why should she worry if she had somehow incurred his displeasure?

And yet how dare Ernest talk to her the way he had? How *dare* he? 'That sort of girl', indeed! Who did he think he was? He was no more entitled to occupy the moral high-ground than she was, and yet he seemed perfectly happy to lay all the blame on her. If he never came back, she was well shot of him. In fact this evening had shown Ernest up in a new light. It was a good thing she hadn't made a permanent commitment before discovering this new and decidedly unpleasant side of him.

So why did she feel suddenly so afraid? As Annie turned towards the house, she shivered. She had a dreadful feeling that she had not seen the last of Ernest.

CHAPTER FOURTEEN

Andrew

'Bad news, I'm afraid. Your cat's dead.'

Your cat. Not our cat, nor even the cat, but *your* cat. Andrew's cat. Tobias. Tobias, whom Janet had always disliked. And now it was she who was breaking the news to him on his return home after a particularly stressful day.

Andrew sat down.

'How? I mean, what happened? He was fine this morning.'

'No, he wasn't. He hadn't been fine for ages. He'd been going downhill for months, and you wouldn't do anything about it. It was inhumane to keep an animal like that alive at his age. Nearly twenty–'

'Seventeen, actually.'

'Well, seventeen, then. Anyway, he'd been having accidents all over the house' (two accidents, and one had happened in Andrew's study, and therefore didn't count) 'and someone had to do something.'

'You mean you.'

'Well, yes, as it happens. Me. Somebody had to take charge, and I knew you'd never get round to it. He managed to get out of your study and made a mess on the sitting-room floor. It was the last straw. We really can't have that sort of thing in the vicarage. I phoned the vet and told him all about it, and he said that what with that and his age, it might be the kindest thing to have him put down. So I took him along this morning, and the vet said I'd done the right thing. Heart failure or kidney failure; something like that. Anyway, he said there was nothing anyone could have done to make him any better, and his quality of life was minimal.'

Andrew felt a swell of grief and rage which amazed even himself, and he clutched the edge of the table to steady himself.

'You mean that you took it upon yourself to have my cat put down when I was out, and when

94

I couldn't be around to give my opinion? You, who have never taken any interest in him at all, decide when it's time for him to die? I can't believe you've done this, Janet. I just can't believe it. I thought even you had a little more – compassion.'

'What do you mean, even me? No one's ever accused me of lacking sympathy! I always do my best to consider other people and do what's best, you know I do.'

'No you don't!' Andrew shouted, beside himself. 'You knew how fond I was of that cat! You've never liked him, and you took the opportunity to – to do this thing while I was out of the house and couldn't do anything to stop you!'

'I tried ringing you on your mobile, but as usual it was switched off.'

'I was taking a funeral, Janet. It would hardly have been appropriate for me to have my mobile switched on during a funeral.'

'Well, it's done now.' Janet turned back to the papers she was sorting. 'There's nothing anyone can do about it now. And I think it's for the best.'

'I don't know how you could do this, knowing how much he meant to me.' Andrew swallowed hard, trying to regain some self-control. He pressed his fingers against his temples, and took a couple of deep breaths before speaking again. 'And am I allowed to know where he is now?'

'Where he is?'

'Yes. His body. Where's his body? What did you do with it?'

'Oh, I didn't do anything with it. I left it at the vet's. He said he'd deal with it.'

Andrew stood up.

'Where are you going now?' Janet asked.

'To fetch my cat,' Andrew said. 'I wasn't allowed to make the decision about his death; I wasn't even allowed to say goodbye to him. I hope I may at least be allowed to decide what to do with his body.'

On the way to the vet's, Andrew wept. It was years since he had shed tears – in fact, quite recently he had wondered whether he was still capable of crying – but now he wept unashamedly. He wept for the tiny rescued kitten who had been brought to his door ('We knew you'd look after him, vicar'), and for the seventeen years of companionship which had followed; for the evenings reading or writing sermons, with the warm softly-purring body twined round his neck (more latterly, curled on his knee, for Tobias in old age had lost his athleticism); for the sinuous twisting round his legs when he managed to smuggle a treat – a little cream, or maybe some sardines – into his study. But most of all, he wept for Janet's total disregard for his own feelings. For if she could do this to him, then it was quite clear that she could no longer care for him at all.

The nurse at the vet's was very pleasant. No, they hadn't disposed of the body yet, and if Andrew would care to wait, she would bring it to him.

Andrew waited. Around him, people sat on hard, waiting-room chairs holding dogs' leads or carrying cages or boxes from which emanated a variety of scratchings and squeakings. Someone even had a glass bowl with an obviously dead

96

upside-down goldfish in it. If this wasn't so awful, Andrew thought, it would be funny. How seriously we all take our pets, we British. Could it be that all these people were, like him, looking for a type of companionship they couldn't get elsewhere? Were they, too, lonely and disappointed?

'Here you are.' The nurse handed Andrew a cardboard box. It felt surprisingly heavy considering the frailty of the body inside.

'Thank you. Can you tell me please, did he, I mean was it, well, fairly peaceful? You see, I wasn't with him when he died.'

'He won't have felt a thing.' The nurse patted him on the shoulder. She smelt of dogs and disinfectant. 'Don't you worry. Mr Evans is very good at this sort of thing.'

Back in the car, Andrew drove round for a bit, and then parked outside the church. On an impulse, he lifted the cardboard box out of the boot, and unlocking the heavy oak door with a key from his pocket, he carried it into the building.

The church was cool and dark, the last of the evening sunlight filtering through the stained glass of the west window and leaving pale lozenges of colour on the worn stone of the floor. The church smelled of old wood and must and the fresh green scent of the flowers which had been arranged in brass jugs on either side of the chancel. Andrew set the box down, and kneeling in one of the pews, he tried to pray.

But for once, he had no idea what to say. Not one to believe in an afterlife for animals, even a much-loved one such as Tobias, perhaps he should simply give thanks for the life which had given him so much comfort. Or perhaps he should ask forgiveness for his outburst of anger, because it could just have been that Janet really had done what she thought best, and that she had had no intention of going behind his back.

But she did know, he thought. She did. This was the ultimate way of getting to him; an act of aggression disguised as a mission of mercy. This was the way it often was. Janet appeared to do the right thing, but now, he realised, there could be more to it; her own aggrandisement, perhaps, or the putting down of another person. It was with a shock that he realised that not only did he no longer love Janet, but that he didn't even like her any more.

It wasn't only today that prayer was difficult. Increasingly, Andrew was finding it hard to make contact with the God to whom he had once dedicated his life. It was as though he was speaking on the telephone to someone who had already replaced the receiver.

Did he still believe? He was no longer sure. Once, it had seemed so obvious; so easy; so *right*. Now, he was filled with doubts; doubts about himself, about his vocation. There was an emptiness in his spiritual life which reflected that other emptiness, the emptiness and pointlessness of his life with Janet. He was not a man given to self-pity. He had seen too much of suffering to think that life was or ever could be fair. But he no longer felt connected with the path he had chosen to follow; with the sermons and the prayers and the services. He felt as though he were acting a part in a drama and that very soon the curtain would come down and all would be shown to have been a sham.

Later on, under a perfect evening sky, Andrew buried Tobias in the vicarage garden. He chose a spot under the prunus tree which Tobias used to climb and which had given him easy access to the flat roof over the study where he liked to bask in the afternoon sun. Janet, watching tight-lipped from the house, had made no comment. Maybe she realised that this time she really had over-stepped the mark.

But it could be that we both have, thought Andrew now, as he marked Tobias's grave with a lichen-covered stone from the rockery. Maybe we have both gone beyond the point of no return and will each of us have to find our own way. It could be that the death of Tobias has marked another even more significant ending: the ending of what little hope is left for our marriage.

He sighed and looked up at the sky. Tiny pin-pricks of stars were already appearing and he could just make out the pale fingernail of a new moon. At least some things never changed.

Brushing the soil from his hands, Andrew picked up his spade and turned back towards the house.

CHAPTER FIFTEEN

Annie's Story

'So where's Ernest these days, our Annie? We don't seem to have seen him in a while.'

It was the question Annie had been dreading, for what could she say? She could hardly tell the truth, and yet Ernest's sudden disappearance had been bound to arouse curiosity.

'Oh, I expect he'll be in touch,' she said.

'It's not like him,' her father persisted. 'Are you sure you've not had a falling out? You'll regret it if you have, you know. You may not have noticed, but there's a bit of a shortage of young men these days. Will be for some time to come, too. You're too fussy for your own good, our Annie, and that's a fact.'

'He'll turn up,' Annie said. 'I expect he's busy at work.'

'Busy at work! These people who work in banks don't know they're born. Nice working hours, and holidays as well. You've upset him, our Annie, make no mistake. I've a feeling we may not be seeing Ernest hereabouts again.'

If only, Annie thought, as she swept out the yard and started on the cow shed. It was true that she hadn't heard from Ernest, but it could be that he was just making her wait. Maybe he was even trying to punish her, and would turn up again once he felt he had kept her waiting for long enough. One thing was certain. If Ernest felt this way now, then whatever feelings he may have had for her certainly couldn't have been described as love.

Annie dreaded seeing him; she dreaded his anger and his disapproval, for although she knew that Ernest was at least as much to blame for what had happened as she was, she felt deeply ashamed that she had allowed things to get so out of hand. She felt soiled and dirty, and knew that she had now joined the ranks of what her mother referred to as girls who were no better than they ought to be.

It was all so unfair. Annie had had to sacrifice her education and any chance of a proper career because of the war, she had worked hard and done her bit, and now, because of a man she didn't care about and a few glasses of cider she had crossed some sort of threshold from which there was no going back. Her mother had always told her that she should save herself for the man she married, and while Annie, in her ignorance, had never been entirely sure what that meant, she had a pretty good idea that she had now become damaged goods. She certainly felt, if not damaged, then at the very least sullied, for who would want her after this?

The harvest came to an end, the trees began to turn, and eventually a short formal letter arrived from Ernest. He regretted that pressure of work and the recent illness of his widowed mother made such demands on his time that he was no longer able to make the trip out to the farm, but he wished Annie and her family well.

Annie was tremendously relieved. She'd had nothing to fear from Ernest after all, even if her father grumbled about the wasted petrol, and her mother mourned the passing of what she appeared to have seen as a golden opportunity for her daughter.

So Annie got on with her life, and before long it was as though Ernest had never been a part of it. She missed their outings and the cachet of having a boyfriend (Mavis, previously unable to conceal her envy, had welcomed Annie's return to the uncoupled state with unaccustomed warmth), but otherwise things were remarkably normal.

Poor Annie. It never occurred to her that her unfortunate fling in the stubble might have more far-reaching consequences than she had could have dreamt of.

While Annie knew a great deal about the animals on the farm, her knowledge about the workings of her own body were sketchy to say the least. She had accepted its growth and development as she accepted everything else around her. Her periods had started when she was thirteen, and like so many of her generation she was at first thoroughly alarmed by what appeared to be a life-threatening condition. Her mother's embarrassed little talk, delivered in haste together with the 'things Annie would need', helped to clear up some of the mystery, but any other questions she might have had remained unanswered. And so it was hardly surprising that she paid little attention when her periods suddenly stopped.

The morning sickness was not so easy to ignore.

'Whatever's the matter, our Annie?' Her father asked, as she fled from the milking shed for the second morning in succession to throw up on the dung heap.

'Must be something I ate,' Annie said, puzzled by these sudden bouts of nausea. 'I expect it'll pass.'

'Morning sickness, eh?' Mavis muttered into the flank of the cow she was milking. 'You're a dark horse, Annie!'

'We're not having that sort of talk, Mavis.' Annie's father, overhearing her, cuffed the back of Mavis's head. 'You get on with your work. And you'll keep a clean tongue in your head, or I'll want to know the reason why.'

But while Mavis's remark had been made in all innocence (if in rather dubious taste) Annie's father evidently paid more attention to it than he had appeared to, for a few days later Annie found that an appointment had been made for her to see the doctor, who after the briefest of examinations pronounced her to be nearly three months pregnant.

Stunned and disbelieving, Annie travelled back to the farmhouse with her father in silence. It couldn't be true. Annie didn't know much about sex, but she did know you couldn't get pregnant the first time. Mavis had told her that. There must be some mistake. There had to be some mistake. This awful thing couldn't be happening to her. She didn't deserve it. Unwanted pregnancies happened to bad girls; girls who asked for it. Poor Annie hadn't asked for anything, and yet here she was, apparently carrying Ernest's baby.

Ernest's baby. It didn't bear thinking about.

'Well, our Annie?' her father finally said. 'What happened at the doctor's?'

What could Annie say? She couldn't tell her father the truth, and yet what choice did she have? And what about her mother? How would it affect her? And Annie herself; what was she to do? Where was she to go? Would she have to leave the farm and go into exile like Doris? Annie burst into tears.

'You're expecting, aren't you?' There was a chill in her father's voice which Annie had never heard before. 'That's it, isn't it? You're expecting.'

'Yes,' Annie whispered.

'And who's the father?'

'Who's the father?' Annie was stunned. What sort of girl did her father think she was? There was only one person who could possibly be the father of her baby.

'Ernest, was it?'

'Yes.' Annie stifled a sob

'You're sure of that, are you? Because if it's Ernest, then he'll have to do the right thing by you. I'll make sure of that.'

'What do you mean? Dad, you can't make him – you can't make us–'

'Oh, can't I?' Her father swung the car into the farmyard and drew up in front of the house. 'If you're expecting Ernest's baby, then Ernest must marry you. It's only right.'

'He won't, Dad. Ernest won't marry me. And I – I don't want to marry Ernest!'

'You should have thought of that before, shouldn't you? It's not going to be about what you want any more. You said goodbye to what you wanted the day you – the day you did this.'

'But you can't make us marry, Dad. You can't! We'd only make each other unhappy.' Annie clung to his arm, weeping.

'And who said you had any right to be happy? There's more to life than being happy, our Annie, as you're about to find out.' Her father shook her free and got out of the car. 'We'll see what your mother has to say about all this.'

'But Dad! You can't tell Mum! Please don't tell Mum!' Annie's mother was so emotionally fragile these days that the family did their best to protect her from anything which might upset her. This latest piece of news would most certainly upset her a great deal.

'I've got to tell her,' her father said grimly, as they reached the front door. 'There's some things that can't be kept from your mother.'

As soon as she got into the house, Annie ran straight upstairs to her room. As she lay on her bed, she could hear raised voices from the room below and the muffled sound of her mother weeping. At one stage, her mother brought her up some bread and cheese and tea, placing them wordlessly beside the bed, but Annie felt too sick and too anxious to eat anything.

In the morning, nothing was said by either of her parents, but there was a new distance in their manner towards her, and she was filled with dread, for she had the feeling that some sort of decision had been made about her future.

'What – what am I going to do, Dad? What's going to happen to me?' Annie ventured, when teatime came and still no one had said anything.

'That all depends on Ernest, our Annie. If Ernest will have you, then you'll marry him. If not, then heaven help you. You give me his address, and I'll write to him tonight.'

'But even if I wanted him Ernest wouldn't marry me. Especially – now.'

'Oh, I think Ernest might be persuaded.' Her father sighed. 'But you've caused us a deal of grief, our Annie. A deal of grief.'

'I'm sorry, Dad. I'm so, so sorry.'

'Too late to be sorry. You've made your bed, our Annie. You're going to have to lie on it.'

'And Mum? What does she think?' But Annie spoke without much hope. Her mother's strict Baptist background would prevent her from going against her husband, especially in a matter as grave as this.

'Your mother? Well, it's the end of all her dreams, isn't it? She always wanted the best for you; a church wedding, everything done properly. Even with the war on, we would have given you a decent wedding. We'd have managed somehow. She – we – saved up for it. Now we may have to put that money to another use.'

'What do you mean?' Annie was fearful.

'You'll see.' Her father's face was grim. 'We'll just have to wait for Ernest now, won't we? It all depends on Ernest now, our Annie. Everything depends on Ernest.'

CHAPTER SIXTEEN

Ophelia

'How?' Billy raged. 'How on earth did you come to lose a job like that? A job which I presume any half-sensible girl could do standing on her head? Exactly how did you manage it, Ophelia?'

He was pacing up and down the cream carpet of the immaculate living-room while Ophelia, who had had this sort of conversation many times before, sat curled up on the sofa.

'I didn't lose it. I left. I gave in my notice.'

'You gave in your notice!' From her father's tone of voice, Ophelia might just as well have burnt down the entire nursing home, and all its unfortunate residents with it.

'But you were so happy, dear,' her mother ventured, entering the room with a tray of coffee.

'I was and I wasn't.' Ophelia uncurled her legs and helped Sheila with the coffee cups. 'I loved the old people, but I didn't get on with the matron.'

'You didn't get on with the matron!'

Ophelia wished her father wouldn't repeat everything she said. It made them sound like some sort of ghastly double act.

'She was an old trout, and she didn't give a fig for the old people.'

'Oh, I'm sure she did, dear,' said Sheila, pouring coffee.

'No, she didn't. And we ended up having this row, and I told her to stuff her job.'

'*Ophelia!*'

'Actually, it was great. I'd been longing to say what I felt. It was worth losing my reference for–'

'Losing your reference!' Now it was Sheila's turn to be shocked. 'Oh, Ophelia! Whatever will you do without a reference?'

'Nearly twenty years old, with no job and no reference. After all we've done for you,' added Billy. This last was an old and familiar refrain, and Ophelia often thought that if she were to predecease her parents, those words would more than likely appear on her tombstone; a reproachful epitaph for a failed daughter.

'I'll be okay.' Ophelia helped herself to a chocolate biscuit, ignoring her mother's raised eyebrows (she was supposed to be trying to lose weight). 'I'll find something.'

'And meanwhile, what are you proposing to live on?' Billy asked.

'They've given me a month's pay, so I've got time to look around. I can get a job waitressing or maybe doing bar work. Something like that. Just to tide me over. Don't worry, Dad. You won't have to keep me.'

'You could go and stay with your grandmother,' Billy said, not without a hint of triumph. 'No excuses now that you haven't got a job to go to.'

'But I ought to be job-hunting.'

'You can leave the job-hunting for a few days. Your grandmother needs you, Ophelia.'

Ophelia forbore to point out that her grandmother had never in her life needed her only granddaughter, and was unlikely to start now.

'How is Gran?' she asked.

'Coping, I think. I haven't been able to get down for a couple of weeks. I rang that priest fellow, but he wouldn't tell me much. He's obviously been going to see her, and I believe she's been talking to him, but he wasn't giving anything away.'

Ophelia began to warm towards the priest fellow. Anyone who could stand up to her father deserved a degree of respect.

'Okay,' she said. 'I'll go.' After all, anything had to be better than suffering her father's wrath and the reproachful murmurings of her mother.

The visit was arranged for the following week. Ophelia was to borrow Sheila's car (her driving test, as Billy frequently pointed out, being the only examination she had contrived to pass first time) and travel down on the Sunday afternoon, returning on the Thursday. Annie had sounded suspicious and uncooperative on the phone, but when Ophelia told her father this, he assured her that it was probably because her grandmother spent too much time on her own. She had been much exercised over the matter of a duvet for Ophelia's bed, and so it had been arranged that Ophelia should bring her own. Sheila provided a casserole to save Annie some of the cooking, and Ophelia bought a potted plant.

The visit got off to an unpromising start. Ophelia was very late, due to a hold-up on the motorway, and when she arrived she found that Annie was already in her dressing-gown and slippers.

'Hello, Gran.' Ophelia kissed her grand-mother's papery cheek. 'So sorry I'm late. The traffic was awful. I've brought you this.'

Annie took the plant and sniffed it.

'It's got no scent,' she said, disappointed.

'I don't think it's meant to have. It's a–' Ophelia consulted the label '–it's a hydrangea.'

'A hydrangea. Fancy that.' Annie paused. 'I don't know much about plants. Ernest did all that sort of thing, you see.'

'And mum sent a casserole.'

'What sort of casserole?'

'I think it's beef.'

'That's all right, then,' Annie said. 'Ernest would never eat pork, you know. He had a Jewish grandmother. The vicar's coming tomorrow,' she added, leading the way through to the living-room.

'The vicar?' That must be the priest fellow her father had referred to.

'Yes. He comes round and I – I tell him about my life.'

'Goodness.'

'Yes. There's things I've never told anyone before.'

'But you tell the vicar?'

'Yes. He thinks it will help me. I'm not sure, though. It can be a bit upsetting.' Annie paused. 'Do you want some of this stew?'

Ophelia had stopped off for a sandwich at a service station, and wasn't particularly hungry.

'No thank you. Just a cup of tea would be nice.'

'Or you could have some whisky,' Annie said. 'I always have one at bedtime.'

'Whisky?'

'Yes. I found some in Ernest's cupboard, and I find it helps. It helps the vicar, too. He told me so.'

'Does Dad know? About the whisky, I mean.'

Annie gave her a pitying look.

'Of course not. And you're not to tell him, either.'

'I wouldn't dream of it,' said Ophelia, much entertained by the idea of her grandmother and the whisky-swilling vicar.

Two large whiskies later ('I only usually have one, but this is a special occasion,' explained Annie), Ophelia and Annie were becoming relaxed and confidential.

'I lost my job, you know,' Ophelia said. 'Dad was furious.'

'I know. He told me,' Annie said.

'I'm a terrible disappointment to them.' Ophelia twisted her glass round between her fingers. She noticed that it wasn't entirely clean.

'Good thing you weren't a boy,' observed Annie. 'Billy wanted you to be a boy, you know.'

'I bet he did. I wonder what they would have called him,' Ophelia mused. 'Siegfried, perhaps, or Horatio.'

'Maximilian,' said Annie. 'They were going to call you Maximilian. Maximilian Ernest William Bentley. What do you think of that?'

Ophelia laughed. 'I think I'm quite glad I'm female. Not just because of the name, either. A disappointing son is somehow much worse than a disappointing daughter, don't you think?' She put down her glass. 'Tell me about this vicar of yours. What's he like?'

'He's nice. I didn't like him at first; I thought he was just interfering. But after he buried the chickens, I felt a bit better about him.'

'What chickens?' A combination of tiredness and whisky, combined with Annie's propensity to leap from one subject to another, assuming complete comprehension on the part of her listener, was beginning to make Ophelia's head ache.

'Ernest's chickens. I starved them. By mistake, of course. But I think it was for the best. I've never been very good with chickens.'

'So I gather.'

'And Andrew's kind—'

'Who's Andrew?'

'The vicar. He's kind and he's – interested. Not many people are interested. I can tell him anything, and he just listens. I've told him things I've never told anybody, and he just takes it all in.'

'What sort of things?' asked Ophelia, intrigued.

'Personal things. Some of them are very personal. I thought he might be shocked, but he didn't seem to be. I've told him the worst part, though, so now it's a bit easier.'

'You don't look the sort of person to have a shocking past, Gran,' Ophelia said. 'It all sounds very mysterious.'

'Not very mysterious really. But such a waste, Ophelia. Such a waste.' There were tears in Annie's eyes which had only a little to do with the whisky.

'A waste of what, Gran?'

'A waste of – of me.'

'Oh, Gran.' Ophelia put her hand on her grandmother's and they sat in silence for a few minutes.

'Everyone would be awfully upset if they knew,' Annie said, blowing her nose.

'Like who? Who would be upset?'

'Well, your parents, Ernest's friends (not that he had that many), his committee people. Billy must have had an idea about some of it, but he never said anything, and Ernest always told me not to tell anyone. "It's private," he said, and perhaps he was right.' Annie looked suddenly fearful, as though the ghost of Ernest were standing behind her shoulder waiting to pounce on her for her indiscretion.

'But maybe now he's dead – well, maybe that changes things a bit?' Ophelia suggested.

Annie smiled, and squeezed Ophelia's hand. 'Maybe. One day I might even be able to tell you,' she said. 'I think I'd like to tell you. One day.'

Later on, as Ophelia lay on the lumpy mattress in the little back bedroom (thank heavens she had brought her own duvet; the musty blankets piled on the chair smelled of mothballs and damp), she felt an unaccustomed surge of affection for her grandmother. There was obviously a lot more to Annie than she had previously thought.

She was surprised to find that she was looking forward to getting to know her grandmother better.

CHAPTER SEVENTEEN

Annie

Although Annie had known that she couldn't put off a visit from Ophelia for ever, she had still been less than pleased when it had finally been arranged. She couldn't quite rid herself of the uncomfortable feeling that Ophelia was being sent as some sort of spy, to assess her progress following Ernest's death, but more than that, having settled into her new routine, she was reluctant to have it disturbed.

For years, Annie's life had been dictated by the needs and expectations of Ernest, and while it had taken her time to adjust to her new freedom, she found that she was beginning to enjoy it. Andrew had recently asked her if she was happy, and Annie had thought it a strange question. After all that time with Ernest, she had long since ceased to expect happiness. There had been small pleasures – a favourite television programme, the feel and smell of a shiny new magazine, a rare evening of bingo, the carefully measured sherries Ernest used to pour for her (Annie had come a long way since those sherries) – but happiness had become a forgotten luxury. And now, in her newly-widowed state, surely she couldn't be expected to be happy, could she? Or could she?

Annie had pondered the question after Andrew

had gone, and to her surprise she had concluded that nowadays, she did experience moments of something approaching happiness. Free from the restraints of running the house to Ernest's exacting standards, and more importantly, free from the fear of any repercussions should she be found wanting, Annie was able to please herself, something she had never in her life been allowed to do before. If she didn't feel like cooking, she opened a tin. If she wanted to stay in bed in the morning, that's what she would do. If she wanted to watch daytime television, then she would watch it, revelling in the tasteless chat shows which Ernest had so deplored. And while she was no longer letting things go in quite the way she had at the beginning, and was managing to resist the temptation to take refuge in the whisky bottle when things got difficult (except, of course, at bedtime), she was in some small way beginning to enjoy herself.

Annie was lonely, but then she had always been lonely. Apart from Billy, she had no family left, and while she had many acquaintances, she had few she could count as friends. Ernest had discouraged her from forming close friendships with other women, anxious that female confidences might lead to indiscreet disclosures on her part, and he himself had hardly been much in the way of company. Since his retirement, his committee work and the garden and his allotment had kept him occupied, and Annie had seen little more of him than she had when he was working. But now, she had Andrew's visits to look forward to.

She anticipated these with pleasure, and was

disappointed on the rare occasions when something else came up and Andrew was unable to call round to see her. Andrew had told her a little about himself, and reading between the lines, Annie had come to suspect that like herself, he had found his life to be less than fulfilling. She didn't know the cause of his sadness, but it was undoubtedly there, and had she been bolder, she might have asked him to tell her more.

Thus, Ophelia's proposed visit had come as an unwelcome intrusion into Annie's new, even cosy, life, and she had done little to prepare for it. If Ophelia wanted to come and stay, she must take her as she found her. She had no idea how she was going to entertain a young woman, or indeed if she was expected to entertain her at all, but that too was up to Ophelia. No doubt they could watch some television together, and Ophelia would probably bring a book to read (as a child, she had constantly had her head in a book). Beyond that, and the purchase of a few random provisions (she was somewhat disconcerted to find on her return from the supermarket that she had bought no less than three tins of anchovies; what on earth did one do with anchovies?) Annie had made no plans whatsoever.

Had she known Ophelia better, things would no doubt have been a great deal easier, but because Annie had had an uneasy relationship with Sheila, the contact between them had been irregular and any visits brief. She and Ernest had very occasionally stayed at Billy's and Sheila's house, but, in rare agreement, had not enjoyed the visits. Annie had hardly dared to sit on the leather sofas

116

in case she disturbed the carefully arranged cushions, and Ernest never liked being away from his allotment and his chickens. As for Ophelia, in the beginning, Annie had looked forward eagerly to being a grandmother and the opportunity of forming a relationship with her new grandchild. The little back bedroom would be ideal for Ophelia when she came to stay, and Annie had even bought a second-hand cot in anticipation of her visits. But Annie, it transpired, was not to be entrusted with the care of a young child, and contact was limited to brief cameo appearances by an uncomfortably overdressed baby closely attended by her overprotective parents. Annie had been allowed to hold Ophelia, and later on, occasionally to read her a story or help her with a jigsaw, but the child was soon swept away in the back of the family saloon car, leaving Annie feeling that she had just experienced a royal visitation rather than a normal family get-together. As Ophelia grew older, Annie still hoped that she might be allowed to come and stay, but when Ophelia wasn't away at her boarding school she always seemed to be busy being improved in some way, and there appeared to be little time for anything else. Gradually, Annie gave up hope, notching up the experience as just one more of life's disappointments, and by the time Ophelia had reached her teens, Annie felt that she hardly knew her at all.

Thus over the years the two families had maintained a certain distance. Billy had kept up regular dutiful contact, and Sheila occasionally telephoned; school photographs arrived and were duly framed and placed on the sideboard; gifts were exchanged at birthdays and Christmas, and the rare, awkward visits had taken place, but otherwise they had played little part in each other's lives. Once, only once, Annie and Ernest had been invited to stay for a never-to-be-forgotten family Christmas, in the course of which Sheila, overwhelmed by all the extra work, had what could only be described as a panic attack, leading to the partial incineration of the turkey, and Ernest and Billy had had a memorable row about, of all things, the timing of the Queen's speech. All things considered, Annie had long since regretfully decided that minimal contact was probably best for all concerned.

But in spite of all her misgivings and her initial annoyance at the late hour of Ophelia's arrival, Annie had been pleasantly surprised by her granddaughter. She appeared to have grown into a thoroughly sensible young woman, with none of the airs and graces of her parents, and very approachable. Of course, she still wasn't much to look at, poor girl, but that wasn't her fault, and she did have nice eyes and a pretty smile. They had had quite a pleasant little chat over their nightcap (Annie had dreaded having to go without her whisky during Ophelia's stay, for she could hardly have sat drinking it on her own), and she thought that they might get along well enough together after all.

It was only as she was preparing for bed that Annie realised that with Ophelia in the house it would be quite inappropriate for Andrew to come tomorrow. Monday was his day off, the day he usually managed to call in and see her, and Annie had been especially looking forward to telling him the next part of her story. In the beginning, it had been a struggle to get started, but now it was as though some torrent inside her had been let loose and needed to continue its escape. When he had left the house the previous week, she had felt almost overwhelmed by the pent-up emotion generated by the vivid reliving of her past, and had hardly known how she was going to wait until his next visit. But she couldn't talk to Andrew properly in front of Ophelia, and she could hardly ask her granddaughter to leave the room. And while it wasn't just the whisky talking when she had told Ophelia that she would like to be able to tell her story to her some time, that time was a long way off and might well never come.

In the event, it was Ophelia herself who brought up the subject over breakfast (crackers and marmalade – Annie had forgotten to buy bread) the next morning.

'If your vicar–'

'Andrew.'

'Andrew, then. If he's coming over today, I can take myself off and have a little drive round.'

'Are you sure?' Touched by such thoughtfulness, Annie was nonetheless anxious not to risk Ophelia's change of heart by any demurral on her own part. 'Are you sure you don't mind?'

'I don't mind at all. It's a lovely day. I've got the car. I can explore a bit.'

Andrew arrived just before eleven, and Annie made the introductions. There was nothing unusual in their meeting – hands were shaken, a few pleasantries exchanged – nevertheless, long afterwards, she wondered that she hadn't noticed what was happening in that room when these two very disparate people met for the first time. But then how could she have?

As everyone knows, love at first sight is a myth, only ever believable to the individuals concerned.

CHAPTER EIGHTEEN

Annie's Story

The week following Annie's visit to the doctor seemed one of the longest of her life. Suspended in a limbo of fear and uncertainty, she went about her tasks with a desperate fervour, feeding and milking, cleaning and mucking-out as though her life depended on it, volunteering to do the jobs she normally eschewed, even giving up her afternoon off so that Mavis could go into town.

'What on earth's got into you, Annie?' Mavis asked. 'Not that I'm not grateful or anything, but I can't help wondering. Looks like you're trying to win some sort of prize.'

And in a way Mavis was right. The prize Annie was working so desperately towards was to be allowed to stay at home. She would work on the farm to the end of her days, and willingly, if she didn't have to marry Ernest. If she could just stay at home she would never complain again. She would prove to her father that she was indispensable. Neither of her brothers would be taking on the farm: Tom was in a military hospital having lost a leg, and would no longer be capable of hard physical work, and Jack was now an officer and had long since decided to stay on in the army and make a career of it, whether or not the war should come to an end. Surely her father would – must – need her. How else would he cope as he grew older? She was cheap and experienced. She was sure he would soon see that he couldn't manage without her.

As for the baby, strangely enough she didn't give it much thought. She had some vague idea that so long as she could stay on the farm, the problem of the baby would sort itself out. Hidden away in the countryside, surely it would be possible for a baby to go more or less unnoticed. Perhaps her mother might even be persuaded to pass it off as her own. Just so long as she could stay where she was, Annie felt that all her other problems would be solved.

Her parents had said nothing further about what was to be done, and Annie didn't dare broach the subject herself. She longed to throw herself on their mercy – literally; to cling and sob and beg; to hold and to be held. She craved reassurance that she was still loved and above all, forgiven, for worst of all was the feeling that she had somehow forfeited her right to be treated as their daughter. Never before had she needed comfort and security as she did now, and her parents had never seemed so distant, although they continued to act almost as though nothing had happened. They went about their work as

121

usual, but her father's tread was heavy and he seemed suddenly older, and more than once there were signs that her mother had been crying. It was as though they too were in a state of uncertainty; they, like her, were waiting. And of course what they were waiting for was a reply from Ernest. What was it her father had said? 'Everything depends on Ernest.' Annie shuddered. If Ernest held her future in his hands, what hope could there be for her?

But then, why should Ernest respond at all? It was quite clear that he didn't love her, and it wasn't Ernest who was to be encumbered with the fruits of his behaviour. Annie began to hope. If Ernest never turned up, then everything would be all right. Things would soon return to normal, and they could all get on with their lives.

But Annie's hope was short-lived. Ten days after he had sent his letter to Ernest, her father received a reply. Annie never found out exactly what was in it, but it seemed that Ernest was prepared to visit her parents to discuss the situation.

'You'll have to keep to your room on Saturday, when Ernest comes, our Annie,' her father said. 'Your mother and I need to talk to him in private. We've things to sort out.'

'Don't make me marry him, Dad! Please don't make me marry Ernest!' Annie begged. 'I'll do anything – *anything* – if you'll only let me stay here with you. I'll work so hard, I'll help Mum in the house too, I'll never grumble again. If only you let me stay!'

'It's too late for that, our Annie. Believe you

me. Your only hope is Ernest. You'd better pray that he wants you, for if Ernest won't have you I don't know what will become of you.'

Ernest arrived just after lunch on the following Saturday. Annie, banished to her bedroom, watched with dread from her bedroom window as he drove into the farmyard, carefully avoiding the mud and the puddles, and drew up in front of the house. All the little mannerisms which she now knew so well – the careful testing of the handle after he'd closed the car door, the wiping of a minute speck of dirt from the windscreen with his handkerchief, the smoothing back of his well-oiled hair, the brief nervous touch to the moustache – now filled her with revulsion. How could she have allowed the relationship to come to this? Why, oh why, hadn't she put an end to it months ago, when her fate was in her own hands rather than those of other people? Annie cursed the vanity which had driven her to accept any boyfriend rather than no boyfriend, dull outings with Ernest rather than evenings at home.

Ernest knocked at the front door and was admitted. Annie didn't know which of her parents had let him in as the door was concealed by the porch, but she could hear the door of the living-room opening and closing, and the sound of voices below. Sick with fear, Annie waited what seemed an interminable length of time while her future was measured out in those muffled voices. Once, her father's voice was raised in anger, and once she thought she heard Ernest too raise his voice, but otherwise the sounds were barely audible. She tried lying on her bedroom floor

123

with her ear pressed to the worn floorboards, but it made no difference. The house was old and well built, used to keeping its secrets. Annie would have to wait a while longer to learn her fate.

Eventually, she heard her father's voice calling her name.

'Annie? Annie! Come on downstairs. Ernest has something to say to you.'

Slowly, Annie walked down the stairs, aware that the next time she ascended them her life might be entirely changed. How many times, she wondered, had she been up and down this staircase in the course of her lifetime? Rushed early mornings, half-dressed, her face still damp and soapy and the taste of toothpaste in her mouth; slow, exhausted bedtimes, when she was scarcely able to put one foot in front of the other. Her mother shouting that breakfast was on the table, and she'd be late for school; her father sending her up to her bedroom in disgrace for some misdemeanour. She and her brothers had dashed up and down these stairs as children in the course of their games of hide-and-seek or sardines (her favourite hiding-place had been the huge airing cupboard, where she would crouch among the clean sheets and towels and breathe in the smell of freshly-ironed clothes). Sliding down the banisters had been strictly forbidden ever since Jack and crashed onto the tiled floor below and broken his arm, but far from deterring them this had simply added to the excitement. It was a long time since Annie had slid down the banisters.

The living-room when she entered it seemed

very quiet, and she stood on the threshold for a moment, not sure what she was supposed to do. Her parents were seated, but Ernest stood up when she came in. He held out a hand, and then seeming to think better of it, let his arm drop by his side.

'Hello, Annie.'

'Hello, Ernest.'

As she held his gaze. Annie felt almost sorry for him. In a way, he too had been caught up by events, and while it appeared that he had a choice in the matter, it couldn't have been easy for him, whatever had been decided.

'Sit down, Annie,' her father said. 'You too, Ernest.'

Annie sat down on the sofa, as far away as possible from Ernest, and folded her hands in her lap.

'Now, Ernest has something to say to you, haven't you, Ernest?' Ernest made a helpless gesture with his hands, and lowered his gaze. 'Well, I'll say it for him then, if that's all right?'

Ernest nodded.

'Ernest is prepared to do right by you, our Annie. You and he will get married. You're a very lucky girl, Annie.'

The silence in the room was tangible. It seemed that everyone was waiting for someone else to speak. Annie felt the blood rush to her head and she heard her heart pounding in her ears. Her eyes were fixed on a loose thread in her skirt and the worn pattern of the carpet beneath her feet. I mustn't cry, I will not cry, she said to herself, over and over again. The clock on the mantelpiece struck three, Ernest coughed, her mother shifted in her chair.

'Well, Annie? What do you say?'

What could poor Annie say? That she was grateful? That she refused Ernest's offer? What did her father expect of her?

She was aware that Ernest was getting to his feet.

'We've never talked of marriage, Annie,' he said, 'but I think you knew how I felt. I've always cared for you. I do care for you. I'll – marry you, like your father said.'

'But what about me?' cried Annie, as the tears came at last. 'What about what I want? Is no one going to ask me what I want?'

'You're not in a position to have what you want, our Annie. Not any more. You have to do what's best, and marrying Ernest is what's best. For everyone.'

'Who says it's best, Dad?' Annie sobbed. 'You? Mum? Ernest? How come everyone suddenly knows what's best for me? How can it be best for me to marry a man I – a man I don't love?'

'That's enough of that, our Annie! You should have thought of that before you – well, before. The alternative is disgrace. Disgrace for you and for the family. Is that what you want?'

'Mum?' Annie begged. 'Can't I stay here with you? *Please?*'

'Your father's right, Annie. We can't make you marry Ernest, but it's for the best, and you'll come to see that it's for your own good. Besides, you can't stay here. We've our reputation to think of. We may only be farmers, but we're – respected. Marrying Ernest is the best thing for everybody.'

126

'We've made – arrangements,' her father said slowly. 'You and Ernest will get married, and you'll have enough money to set up home together. You won't be rich, but Ernest's hoping for promotion, and you should be able to put a deposit on a place of your own before long.'

'You mean – you mean you've *paid* him to marry me?'

'We've a bit put by. It'll make it easier for him to take on a wife and family. It's the best we can do, our Annie. We can't do any more.'

Annie thought she saw tears in her father's eyes, and for a moment she wondered whether it might still be possible to fling herself into his arms and beg him to change his mind, but she knew that it would be of no use. Besides, her parents had a point. This situation was not of their making, and they were trying to do their best for her. She knew that she had let them down badly. Her only way of making reparation was to do what they asked, and marry Ernest. Perhaps, after all, she owed them that.

'When?' she whispered.

'As soon as possible, naturally. Under the circumstances.' Her father stood up. 'And now, perhaps we'd better drink a toast to the two of you. Fetch the sherry, our Annie.'

Wordlessly, Annie left the room and went into the kitchen, where she brought out the sherry bottle from the cupboard in the dresser. Wiping the bottle with a tea towel (it hadn't seen the light of day since Christmas, and was filmed with dust), she set it on a tray, together with four glasses, and returned with it to the living-room.

This wasn't how it was meant to be, she thought wretchedly. In her worst dreams, she had never imagined that her engagement – for she supposed that was what this was – would be anything like this. There should have been love and romance, a proper proposal, an engagement ring and a joyful announcement. And happiness. Most of all, happiness.

As she looked across the room at Ernest, their eyes met, and she was shocked at what she saw in his gaze. Beyond the sombre expression and respectful demeanour, there was a light in Ernest's eyes which could only be described as triumph.

CHAPTER NINETEEN

Annie's Story

The wedding of Annie and Ernest was arranged for the following week. Hasty marriages had become a normal part of life, and even though Ernest wasn't engaged in active service, and had no war to hurry back to, few local eyebrows were raised. If there was any gossip, no one at the farm got to hear about it. Tom, now home recuperating and trying to accustom himself to an artificial leg, was too absorbed in his own problems to worry about his sister, and more distant members of the family were to receive the news of the marriage as a fait accompli, with a date carefully amended to take into account the arrival of Annie's child.

Mavis, however, never one to miss a trick, was triumphant.

'I knew it! You're expecting, aren't you? After all you said about Ernest, too! Well, that's one way to catch your man, I suppose, though I wouldn't want to be married to that one myself, I can tell you. Still, the best of luck to you, Annie. At least you've found yourself a husband, which is more than can be said for me.'

'I don't want to marry Ernest,' Annie confided. 'I never wanted to marry Ernest, but now it seems I've got no choice.'

'Never mind,' Mavis said. 'It mightn't be that bad, and at least you'll be getting away from the farm. If I never see another smelly animal again, it'll be too soon. I'll miss you, Annie,' she added, with unaccustomed warmth. 'Who will I have to talk to when you've gone? I can hardly have a laugh with the pigs, can I?'

The wedding took place on a damp November afternoon. The only people in attendance were Annie's parents, Mavis and poor Derek. Derek couldn't be trusted to be left on the farm on his own, and in any case, his wits were too fuddled to allow of any indiscretion on his part. Ernest, it seemed, had no one he wanted to invite (his mother was in poor health, and unable to make the journey, and he had no brothers or sisters), and so Tom, a reluctant participant in his wheelchair, filled the role of Best Man.

Annie remembered her wedding day as a solemn, even grim occasion. The single photograph portrayed her in a loose summer frock and a jacket borrowed from her mother, and carrying a posy of late roses from the garden. Ernest, dapper as ever, wore his best suit. Both looked as though they were facing a firing squad rather than a lifetime of marriage.

The wedding breakfast was taken back at the farm, for as Annie's father pointed out, they had more and better food at home than any hotel might have to offer. And indeed Annie's mother, perhaps touched at last by the plight of her only daughter, did her best to provide a festive meal. But apart from Mavis and Derek, no one was very hungry, and much of the meal went untouched. Finally, after a half-hearted toast and a piece of the wedding cake (a chocolate sponge, but without any decoration, for even their combined sugar rations didn't stretch to an iced cake), Annie and Ernest adjourned to the inn in the village where they were to spend their wedding night.

'I won't be – bothering you, Annie,' Ernest said, as he sat on the edge of the bed to take off his shoes. 'Not until the – well, not until afterwards.' He placed the shoes neatly side by side, just as Annie had known he would, tucking his socks inside them. 'It wouldn't be right to – to bother you.' For the first time that day, he turned to look at her properly. 'I did – do – care for you, you know, Annie,' he said, reaching out to touch her arm. 'We must make the best of things.'

Perhaps Annie might have been touched by Ernest's words if he had at least volunteered to marry her, but the humiliation of having been as it were handed over to him with a dowry of her parents' precious savings was still too painful. Annie give him a tight little smile. Her jaw ached with holding back the tears which had been threatening all day, and she longed just to lay her head on the pillow and weep; to weep for the girlhood she had left behind, for the missed opportunities, for her own familiar bedroom and for the forlorn little group who had waved them off at the farmyard gate. She envied Tom, who was safe at home, who was loved and cared for. She would gladly have given one of her own legs to change places with him.

By tacit agreement, they took it in turns to undress in the bathroom across the corridor. Ernest's striped pyjamas looked crisply new, and for a moment, Annie was touched. Her own nightdress was the best she had, but not new. There hadn't been time to make one, and she preferred to save her precious clothing coupons for more practical use, especially in view of her burgeoning pregnancy.

Later on, in the sagging double bed with Ernest lying stiffly beside her, Annie thought of the lifetime of bedtimes to come, and of the attentions which she was to receive once she had had her baby. She had no idea how often married people indulged in sex, but imagined that it must be pretty often, and she was not looking forward to it. Of course, she wouldn't refuse Ernest when the time came. She accepted that sex must be a part of married life. She knew from her occasional chats with Mavis that sex was important to men, and no doubt Ernest was no different from any other man in this respect, but she couldn't for the life of her imagine why anyone would want to do anything so peculiar and so downright uncomfortable unless they really had to. Perhaps in time she would get used to it. In the meantime, she was relieved and grateful that their sexual relationship was to be postponed for the time being.

A pencil of moonlight filtered through a gap in the blackout curtains, laying a pale stripe across the counterpane. Beside her, she felt Ernest relax and heard the sound of his gentle snoring. Annie turned her face into her pillow, and wept at last.

CHAPTER TWENTY

Andrew

Andrew found the tale of Annie's marriage, together with the events leading up to it, extraordinarily moving. In many ways it was a common enough tale, but Annie brought her story to life in such a way that it was as though she were speaking of events which had happened a few weeks, rather than half a century, ago. And while Annie expressed great sadness, she seemed to be altogether without bitterness or self-pity. He was fascinated by the glimpses of the young Annie; of a girl who had her share of romance and vanity and mischief, and who was yet capable of being both hardworking and practical. Looking at her now, it was hard to imagine that the woman who had managed to starve eight chickens to death was the same person who had milked cows and mucked out pigsties on the family farm all those years ago. Age and events had changed Annie as they did most people, yet Andrew was beginning to see the links which bound the lively country girl to the disappointed widow. Sometimes, as she spoke of her younger self, it was almost as though it were the young Annie rather than the old who was talking; there were touches of humour as well as sadness, of hope as well as despair, but above all a wistfulness which was at times almost heartbreaking.

'Do you think I should come to church?' she had asked unexpectedly, just as Andrew was about to take his leave. 'You being the vicar.'

'I think that's up to you,' he'd replied, somewhat taken by surprise. Oddly enough, Annie had never mentioned church before. 'You must do what you feel is best.'

'I haven't been to church for years,' Annie mused. 'The last time must have been Ophelia's christening.'

'An unusual name,' Andrew remarked.

'Typical of Billy and Sheila,' Annie said. 'They couldn't have a Mary or a Jane, could they? Had to be something posh; something unusual. Poor girl. Doesn't suit her, does it?'

'I rather think it does,' Andrew said, and he meant it. Certainly, Ophelia wasn't beautiful in any conventional sense, but her clear skin, fine grey eyes and the directness with which she had spoken had strangely disturbed him, and when they had shaken hands – her hand firm and cool in his own – he had felt something in him respond which he had thought long since dead. 'Has she – a boyfriend?'

133

Immediately, he regretted the question. What on earth had it to do with him, and why did he want to know, anyway?

'Oh, I shouldn't think so,' Annie said. 'Ophelia isn't the sort to have boyfriends.'

'And what sort would that be?' Andrew asked, in spite of himself.

'More glamorous, I suppose. She doesn't make the most of herself, does she? That skirt looks as though it's been cobbled together by a child.' Annie sniffed. 'When we were young, we knew how to sew. Had to, what with the war and everything.'

Driving along the lanes towards home, Andrew thought of the long gypsy skirt Ophelia had worn that morning, her sandaled feet, her bare arms with their dusting of blonde hairs and her complexion which owed nothing to the artifice of make-up, and thought she was precisely the sort of girl to have boyfriends. How odd that he should remember exactly what Ophelia was wearing, when he would have been completely unable to recall what had been worn by the woman with whom he had breakfasted that morning. Janet had always said that he was unobservant, and on the whole, that was true. But it was as though Ophelia had not only imposed herself on his consciousness but had, as it were, painted herself onto his memory. Her smile, her hair, the tone of her voice, her hands (small, square, with short unvarnished nails), her slight air of diffidence – he could remember them as clearly as if he had known her all his life.

I'm lonely, he thought, as he pulled onto a grass

verge and switched off the engine. That's what all this is about. I'm a lonely, unsuccessful man on the borders of middle age, fantasising about a girl whom I have only just met and who is young enough to be my daughter.

Was it lust that he felt for Ophelia? Andrew was reluctant to think of her in those terms, and yet if this wasn't lust, then what was it? Not love, certainly. Not even friendship, for he'd barely spoken to her. He tried to think when he had last lusted after anyone, and couldn't remember. As a schoolboy, he had certainly experienced lust. He well remembered the excitement engendered by Angela Drew, a big blonde hussy of a girl, whose enormous breasts rolled and bounced in un-fettered glory inside her aertex shirt during PE, like giant melons endowed with lives of their own. Andrew had never quite been able to bring himself to speak to Angela, but the soft magnifi-cent promise of those breasts had haunted his dreams and provided material for many a boy-hood fantasy.

But that was then. Now, he felt that lust would have been far easier to cope with than the emotions aroused in him by Ophelia, which were more complex and held within them the potential to be infinitely more dangerous. There was tenderness and a sense of kinship, but also a desire to look after her, which was ridiculous, because no doubt Ophelia was perfectly capable of looking after herself.

Andrew looked at his watch. It was still only midday, and he had the rest of the day ahead of him. He had plenty of paperwork and reading to catch up on, but he didn't want to go home yet. Janet was holding some sort of meeting in the vicarage – a 'working lunch', she called it – and he knew the house would be swarming with those loud, upholstered but well-meaning women upon whom the church depended for so much but whom he found so wearying. Since the death of Tobias, he had found his home even less welcoming than it used to be. Apart from the days when the loyal and adoring Josephine was working, there was no one to greet him when he returned, unless you counted Janet's 'Is that you, Andrew?' (who else could it possibly be?), or the numerous answerphone messages, all, it seemed, from people demanding his immediate attention. In an attempt to build at the very least a small bridge, Andrew had suggested that he and Janet do something together this afternoon, but the idea had been brushed aside, its good intention unacknowledged. Janet, it seemed, had more important things to do.

But we can't go on like this, he thought. The death of Tobias had marked a crisis in their marriage, and yet neither he nor Janet had mentioned it since. Tobias in death was far more of a threat to their relationship than he had ever been in life, and Andrew was aware that now they both tiptoed round the subject, anxious not to disturb it in case it should explode and wreak further damage. If he was honest, he thought that Janet probably regretted what she had done, but she had never been much good at apologising. As for Andrew himself, he thought that if he were ever to allow himself the luxury of saying all the things he wanted to say, he might never stop. It seemed that all the anger and resentment and disappointment he had ever felt in his marriage was concentrated on that single act of betrayal. Now, when he said the Lord's Prayer, he found himself unable to complete those most-familiar of words, 'as we forgive them...' He would get so far, and then falter, for try as he might, he couldn't forgive Janet. He had prayed about it; he had tried to see the situation from Janet's point of view; he had even spoken about it to Father Matthew, the gentle elderly priest who was his spiritual adviser. But the forgiveness wouldn't come. It had become a sticking-point not only in his marriage but in his fragile relationship with his God; perhaps the last straw for both.

Ophelia wouldn't have done a thing like that, he found himself thinking, and was shocked at himself. Ophelia again. What was Ophelia to him? She was simply the granddaughter of an elderly woman he visited. He had met her once, and then fleetingly. He met many young women in the course of his work, and didn't give them a second thought. Some of them even he could see were more beautiful than Ophelia could ever hope to be; many were more successful (Annie had told him of Ophelia's abrupt exit from the nursing home), but there had been something about her which he had found irresistible.

But I must resist, he thought, as he turned on the engine and started up the car. Life was quite difficult enough without inviting further complications. Andrew determined that he would make sure that he never saw Ophelia again.

CHAPTER TWENTY-ONE

Ophelia

'He's nice, your vicar,' Ophelia said casually, as she sliced tomatoes for lunch.

'He's been very good to me,' Annie said, getting plates out of a cupboard.

'How did you get on this morning?'

'It was difficult.'

'In what way difficult? He seems very – approachable.'

'Oh, he's easy enough to talk to, but it's what I have to say that's difficult. Painful, I suppose. Going over the past. But there's worse to come, and that's something I've never talked about.'

'Haven't you ever told anyone at all?' Ophelia grated some cheese. It was hard round the edges, and there were slight traces of mould. She scraped them off.

'No one at all. No. Ernest – Grandad – wouldn't let me.'

'Did you always do what he told you to?' Ophelia asked.

'Didn't have much choice.' Annie paused in what she was doing. 'You're asking a lot of questions.'

'Sorry. I suppose I'm interested. Family history and all that. We don't really know each other, do we, Gran?'

'I suppose we don't. I did try, though. When you were little. But I don't think your mum trusted me.'

Ophelia laughed. 'Mum didn't trust anyone. She used to turn up unexpectedly at school. There was always some excuse, but I think she was trying to catch the teachers out, though what she thought they might be up to I've no idea. Is there any pickle?'

'There might be some in the larder.'

Ophelia hunted through the jumble of half-empty jars and bottles and unearthed an ancient jar of chutney.

'That was your grandad's favourite,' Annie said.

'It's a bit – old.' There was an unpleasant black crust round the rim of the jar and the contents smelt unappetising.

'Well, he's been dead a few months now, hasn't he?'

They both laughed.

'Oh dear. We shouldn't laugh, should we?' Annie said, looking suddenly stricken.

'Oh, I don't know. It's not as though we're doing any harm, are we?'

'I suppose not. We didn't laugh much, your grandad and I.'

'Were you – were you very unhappy?' Ophelia ventured, aware that she could be treading on sensitive ground.

'A lot of the time, I suppose. Yes, I was. I think I've only recently realised how unhappy. Talking to Andrew's made me understand much more than I did.'

'Will you tell him – everything?' Ophelia asked.

'I'm not sure, but I think I might. It was difficult at the beginning, but now I've got started it's getting much easier. Did you buy any bread?'

'Yes. It's unsliced, I'm afraid. All I could get.'

'That's all right. Your grandad wouldn't eat the other sort.'

How odd, Ophelia thought. In some ways, she still behaves as through Grandad's alive; she's still pandering to his little idiosyncrasies. Ophelia wondered whether Annie had got rid of any of Ernest's things, and rather doubted it. She had noted the raincoat hanging in the hallway, the wellington boots in the porch, a worn shaving brush in the bathroom.

'And Andrew,' she said now, buttering a slice of bread. 'How often do you see him?'

'Once a week usually. Occasionally twice, if he happens to be passing. Depends what he's doing.'

'Am I – am I likely to see him again?'

Annie eyed her sharply.

'You might do. Why?'

'I just wondered,' Ophelia said, puzzled as to why it was she was having such trouble getting this stranger out of her head.

Ever since she'd met him that morning, something about him had haunted her. His pale, sensitive face, his grey-green eyes, the way his hair (mouse-brown like her own) flopped over his forehead, the affectionate embrace he had given Annie when he'd arrived (when had anyone last embraced her grandmother, she wondered?). Perhaps it's just that I automatically take to anyone who shows real kindness to elderly people, she thought. Maybe that's it. The old are so often sidelined; treated as though they are invisible. This man really seems to care. This man is *kind*.

'Has he got children?' she asked now. It seemed a bit less direct than asking if Andrew had a wife.

'No. But he is married. Not very happily, reading between the lines. But then, who is?'

Ophelia thought of her own parents. Were they happy? Certainly, their marriage appeared to work. At any rate, they were still together. They didn't have rows. Each had their role in the relationship, and nothing was allowed to rock the boat. If they had a difference of opinion, the subject was immediately closed, as though allowing it to be aired might pose some threat or, at the very least, upset the carefully balanced status quo. They had their separate interests, but always holidayed together, although Billy hated going abroad (Sheila's choice) and Sheila disliked hill-walking and golf (Billy's). Another child might have helped (it would certainly have helped Ophelia to have someone to share the load of parental expectation), but none had been forthcoming, although Sheila made no secret of her disappointment and Billy would certainly have liked a son.

'Have you met his wife?' Ophelia asked.

'No reason to,' Annie said. 'They live in town, of course, and I don't got to church, so our paths don't really cross. I have to admit, though, I'm curious.'

Ophelia, who was also curious, but for quite different reasons, wondered how she could engineer a visit to church for the two of them without arousing suspicion.

'Is it a nice church?' she asked.

'The little one in the village isn't much, but it's only used about once a month. The main one's in town. Quite nice, I think, but I've only seen it from the outside. I never did know much about architecture.'

'We could go and see it while I'm here, couldn't we? I've got the car,' Ophelia said. 'It would be nice if you were to show an interest, after all he's done for you,' she added.

'You seem to be showing quite an interest yourself,' remarked Annie.

'Nothing wrong with exploring a bit. We could go this afternoon if you've nothing else planned. And then maybe find somewhere to have a cup of tea,' Ophelia said, cutting the sandwiches she had made into neat triangles. 'Let's have lunch, shall we?'

Later on that afternoon, when Annie had had her customary nap and Ophelia had washed up the lunch things, they set off together in the car.

'You're lucky living here,' Ophelia said, as they drove past fields of black and white cows and ripening wheat. 'I'd love to live in the country.'

'It's pretty lonely,' Annie said. 'When we first moved here, there was a shop and a post office. You could meet up with people and have a chat. Now there's nothing.'

'But you were brought up in the country, weren't you?' Ophelia knew little about the countryside and had romantic ideas about rural life, which she imagined to be an idyll of meadows and sunsets and the trilling of skylarks

(Ophelia had never heard a skylark, and wouldn't have recognised one if she had). She couldn't imagine wanting to exchange all that for the noise and bustle of crowds and shops and traffic.

'That was different,' Annie said. 'I was useful then. I'm not much use to anyone now, am I?'

She's right, Ophelia thought, remembering the residents in the home. It's being needed that people miss as they get older. However much help they are given, however many treats may be arranged for them, nothing compensates for being unable to make a contribution themselves. She recalled last Christmas, when the old people had been loaded onto a coach to be taken to, of all things, a pantomime. The other staff had thought it a charming idea, but the expressions on the residents' faces had told a quite different story. One elderly woman, who had bravely refused to join the party (although she was accused of being awkward and ungrateful) had defied the health and safety regulations to spend what had seemed to Ophelia to be a far happier afternoon helping the kitchen staff prepare vegetables for supper.

'You're of use to me,' Ophelia said now, patting Annie's hand.

'What use?'

'If I hadn't come to stay with you, I'd be at home listening to Dad telling me what a dreadful disappointment I am.'

'We're both dreadful disappointments then, aren't we?' Annie said. 'Your grandad was pretty disappointed in me. I don't think I was at all the sort of wife he'd hoped for.'

143

They both laughed.

'Well, we'd better make sure we don't disappoint each other,' Ophelia said. 'This must be the church.'

Rising from sturdy Norman origins, the church sported various later additions and some spectacular stained glass.

'It's rather beautiful,' Ophelia said, impressed, as they wandered together down the nave. Two women were dusting the pews, and a third was arranging flowers on the altar. She wondered whether any of them could be Andrew's wife, but there seemed to be no subtle way of finding out.

'You were christened here,' Annie said.

'Was I?' Ophelia was surprised.

'Your grandad had just had his hip done, and couldn't travel,' Annie said. 'You wore frills and screamed a lot,' she added.

'Why do you suppose they had me christened?' Ophelia asked. As far as she knew, her parents had never been churchgoers and held no particular religious belief.

'Probably to be on the safe side,' Annie said. 'Like an insurance policy. I'll say one thing for your parents. If there was anything going, they wanted you to have it.'

After Ophelia had prolonged the visit for as long as she reasonably could (no sign of Andrew or, as far as she could tell, his wife), they adjourned to a tea shop for refreshment.

'My treat,' Ophelia said, ordering chocolate éclairs.

'I thought you were out of work,' Annie said.

'I am. I'm also supposed to be trying to lose

144

weight. But what the hell?' She grinned. 'Hey, Gran. I could do your hair for you if you like. I'm quite good with hair.'

'What's wrong with my hair?' For years, Annie had made a fortnightly trip into town to have her hair shampooed and rolled into rows of identical grey curls. Every three months, she had a cut and perm. It had never occurred to her to have it done any other way. Besides, who was there to care what she looked like?

'Nothing's wrong with it. It's just that it looks – old. Like everyone else.' Ophelia had often wondered why the residents in the home had all seemed to go for the same stereotypical grey perm, emerging from their weekly hairdos (a hairdresser visited the home on Thursdays) like so many elderly clones.

'Well, I am old.'

'Not that old, you're not.' Ophelia took a bite of her éclair. 'What colour did it used to be?'

'A sort of strawberry blonde, I suppose. Not a bad colour at all. I used to be quite proud of it, though Ernest always said he preferred brunettes.'

'We could rinse a bit of that blonde back in if you like,' Ophelia said. 'Not too brassy, but just a hint, to liven it up. What do you think?'

'I think,' said Annie, wiping cream off her chin, 'it's a mad idea, but what have I got to lose?'

'Good for you, Gran! And now, shall we have another éclair?'

CHAPTER TWENTY-TWO

Annie

The following evening, Billy phoned.

'How are things, Mother?' he asked. 'How are you coping with Ophelia?'

'You don't usually phone on a Tuesday,' Annie said. Saturday was Billy's day for phoning her. He always rang at five o'clock on the dot, so that he and Sheila had time to prepare for any social engagement they might be planning, and Annie and her son usually spoke for about ten minutes. They rarely had much to say to one another.

'Well, I'm phoning tonight.' Billy's voice had that patient tone that Annie found so patronising. 'How are you and Ophelia getting along?'

'Fine. We're getting along very well.'

'And?'

'And what?'

'How's she been? Is she behaving herself? Has she given you any idea of what she wants to do?'

'Well, yesterday she made some lovely cheese and tomato sandwiches for lunch. We didn't bother with pickle, though, because it looked a bit–'

'No. I mean *what she's going to do*. With her life. A career. That sort of thing.'

'Oh, I don't think she wants to do anything. She hasn't said, anyway.'

'That's what I was afraid of.' Billy sighed. 'Perhaps you can talk some sense into her.'

It was a long time since Annie had been invited to talk sense into anyone, and she certainly wasn't going to jeopardise this new relationship with Ophelia by trying to subject her to anything of that sort.

'I don't really think it's my job,' she said. 'Besides, Ophelia seems a very sensible girl. Probably more sensible than me, if the truth be told.'

'Quite possibly.' There followed a silence in which Billy's exasperation was palpable. 'And when is it she's coming home?'

'I think she said Thursday. That's right, isn't it?' Annie turned to Ophelia, who was listening in to the conversation with some amusement. 'You're staying until Thursday?'

'Make it next Thursday,' said Ophelia recklessly. 'If you'll have me, that is.'

'Next Thursday,' Annie told Billy. 'She's not coming home until next Thursday.'

'But she told us this Thursday!'

'Then why did you ask?'

'I was just making sure. Finalising, you could say. Just as well I did, as it happens. But she can't possibly stay an extra week. It will be far too much for you having a visitor for all that time, and her mother needs the car.'

'Your mother needs the car,' Annie told Ophelia.

'Tell him you need my company,' Ophelia said. 'Tell him it's a shame to come all this way for such a short time.'

Annie relayed the message.

'He wants to speak to you,' she said, handing Ophelia the phone.

'Hello, Dad.'

The receiver buzzed angrily for several minutes.

'No, Dad. I'm staying here with Gran. I feel it's the least I can do. You said so yourself.' Ophelia winked at Annie.

There was more buzzing, punctuated with tinny growling noises.

'Well, I'm sorry you feel like that, Dad. But it makes sense to stay on a bit longer now I'm here, and I'm sure Mum will understand about the car.'

The buzzing reached fever pitch.

'I've got to go, Dad. Gran needs me. Love to Mum.' Ophelia replaced the receiver. 'Well, that's that sorted.'

'He was a bit cross, wasn't he?' observed Annie, who was much impressed with the way Ophelia had stood up to her father. She herself would never have dared to speak to him like that.

'He'll get over it.' Ophelia sank into a chair and grinned at Annie. 'Are you sure it's all right?'

'What's all right?'

'Me staying on. It was a bit of a cheek springing it on you like that, but I couldn't resist it. Dad expects everyone to do things according to plan, preferably his plan, and I think it does him good to find that he can't always have things his own way.'

Anne thought it unlikely that Billy often had things his own way with his daughter, but refrained from saying so.

'Of course you can stay,' she said, 'if you really want to. It's nice having the company.'

148

'We've had a bit of fun, haven't we?' Ophelia said.

'Yes, we have. I wasn't expecting it, though.'

'Neither was I. That's what's so nice about it.'

'You could – stay longer,' Annie ventured. 'If you've nowhere else and you don't want to go home. You could even get a job here. We could make the room nice, and you could come and go as you like.' She paused, thinking that perhaps she had spoken too soon. After all, Ophelia had only been with her for two days. They still had a lot to find out about each other. And Ophelia might start to find Annie's habits irritating (Annie had forgotten what her irritating habits were, but Ernest was always complaining about them, and Ernest was usually right).

'You know, that's rather a good idea,' Ophelia said. 'Thanks, Gran. Let's see how the next week or so goes, and then we could think about it. It would certainly get me out from under Mum's feet, though she'd want her car back.'

'But there's your grandad's car!' Annie exclaimed. 'You could have that!'

She had entirely forgotten about Ernest's car. In fact, she hadn't been inside the garage since Ernest had died. It was one of a little row of garages round the corner from the house, and in addition to the car it housed Ernest's tools which were neatly arranged on hooks and shelves at the back. Annie had never had any reason to go in there, and Ernest had discouraged it. She had never learnt to drive, either. Some people were natural drivers, Ernest had told her. Annie, it seemed, was not (although she had never so

149

much as sat behind a steering wheel, so how could he tell?).

'It probably won't start,' she said now. 'Ernest made sure to drive it at least once a week. To keep it ticking over, he said. He used to clean it on Sunday mornings, even when it wasn't dirty. He was very particular like that, your grandad.'

'Let's go and have a look at it,' said Ophelia.

The up-and-over door of the garage was reluctant to go either up or over, and Ophelia and Annie struggled with it for some time before they managed to get it to work. Once inside, they switched on the light and surveyed the garage's dim interior.

There was an air of dusty neglect probably unheard of in Ernest's lifetime. Cobwebs festooned the walls and corners, and were draped over the wing mirrors and bumper of the car. They were the kind of cobwebs Annie always thought of as Halloween cobwebs; dense and blankety and unpleasant. Not at all like the pretty dew-spangled ones on the bushes outside. The car itself was thick with dust ('CLEAN ME' Ophelia wrote on the bonnet with her finger, and then, because the job would more than likely fall to her, added 'PLEASE OPHELIA').

'And I shall,' she told Annie. 'Tomorrow, I shall give it a proper makeover. Worthy of Grandad,' she added, because after all, in a way it was still his car. Annie didn't drive, and much as Ophelia would love to own it herself, she had long since learned never to count her chickens.

The following morning, they returned with the car keys.

'I'm not insured,' Ophelia said. 'Do you think it matters?'

'You're only driving it out into the road. That hardly counts,' said Annie, who knew nothing at all about car insurance, and cared even less.

Gingerly, Ophelia opened the car door, and slid into the driving seat. It was odd to think that the last person to drive the car had been her grandfather (apart from whoever had driven it back from town after his death). His driving gloves were still tucked into the glove compartment (where else?), and there were also a tweed cap, a road map, a packet of Polos and a half-eaten bar of chocolate. How odd, she thought, that however old we are, we go through life behaving as though we have plenty of time. Does anyone, she wondered, end their life with all the chocolate eaten, the toothpaste used up, bills paid, letters answered and the dustbins outside the gate awaiting collection? Even people who know they're going to die soon probably leave loose ends and unfinished business, just in case they're granted a last-minute reprieve. Or maybe it's just that when it comes to it, no one really believes they're going to die. Her grandfather had expected to wear those gloves again and finish his bar of chocolate; he had anticipated journeys using his road map, and perhaps eating his Polos. He had expected to stay *alive*.

'Are you all right?' Annie mouthed through the dusty window.

'Fine. Just thinking,' Ophelia called back, and switched on the ignition.

Amazingly, the engine coughed into action

after only a few attempts on Ophelia's part. She gave the thumbs up to Annie and very carefully inched the car out of the garage, parking it neatly by the kerb.

'That tyre's a bit flat,' observed Annie.

'It's completely flat,' Ophelia said, 'and the others aren't looking too good, either, but there was bound to be something wrong after all this time.'

'Are you any good with tyres?' Annie asked. 'I think there's one of those jack things in the boot.'

'All cars have a jack thing in the boot,' Ophelia told her, 'but unfortunately I've never used one. If we can change that very flat tyre, it can be driven to a garage to have the rest pumped up. What we need is a man. The kind sort, who doesn't mind helping out and getting his hands dirty. But I don't suppose we're likely to find one of those.'

'There's Andrew,' said Annie. 'I'm sure he'd help. I'll give him a ring, shall I?'

CHAPTER TWENTY-THREE

Andrew

'Annie Bentley's been on the phone again,' Janet said, when Andrew came home at lunch time. 'Something about a flat tyre. I asked her if she'd thought of ringing the garage, but she said she was sure you'd sort it out. She said could you ring her back. Really, Andrew, I do wish you wouldn't keep running round after that woman. You've more important things to do with your time.'

Andrew wondered why it was that whatever Janet said to him these days, she managed to make it sound like an accusation. (He also wondered what Annie, who as far as he knew neither drove nor owned a car, was doing fussing about flat tyres.)

'I don't, as you put it, run round after Annie Bentley, Janet. I visit her once a week, usually on my day off. As to the things I've got to do, I think I've a better idea of what those are than you have.'

'Which means, I suppose, that you'll go.'

'Which means that I might,' Andrew said, making off in the direction of his study. 'I'll have to check my diary first and then find out exactly what it is that she wants doing.'

Josephine had been at work that morning, and the usual chaos of papers which accumulated between her visits had been organised into tidy piles, together with a list of telephone messages in her neat copperplate handwriting. She also appeared to have been doing a spot of dusting, and had brought him a new pot plant for his desk. Andrew noted with amusement that it was a cactus; unattractive, but indestructible (its predecessor, a wispy spider plant, had succumbed some time ago after two years of neglect).

He glanced through the messages. An afternoon appointment had been cancelled, and Communion at the old people's home had been postponed because of an outbreak of some bug. He could make it to Annie's at a pinch, provided it was important enough.

But of course Ophelia would still be there, and he had vowed that he wouldn't see Ophelia again. Thinking about it now, perhaps he had over-reacted. It seemed a rather dramatic decision to have taken on such a brief acquaintance. Monday had been a bad day, and he had been feeling tired and vulnerable. Today might be different. It was true that he had thought about her a great deal since their brief meeting, but it was also possible that he had exaggerated whatever it was about her that he had found so attractive. If he saw her again it was more than likely that he would see her for the entirely ordinary girl she almost certainly was. In fact, it might be a good thing if he did see her, then he could put the whole silly business behind him.

Andrew picked up the telephone.

'What's this about a flat tyre?'

'Ernest's car.' Annie sounded breathless and excited.

'I didn't know he had one.'

'Neither did I. Well, anyway, I'd forgotten about it. But he has – had – and it's a bit dusty and it's got a flat tyre, and I want to give it to Ophelia.'

'Goodness!'

'Yes. Isn't it a good idea?'

Andrew agreed that it was.

'And we – I – thought that you might come and have a look at it.' Annie paused. 'Your wife didn't sound very pleased.'

'Well, she has a point,' Andrew said. 'I'm not a mechanic, and I do have a job to do.'

'It wouldn't take long,' said Annie, who had no idea how long it might take to change a tyre.

154

'And we can all have a nice a cup of tea together afterwards.'

Andrew looked at his watch. 'I'll be round some time this afternoon. I can't guarantee exactly when, and if there's anything complicated wrong with the car, you'll have to call the garage. But I think I can just about cope with a flat tyre.'

I shall be businesslike, he told himself as he replaced the receiver. I shall go round, change the tyre and come straight home. I shall refuse the cup of tea, and I shall say as little as possible to Ophelia. What could be more straightforward?

They were both outside the house when he arrived, Annie holding a bucket and Ophelia sloshing soapy water over an elderly but very respectable Mini. Annie's hair appeared to have changed from grey to an interesting pinky-blonde, and had it not been for her familiar flowered pinafore he would hardly have recognised her. Ophelia was wearing jeans and a tee shirt and was very wet.

'Here's Andrew!' Annie cried, putting down her bucket. 'I knew he'd come.'

'I said I'd come,' Andrew said. 'I – like the hair.'

'Isn't it lovely? Ophelia did it. I wasn't sure at first, but I'm getting quite used to it now. It used to be this colour once, you know.'

'Yes.' Andrew was very aware of Ophelia standing with her sponge, waiting for him to say something to her.

'Hello again, Ophelia.'

'Hello.'

Ophelia pushed her hair out of her eyes with the back of her hand and smiled at him.

155

'It's really kind of you to come,' she said, and he noticed for the first time that her voice was very slightly husky. Her shirt clung damply to one breast and she had a streak of dirt across her cheek. 'If we can just get this tyre changed, then I can take it to a garage to be checked over.'

'Are you insured to drive it?' Andrew asked. She's really quite plain, he thought. Almost dumpy. Whatever was I thinking of to get so worked up?

'No, but I will be.'

'That's good. And the tax?'

'Oh.' Ophelia looked crestfallen. She peered through the soapy windscreen. 'It's expired,' she said, disappointed. 'But never mind. We can re-new it, and then Gran says I can have it. Isn't that great?'

'Great,' Andrew agreed. It was no good. Ophelia was neither plain nor dumpy. She might be scruffy and wet, her hair might be all over the place and her face dirty, but she looked utterly enchanting. Andrew dragged his gaze away from her and turned his attention to the rogue tyre.

Fifteen minutes later, the three of them were sitting in Annie's kitchen and Ophelia was making tea (Andrew had decided that he couldn't really refuse. It would have been churlish, and they were so grateful to him for changing the tyre).

'How long are you staying?' Andrew asked Ophelia, aware that he had probably already been told, but hadn't taken in the answer.

'Thursday. Next Thursday.' Ophelia took milk from the fridge and poured it into a jug. 'And I might stay longer, if I can find a job.'

'You mean you might live here?'

'Yes. Gran's got the room and we seem to get on. And I can drive her about when she wants, once we've got the car sorted.'

Andrew watched Ophelia as she brought the teapot to the table and poured tea into three cups. She was so close that he could breathe in the smell of her – oil from the car mingled with soap and freshly-washed hair – and could see the fair down on her upper lip and the pale curve of her throat. He could almost feel her breath on his cheek when she handed him the cup, and found himself unable to meet her eye.

'That sounds like a really good idea,' he said, staring down into his teacup. The tea was still swirling from where Ophelia had stirred it, and he wondered how she had known that he took sugar.

'She can paint the bedroom whatever colour she likes,' Annie said, dunking a biscuit in her tea.

'I've never been allowed to choose my own colours,' Ophelia said. 'Mum likes pale blues and pinks and yellows for bedrooms, with flowery curtains and matching duvet covers. All very pretty and frilly, but not really me. When I was fifteen, I wanted to paint my bedroom black, but she wouldn't let me.'

'Do you want black?' Annie sounded alarmed.

'Of course not,' Ophelia laughed. 'I'm not fifteen any more. But something – exciting. Something different. I want a room that's me, not Mum. Not that awful bed-sit, either. And posters. Can I have posters, Gran? Mum would never let me have them. She said they made marks on the walls.'

Andrew felt dizzy and slightly sick. Ophelia

wanted posters on her walls. He was lusting – when all was said and done, that was the word, wasn't it? – after a girl still young enough to get excited about putting up posters on her walls. A kid, really. A *child*. He took a gulp of tea and replaced his cup carefully on its saucer. The patterned oilcloth of the kitchen table was marked with brown rings from previous teacups, and there were some stale-looking crumbs and a smear of something which looked like ketchup. Someone had placed a jam jar of wild flowers in the middle of the table, and Andrew watched as a tiny insect crawled along a stem. He was aware of Ophelia moving away towards the sink, running a tap, saying something to Annie, laughing. Out of the corner of his eye he could see her feet (rubber flip-flops) and the worn hem of her jeans.

'What kinds of posters?' he asked, looking up at last. 'What sorts of things are you interested in?'

Ophelia met his gaze and held it for a moment, unsmiling, her grey eyes serious, and for just a moment, it was as though there were no one and nothing else in the room but the two of them.

'Oh, birds, flowers, wild animals, anything really,' she said, moving back to the table. 'Not pop stars or football players, if that's what you're thinking.'

'I wasn't thinking anything of the kind.' Andrew laughed, but his laugh sounded hollow and artificial, and he immediately regretted it.

'I don't really look the pop star type, do I?' Ophelia said.

'Well–'

'I think these pop stars get paid far too much,'

Annie said, unaware of any atmosphere. 'I can't see the point myself.'

Whether she meant the point of pop stars or of their pay was not clear, but Andrew was relieved that the conversation had taken a turn in what seemed to be an altogether safer direction.

'They're certainly a lot better paid than I am. Talking of which, I'd better be going,' he said, getting up from the table. 'Paperwork and sermons call.'

'I'll see you out.' Ophelia took his cup and saucer and put them on the draining board. 'Thanks so much,' she said as they made their way to the front door. 'I really did suggest the garage for the tyre, but Gran seems to think you're the answer to everything. She's very fond of you, you know,' she added, as Andrew got into his car.

'I'm fond of her,' Andrew said. 'She's a brave woman. You take good care of her.'

'I intend to,' Ophelia said, and smiled, running her fingers through her tangle of hair and thrusting her hands into the pockets of her jeans. 'See you soon, I expect.'

'Yes. See you soon.'

'I don't know what you're smiling about, I'm sure,' Janet said when Andrew returned home late for tea.

'I wasn't aware that I was.'

'You've had that silly grin on your face ever since you got home.' She placed shepherd's pie on the table in front of him.

Andrew thought about it. It was true. He did feel ridiculously happy. But it was also true that it was a dangerous and fated happiness; a happiness which couldn't possibly last; a happiness, furthermore, which could be bought only at the expense of other people's. But I'll make the most of it, he thought, helping himself to cabbage. Surely there can't be any harm in simply feeling happy, even if – especially if – it never leads to anything more. And of course, it can't lead to anything more. It would be out of the question. But just for now, just for today, I shall enjoy being happy.

Andrew looked up and smiled at Janet.

'Lovely shepherd's pie,' he said.

CHAPTER TWENTY-FOUR

Annie's Story

Annie and Ernest started married life in the tiny flat Ernest rented above an antiques shop in the town. The two rooms were modest, and the bathroom and kitchen shared with the landlady, Mrs Stubbs, a pinched-looking widow of uncertain age, who was in frequent attendance to ensure implementation of blackout regulations and the strict rationing of bathwater. While she was clearly very fond of Ernest, it was obvious that she did not approve of his wife or the ill-timing of her condition, for which she appeared to hold Annie solely responsible.

Annie was desperately unhappy. Homesick for the farm and her family, missing the outdoor life and the work she was used to, she was bored and lonely. Ernest, meanwhile, made it clear that while he was responsible for earning their living, he expected high standards from his new wife in the housekeeping department. In this, he was soon to be disappointed.

Apart from her tendency to daydream, Annie had always been a practical girl, but since the war her skills had been mainly restricted to the farm. At home, her mother had seen to the housework and cooking, helped two mornings a week by the daughter of neighbouring farmers, and thus Annie had little experience of washing, cleaning and cooking. She was used to making her own clothes, such as they were, and she could prepare a simple meal and light a fire, but that was about all. Now, her sewing skills were certainly required, not least because her increasing girth needed to be accommodated, but there was no fire to light, and Ernest told her that he expected something both palatable and substantial for his tea when he got home from work.

Used to the luxury of fresh produce from the farm, Annie was bewildered by some of the ingredients from which she was supposed to make meals. Unaccustomed to queuing for her supplies, she was often too late to buy anything but the cheapest cuts of meat or the most dubious-looking sausages (Ernest was very fussy about sausages, as he suspected – probably rightly – that in these hard times, they were likely to be the repository for all the more distasteful by-products of the butcher's trade). The pink rubbery texture of Spam revolted her (there had been no need for it at home), and her attempts to incorporate dried egg into her cooking were a disaster. How on earth did other people manage, she wondered, endeavouring to cobble together a stew with a few scraps of scrag-end of lamb and a handful of lentils? Who had taught all those bustling queuing housewives what to do with their meagre purchases once they got them home?

It didn't help that her struggles in the kitchen were often observed by Mrs Stubbs, who had a disconcerting habit of standing in the doorway with folded arms, commenting on Annie's efforts.

'You'll not get that to work,' she said with satisfaction, the first time Annie tried to make pastry. 'You've added too much water.'

'Well, what can I do?' Annie wailed, trying to scrub the sticky dough from her hands.

'You'll have to scrap the lot and start over.'

'But I've no more flour, and I promised Ernest a pie for his tea.' Annie was almost in tears.

'He likes his pies, does Ernest.' Mrs Stubbs seemed to enjoy airing her superior acquaintance with Ernest's gastronomic requirements. 'He used to enjoy my steak and kidney pies, I can tell you. Steak and kidney pie and a bit of mashed potato. That was one of his favourites.'

Annie longed to hurl the ball of sticky dough at the sour smug face of Mrs Stubbs. She also wondered how the wretched woman managed to get hold of steak and kidney, but she certainly wasn't going to give her the satisfaction of appearing to need her advice. She couldn't even ask Mrs Stubbs to leave her on her own when she was using the kitchen, because it was Mrs Stubbs's kitchen and Mrs Stubbs's house, and inexpensive digs were hard to come by. As for Ernest, he wouldn't hear a word against the woman who he said had been 'like a mother' to him.

Once a fortnight, Annie and Ernest visited the farm, where the food was as good as ever and where they were afforded a surprisingly warm welcome. Annie's condition was now openly acknowledged, her married state having apparently afforded it the respectability it had previously lacked, and Annie's mother appeared to be anticipating the new arrival with considerable excitement. Old towels were brought out to be cut up and hemmed as napkins, and the ancient pram which had been used for Annie and her brothers was rescued from the loft.

'I remember pushing you up and down the hall in this, our Annie,' her father said, as he cleaned and oiled the wheels. 'To get you to drop off so we could have a bit of peace and quiet. We never thought then – well, we never thought one day you'd be pushing your own babby around in this pram.'

Ernest himself rarely referred to Annie's pregnancy. It was as though he considered the baby as well as its begetting to be Annie's fault and therefore her responsibility. If the subject had to be addressed, it was left to Annie to bring it up. Otherwise, his manner towards her was on the whole courteous, occasionally even tender, but frequently tempered with irritation and a resentment which he had difficulty in concealing. He rarely touched her, restricting any physical contact to a peck on the cheek when he left for work in the mornings, and the occasional brief squeeze of her hand or arm. In her more charitable moments, Annie was able to feel some pity for him. Poor Ernest. Trapped into this marriage, just as she had been, he was probably regretting it as much as she was, for no amount of money could be compensation for a life which was going to be at the very least unsatisfactory.

Had Ernest any feelings left for her? Annie often wondered, and concluded that he probably didn't. It seemed that the episode in the cornfield had toppled her off her pedestal as surely as if she had contrived to seduce half the county, and it wasn't as if she had ever asked to be placed on a pedestal in the first place. It was all so desperately unfair. If only the fact that they shared the same fate could somehow bring them together, something might be salvaged from the whole sorry mess, but Annie knew that this could never happen. They were both in their separate ways too stiff-necked and strong-minded, victims of their personalities as well as of their fate.

Ernest never got his promotion, but in the new year, he was asked whether he would be prepared to be transferred to a branch in the Midlands. The idea appalled Annie, who had hoped that at least they might be able to remain near her home, but Ernest said that it was too good an opportunity to miss. He welcomed the idea of a new start, and besides, property would be cheaper and they would be able to afford a home of their own. So the decision was made. Ernest found a small flat in town, and used the money from Annie's parents as a deposit. There was also enough to buy a few pieces of utility furniture, and with bedding and linen from the farmhouse and a few pots and pans Annie's mother no longer needed, they were able to set up house.

For the first time since their marriage, Ernest seemed genuinely excited.

'Our own home, Annie. Just think of that! We'll be able to do just as we like, and I know you'll make it nice.'

Annie did her best. She made curtains and cushion covers, she decorated the living-room and white-washed the tiny kitchen and polished the cheap veneer surfaces of the new furniture, but her heart ached with a dull despair. Miles away from her family, the farm, everything and everyone she had ever known and loved, she felt utterly abandoned. She wrote to her parents every week, begging for news, but neither of them had ever been much good at letter-writing, and besides, they were busy, so such letters as they did write were infrequent and brief. It is true that Tom, perhaps understanding her situation better than she had given him credit for, did his best to keep in touch, writing rambling stilted letters about leaking roofs and premature lambs and the pain in his leg, but there was no warmth, no chat, none of the gossip Annie longed for. Mavis did write once or twice, but her letters were full of envy rather than the sympathy Annie craved:

How lucky you are, Annie! A house of your own, and a baby on the way! You are quite the grown-up lady, now, I'm sure, and would not want to get your hands dirty working with us on the farm. I'm using your wellingtons now. I don't expect you'll want them any more, and they haven't got so many holes as mine.

If only Mavis knew. Annie would cheerfully have given up home, marriage, baby and all to be able to wear those wellingtons again and get cold and muddy delivering lambs by torchlight, returning home in the small hours for a mug of hot cocoa and a warm-up by the kitchen range.

Spring came, although to Annie it seemed barely noticeable. Accustomed to life in the country, she was amazed at how little the town was affected by the changing seasons. At home on the farm, the first signs of spring had been heralded by early lambs, the flowering of snowdrops and aconites and the starkly white blossom of blackthorn in the hedgerows. Here in the town, bulbs sprouted and flowered in tidy clumps in the gardens, blossom appeared in organised sequence, the weather grew milder, but everything seemed colourless and muted; there was none of the exuberance and extravagance of light and colour and sound that accompanied spring in the countryside. Even the dawn chorus seemed subdued, almost apologetic, as though the birds were reluctant to disturb the busy self-importance of town life.

Annie's baby was due in the middle of May, and she was filled with fear, for how could any-thing as big as a baby (and this baby was certainly big; the doctor had told her so) possibly get out of a body as small and slight as Annie's without causing terrible damage? Despite her experience with the farm animals, she had little idea of what to expect, and there was no mother nearby to advise and support her. She didn't like to confess her fears to Ernest; she felt sure that he would find the subject distasteful if not embarrassing. Annie herself would certainly have found it very embarrassing indeed.

But unprepared as she was for the actual birth, Annie had made all the necessary preparations. She had purchased a second-hand crib, and with the help of her additional clothing coupons and some advice from a kindly neighbour, she had assembled a basic layette, but none of these things seemed to bear any relation to the child she was carrying. Fingering the tiny garments, she couldn't imagine them ever being actually worn by her own baby. She tried to envisage herself fastening napkins and tying the ribbons on miniature vests and nighties, holding and cuddling and feeding this unwelcome stranger, and her imagination failed her.

Would she love her baby? Mothers were supposed to love their babies, and it would seem that many of them managed it without much effort, but Annie was not particularly maternal, and this baby had caused her so much heartache that the only feeling she had towards it was resentment.

Annie went into labour a week early in the small hours of the morning. Ernest, shocked into unaccustomed concern, fussed and fretted while they awaited the arrival of the ambulance, and actually held Annie's hand on the short but bumpy journey (although Annie, who hadn't expected everything to happen so suddenly and painfully, would much have preferred to have been on her own). As anticipated, the baby was big, and the labour long and hard, and Annie, terrified beyond endurance, fought and screamed until she was exhausted. In her few calmer moments, she remembered the easy slithering of the pinkly polished forms of new piglets as they entered the world, and wondered at the contrast of the protracted agony of childbirth.

'Mother's not being very brave,' remarked the midwife unhelpfully, performing her excruciating and intimate examinations of Annie's writhing body. 'We're not helping baby by behaving like this,' she added, pulling on an enormous and very businesslike looking pair of rubber gloves. 'Baby can't be born unless you help him, you know.'

Annie's son finally arrived almost twenty-four hours later. He emerged, blue and bald and howling, while the wind flung rain like handfuls of pebbles against the window outside.

'A lovely baby boy,' announced the midwife with satisfaction, almost as though this happy outcome were purely a result of her own efforts.

'Is he supposed to be that colour?' Annie whispered, glimpsing the furiously flailing limbs of her son as he was wiped and weighed and wrapped, almost as though he were some pur-chase at the butcher's.

'He'll be fine as soon as he's got some oxygen into his lungs. Would you like to hold him?'

Annie shook her head. Tired beyond all tired-ness she had ever known, dishevelled and damp with sweat, all she wanted to do was to sleep. Thank God she would never, ever have to go through anything like this again.

The following afternoon, washed and tidied

and sitting up in bed in the bed-jacket her mother had knitted for her, she received her first visit from Ernest.

Annie was surprised at how tired he too seemed to be, and touched at the way he tiptoed into her room.

'How – are you?' he asked, placing a bunch of roses on the bedside table. 'How was it?' He stooped and pecked her cheek.

'Awful.' Annie grimaced. 'Thank you for the flowers.'

'A boy. That's good,' Ernest said. 'Congratulations.'

'Thank you.'

There followed a brief silence in which neither of them seemed to know what to say. Ernest shuffled his feet and coughed. 'Have you seen him?'

Annie shook her head. 'Not properly,'

'I have.' Ernest spoke almost shyly. 'He's – beautiful. They let me see him through the glass. I think he's going to have fair hair. Like yours.' He paused. 'What would you – what shall we call him?'

Annie noted the 'we', and was grateful, for up until now, Ernest had seemed reluctant to acknowledge his role as father of her baby. But she hadn't thought of a name. The matter had never been discussed between them. She had vaguely thought of calling the baby after her mother if it were a girl, but a boy? She had no idea. For some reason, she hadn't expected the baby to be a boy.

'I like William,' Ernest continued. 'I've always liked William. A nice sensible name. We can call

169

him Billy for short.'

'Fine. We'll call him William,' Annie said.

'Perhaps – William Ernest?'

Annie opened her eyes and looked at him. Ernest's expression was eager, almost boyish, and for a moment Annie felt an unexpected wave of affection for him. Could it be that this baby was going to mark a new beginning for them? Maybe – just maybe –there was a chance for them after all.

She nodded and gave a small smile.

'William Ernest,' she agreed. 'William Ernest Bentley.'

CHAPTER TWENTY-FIVE

Ophelia

Ophelia sat on the bed which had been hers for the past week, and wrote in her diary.

She had been keeping a diary ever since she was ten, when a godmother had given her a five-year diary as a Christmas present. At first, she had been wary of this unexpected and to a large extent unwanted gift. To invite someone to keep a record of a year's activities seemed a tall order; of five years' (half her lifetime so far), almost impossible. But in the end, Ophelia, possibly spurred on by her father's comment ('well, she'll never keep *that* up') had risen to the challenge, and apart from the few occasions when she had been ill or overtaken by such events as the dismal failing of examinations, she had managed to keep it going. That first diary was, of course, long finished, but each year Ophelia bought a new one, and was now well and truly hooked, not only on the actual process of writing – of watching the words unfurl across the page in flowing black biro (Ophelia had nice handwriting) – but also on the immediate access it gave her to the past.

Now, she paused, sucking her pen and wondering how much she ought to entrust to pages which could, despite her best efforts, fall into the wrong hands. She had always been careful what she wrote, using codes for anything too personal or damaging, but what code could there possibly be for a violent and passionate infatuation with a married man?

Infatuation. Ophelia considered the word, and then drew a line through it and substituted the word *love*. Of course, it was usually accepted that it was not possible really to love someone unless you knew them well, but what other word was there to describe the feeling of recognition, of coming home after a long journey, the sensation of wordless communication which she felt when she was with Andrew? As far as Andrew himself was concerned, she could be quite wrong; she knew that. It was more than possible that he was completely unaware of what was happening to her, for certainly nothing had been said. Such conversations as had taken place between them had been limited to mundane exchanges on safe subjects, nearly all of them in the presence of Annie. And yet there had been those few, precious occasions when they had looked at each other, and everything else had simply melted away and ceased to matter; when Ophelia had felt completely understood, almost as though she and Andrew, for those brief moments, had merged into one. There was physical attraction, certainly, but this seemed secondary to that other deeper magnetism, which was something she had never experienced.

But of course it couldn't be. It must never be. Whatever Andrew might think or feel, his position made the whole situation untenable. Ophelia turned to the back of the diary to the Notes section, and made a neat list.

1. *He's married (probably unhappily, but could be wrong. Don't know for sure).*
2. *He's old enough to be my father (40? Difficult to tell).*
3. *He's a vicar and I don't go to church.*
4. *He's Gran's friend, and I don't want to spoil things for her.*

Of course, the last three objections could be overcome. Age didn't matter so very much, although her parents would object (but then they would probably object to anyone Ophelia fell in love with). Besides, Ophelia knew that in many ways she was quite mature for her age; being an only child had helped, but having to stand up to her parents had done even more. For with Sheila and Billy, there had been only two options: toe the line, or be yourself. Ophelia had long since chosen the latter.

Going to church needn't be such a problem, either. Ophelia had often thought that attending church must be a nice comforting thing to do, provided you could persuade yourself that there was something in it. When she was fourteen, she had spent two terms at a Catholic boarding school (her parents had heard that it did wonderful things with under-motivated girls), where she had been much taken with the gliding tranquillity of the nuns, and had even toyed with the idea of becoming one herself. She had imagined herself becoming sickly and spiritual, like St Thérèse of Lisieux, dying young and going on to perform posthumous miracles of healing and enlightenment for the benefit of those left behind. Her parents would at last realise how special she had been, and would weep with remorse at her graveside, and she wouldn't have to pass any more exams. Unfortunately, all these plans were put paid to when she and one of her classmates were summarily expelled for smoking behind the chapel after Sunday Mass.

Lastly, there was her grandmother. Andrew was really Annie's discovery, not hers, and Ophelia was reluctant to trespass on this new and evidently highly valued territory. But perhaps they could share him? After all, their interests in him were very different, and could be compatible, and Ophelia and Annie were becoming quite close. Annie might even approve.

But there was still the married thing, and there was little Ophelia could do about that. There were no children, which made it slightly less problematic, but she had never thought of herself as the kind of person who would willingly break up another person's marriage, even if that marriage were less than satisfactory. And a priestly marriage must, of its essence, be more sacred and thus its downfall more damaging than a secular one.

Ophelia sighed. Maybe it's just a stupid crush, she thought. I haven't enough to think about at the moment, with no job and no real home of my own. I'm just treading water, keeping my widowed grandmother company, spending my days doing footling jobs about the house and getting excited about an old car I can't afford to keep. From downstairs, she could hear the distant sound of her grandmother's voice. Andrew had come round for another of their mysterious chats, and after making tea for them both, Ophelia had made herself scarce. She looked at her watch. Andrew had been here for over an hour. Should she offer more tea, or leave them to it? Ophelia was very curious as to the content of these conversations, but respected her grandmother's privacy. It was true that Annie had started to take her into her confidence over the past few days, and Ophelia had learnt quite a lot of things she hadn't known before, but the secrets which had been hinted at had so far remained secrets.

Ophelia closed her diary and placed it on the bedside table. Lying back on the bed, she picked up a book, and leafing through the well-thumbed pages, began to read. It was a battered copy of *Pride and Prejudice*, its brown paper cover ripped and smudged with ink, its margins marked in pencil where the schoolgirl Ophelia had made her notes. On the label inside was her name: 'Ophelia Bentley, form Vb'.

Ophelia Bentley. Ophelia Rose Bentley, to be more precise. Her initials – O.R.B. – had given rise to a series of nicknames: The Orb, of course, (not least because she had a tendency towards what her mother unkindly referred to as puppy fat) but then, following on in logical sequence, The Ball, Balloon, Balloony and finally, triumphantly, Loony. Loony Bentley. Poor Ophelia had been known as Loony for the last three years of her school career, only shedding the hated label on the day she finally stuffed her school skirt and blazer into the dustbin.

But she had hung on to *Pride and Prejudice* (after all, surely that wretched school owed her something), a novel of which she never tired. She dreamed of having the sweet nature and the looks of Jane and the sharpness and wit of Elizabeth, comforted herself that these girls had had to put up with a mother even worse than her own, and dreamed of Mr Darcy in the same way that her friends had dreamed about pop stars. When she first made their acquaintance the Bennet sisters had almost certainly been older than she was, but now she had probably overtaken Elizabeth, if not Jane, and was certainly older than Lydia (who had even managed to find herself a husband, albeit a scoundrel). These heroines would remain forever young and beautiful and full of hope, and would certainly never fall into the trap of loving a married man. To Ophelia, the heroines of Jane Austen inhabited the golden age of romance, when men swooned at the sight of a well-turned ankle, no girl was ever expected to show her legs, and no one tried to put their hand (or, come to that, anything else) inside your knickers.

A door opened, and she could hear voices in the hallway. If she was to have another glimpse of Andrew, Ophelia would have to get a move on. Forgetting that she had resolved to try and avoid seeing him any more than was necessary (and this was hardly necessary), she threw aside her book and ran down the stairs.

'Ah. Ophelia.' Andrew said. 'Thanks again for the tea.'

'Would you like some more?'

'No, bless you. I have to be getting back. Janet's expecting me. We eat early on a Monday because of her women's group.'

So her name was Janet – not a name Ophelia liked much (but then she wouldn't, would she?) – and she was the kind of woman who went to meetings. An ideal wife for someone like Andrew then, she thought sadly, wondering what the sex was like.

'But perhaps I'll see you again, if you're staying on?' He was looking at her now, with that half-smile she found so irresistible.

Ophelia swallowed. 'Yes. Yes, of course. Of course you'll see me again. In fact I was thinking of coming to your church,' she added, surprising herself, because up until a few minutes ago she had been thinking of no such thing.

'You never said you wanted to go to church,' Annie said.

'Didn't I? Well, now that I've found out that I was christened there, it seems a good time and place to give it a go.' Ophelia blushed, realising that this was hardly a mature approach to church attendance. 'Perhaps you'd like to come with me?'

'Well...' Annie didn't look too sure. 'It's been a long time.'

'All the more reason to start again now.' Ophelia turned to Andrew. 'What time are the services?'

'Nine-thirty Communion at St John's, eight-thirty once a month at your little church. Matins every third Sunday. Oh, and Evensong, of course.'

'We'll be there,' said Ophelia, showing him out. 'It's the least we can do,' she added, as she walked with him to his car.

'The least you can do?'

'After all your help. Looking after Gran, and changing the tyre and everything. We owe you one.'

'You owe God one, more like.'

'Do you believe in God?' Ophelia asked.

'What an extraordinary question! Of course I do. You could say that my job depends on it.' Andrew laughed, then turned to unlock the door of his car. Ophelia noted that the car itself was in need of a good clean, and wondered whether she might offer to do it for him.

'I suppose so. But what on earth would you do if you stopped believing? I guess you'd have to pretend. Like the royal family.'

'Do you think they pretend?' Andrew lowered himself into the driving seat and wound down the window.

'I'm sure some of them must do. After all, they can't all believe, can they? They're more – born to it, like unveiling things and watching tribal dances and making speeches. It's part of what they do, poor things,' said Ophelia, thinking of the orderly processions of hatted and gloved royals photographed attending morning service at Sandringham.

'You may be right.'

'I'd hate to be one of them, anyway,' Ophelia said, prolonging the conversation as long as she could.

'I thought all girls dreamed of being princesses,' Andrew smiled, starting up the engine.

'Not this one. I had enough trouble living up to being my parents' daughter. Royalty must be sheer hell.'

'I really have to go now.'

'Yes.'

There was a moment's silence. Andrew started doing up his seatbelt, then seemed to hesitate. 'I wonder – I mean would you–'

'Yes?' Ophelia felt the blood rush to her face.

'Nothing.' Andrew sighed, and his shoulders seemed to sag. 'It doesn't matter. It was just a silly idea.' He looked at his watch. 'Goodness. I really must be off. I'll be in trouble if I don't get a move on.'

'Yes.'

'Goodbye, then.'

'Goodbye.'

But not goodbye. Not really, Ophelia thought gleefully, as she made her way back into the house. He had been about to ask her – what? If he could see her on her own? Take her out? Something, anyway. There had been another of those moments between them; another wordless communication of mutual attraction and, on Ophelia's part at least, of longing. And while Andrew had obviously thought better of whatever it was he'd been about to say, there would be other opportunities, of that she was sure.

'You took your time,' Annie said, as Ophelia closed the front door behind her.

'We were just talking.'

'What about?'

'Oh ... God, the royal family. That sort of thing.'

'Hmmm.' Annie turned back to the vegetables she was preparing.

'What do you mean, hmmm?'

'Just hmmm,' said Annie, plopping a potato into a saucepan of water. 'I'm not as daft as I look, you know. You be careful, my girl, that's all. You just be careful.'

'Careful?' Annie patted her grandmother on the back. She could almost feel the disapproval filtering through the robust cotton of the flowered pinafore. 'I can't think what you mean.'

'Oh, I think you can.' A more aggressive plop this time, splashing the draining board and Annie's own sleeve. 'You're not stupid either, Ophelia. I rather think you take after me.'

CHAPTER TWENTY-SIX

Annie's Story

The infant Billy screamed and screamed. It seemed to Annie that he barely paused for breath between one fit of enraged crying and another. Red-faced and rigid, his tiny fists clenched in fury, he yelled as though all the hounds of hell were after him, and nothing Annie did seemed to make any difference.

Ernest, meanwhile, did little to improve matters. His manner towards Annie had softened since Billy's birth, and he was obviously proud to have fathered a son, but he also made it clear that the baby was her responsibility,

'Can't you quieten that child?' he would ask, from behind his newspaper. 'You must be doing something wrong. I'm sure babies aren't meant to cry like that.'

Annie, who had never in her life had any sort of contact with babies, had no idea what they were meant to do, but she too felt that it couldn't be normal for any human being to display so much misery at so young an age, for nothing in his life seemed to give Billy any pleasure or her any respite. He cried when she dressed or changed him; he cried when she bathed him, his soapy wriggling body nearly slipping from her inexperienced hands; he cried when she took him out in his pram. He even managed to cry when she was feeding him.

Annie often wondered whether she had been wrong to opt for bottle-feeding, but Ernest had told her that the whole idea of breastfeeding was distasteful to him, and at the time she hadn't felt that it was a matter worth arguing about. But now she thought that perhaps Billy might have derived some small comfort from the warmth and softness of her breasts rather than the hard glass bottles with their rubber teats which seemed to bear so little resemblance to her own nipples.

The nights were particularly difficult, for Ernest expected to get his full ration of sleep; as he explained to Annie, he had a job to go to. She only had to look after the house and the baby; he had a living to earn. So not only did Annie have to forego much-needed rest, but she had the added problem of trying to keep Billy quiet.

One night, when Annie was almost at her wits' end, Ernest stormed out of the bedroom, and took the baby from her.

'For goodness' sake, Annie! Can't you see you're not doing him any good? Let me have him.'

Annie gaped. Ernest had only held Billy a couple of times since she had returned home with him, and she had assumed that that was the way it was going to be. And now here he was, walking up and down the room with the baby over his shoulder. And Billy had stopped crying.

'There. You see? You just weren't doing it right,' Ernest said, doing another circuit of the small living-room. 'He's fine now.'

'But that's just what I have been doing!' Annie

said. 'I must have walked miles with him. He's probably worn himself out.'

'He just needs a bit of love, that's all,' Ernest said, patting Billy's back as though he'd been soothing small babies all his life. 'Just a bit of love.'

And maybe he had a point. Annie hadn't really thought much about her feelings for the baby, so occupied had she been with the job of looking after him, but Ernest was right. If she was honest with herself, she didn't love Billy. She found herself unable to hug him to her in the way she had seen other mothers hug their babies; her kisses were dutiful rather than affectionate. She cared about him, and she certainly wished him no harm, but such feelings as she had couldn't really be described as love.

'Are you – are you glad we had him? Are you pleased with Billy?' she asked now. It was a question she had often wanted to ask, but hadn't liked to for fear of what Ernest's answer might be.

Ernest looked down at Billy, who was now fast asleep in his arms.

'He's my son,' he said, his face softening as he touched the baby's cheek. 'Of course I'm pleased with him. He's a bit noisy, but he'll be all right, will our Billy.'

Annie was touched, and opened her mouth to say something; to thank Ernest perhaps for his acceptance of this child he had never wanted, or simply to show her appreciation for his help. But she decided against it. Maybe it would be unwise to make an issue of what was, after all, a relatively unimportant exchange. It was enough that Ernest was happy with Billy; perhaps even happy that they were now a proper family. Once again, she wondered whether Billy just might be the making of this ill-fated marriage, as well as its cause.

That night proved a turning point in Ernest's relationship with Billy. It was as though they had each found in the other something they had been searching for, and while Billy began at last to settle down and find a degree of contentment, Ernest too seemed more cheerful.

Annie didn't know what to think. On the one hand, she was grateful and relieved to have Ernest's help, but she soon began to feel excluded.

'Where's our Billy, then?' Ernest would say when he arrived home from work, and he would pick the child up and hug him and throw him in the air. Billy would laugh and crow, and pat Ernest's face with his fat little hands. He hardly ever smiled for Annie.

'So what's he been doing today? What's new?' Ernest wanted to know, and he would nod and smile over each little development, almost as though Billy's small achievements were his own.

'But I've not had such a good day,' Annie ventured once, hoping that perhaps Ernest might show a little interest in Billy's mother as well as Billy himself.

'So your mother's complaining again, is she? What's she got to complain about, with you to play with all day, eh?' Ernest tickled Billy under the chin, and the baby laughed delightedly,

'I'm not complaining,' Annie said, the tears springing to her eyes. 'It's just that I've hardly spoken to a soul all week, and the only person you seem interested in nowadays is Billy.'

'So you're jealous! Is that it? You're actually jealous of your own baby! He's just a helpless mite. You should be ashamed of yourself, Annie!'

Annie forbore to say that the helpless mite had spent much of the day grizzling, had spat out all the food she had painstakingly prepared for him and had then contrived to vomit all down his clean smock. Ernest wouldn't understand that looking after a small baby on her own, day in day out, queuing for food with the restless Billy squawking for attention, trying to clean the flat while he had his nap when she would much have preferred ten minutes to put her feet up, added up to a life which was humdrum, exhausting, and at times deeply boring.

But whatever Ernest might say, Annie was determined that he would never be able to find fault with her as a mother. She might not be the most doting of parents – after all, she couldn't help how she felt, could she? – but Billy would want for nothing if she could help it. She kept him scrupulously clean, fed him the best food she could afford (and find) and made sure he had a daily outing in his pram, whatever the weather.

And Billy thrived. He might not have been the happiest of infants, but he put on weight and reached all his milestones in record time. Annie's mother, who had at last managed to find the time to make the long train journey up to visit them, was impressed.

'Well, you're certainly doing a good job, our Annie,' she said, as she held her new grandson on her lap. 'He looks very well.' Billy cooed obligingly and played with the buttons on her blouse. 'And how are you and Ernest? How's married life? You're certainly looking very well on it.'

'Am I?'

'Of course you are. And so you should. A nice little flat all of your own, and this lovely baby. You're a very lucky girl, our Annie. When I had all of you, I was helping your father out on the farm as well as everything else. You're quite the lady of leisure.'

Annie bit her lip. She could see that there was no point in telling her mother of the loneliness and isolation she felt, of her longing for her family and her hopes and fears for her marriage. Her mother would only hear what she wanted to hear, and that was that she and Ernest and Billy were well and happy, The hasty marriage and the events leading up to it had, it seemed, been conveniently forgotten.

Meanwhile, Annie's mother was full of news, and Annie was eager to hear it. Tom was doing well with his artificial leg, and Jack was expected home on leave. Derek had mysteriously disappeared, but was not much missed ('I never trusted that one') and Mavis was engaged.

'Engaged! I never knew! Who to?' Annie asked.

Annie's mother mentioned the name of a local pig farmer, and Annie was much entertained. Mavis with her lofty ideas and her thorough dislike of pigs! How would she manage? Hers must be a love match indeed.

Annie missed her mother after she had gone. Starved of company, she felt lonelier than ever, and while Ernest did seem to be making some effort, there was no real companionship between them.

Once, only once, did he refer again to the circumstances surrounding her pregnancy and the timing of their marriage.

'No one is to know about it. No one. Do you hear me? I come from a respectable family, and I've my reputation to think of. As far as anyone else is concerned, Billy arrived – early. If my mother ever came to hear about it, it would kill her.'

Annie couldn't help smiling. Even she knew that eight-and-a-half pounds was on the heavy side for a seriously premature infant. Besides, wasn't Ernest being a little over-dramatic? After all, they were married, weren't they? Did it really matter that Billy had been conceived before rather than after the event? As for what people would think, they had few friends, and most of those lived many miles away, and Ernest's mother still lived up in Yorkshire. Annie had never so much as met her. But she readily agreed to comply with Ernest's wishes. She certainly wasn't going to do anything to endanger the fragile peace which had been established between them.

How could she have guessed that one day she would come to look back on the first six months of Billy's life as a period of relative happiness?

CHAPTER TWENTY-SEVEN

Andrew

'I have fallen for someone. I have fallen for a girl half my age, and I don't know what to do.'

Andrew's words broke the still atmosphere of the small study, seeming to interrupt the gentle ticking of the clock on the mantelpiece and the sound of birdsong from the garden outside. How many times had he sat in this room with this kindly, spiritual man, discussing his struggles to enliven the sleepy parish of mainly elderly churchgoers who constituted his flock, and his own rather uncertain spiritual journey? Up until now, he had looked forward to these sessions, and usually came away feeling invigorated and at peace. There was no one else who would listen to him the way Father Matthew did; no one who seemed to understand quite as well or whose wisdom he so respected.

But today, as he sat looking down at his hands, unable to meet Father Matthew's eyes, he was filled with apprehension and, for the first time, a deep feeling of shame. He had let his mentor down, of that there was no doubt, and he dreaded losing the respect of someone who had indeed come to be a kind of father to him.

'You don't know what to do,' Father Matthew repeated.

Andrew shook his head.

'Who is this girl?'

Andrew told him about Ophelia; of how he'd met her, of his feelings for her, and how his thoughts of her were beginning to dominate his life.

'I can't seem to escape her,' he said now. 'I can't read, I can't pray, I can't sleep. Everything I do, everywhere I go, it's all Ophelia. Which doesn't really make sense, because we've never been anywhere or done anything together.'

'So there's no harm done.' There was humour in Father Matthew's voice although his tone was serious.

'Well, no, I suppose not.'

'But?'

'But.' Andrew sighed, and looked up. His companion's gaze was level and untroubled. There was none of the surprise and disappointment he had expected, and he took courage. 'But I can't – I can't keep away from her. I simply can't.'

'Can't you?'

'Well, of course I can, but – and I know this sounds ridiculous – she offers hope. My life's a mess at the moment, and she's become the light at the end of the tunnel. I may get to the end of the tunnel and find there's nothing there – no light, no hope even – but I have this compulsion – this *longing* – to go after it. In case.'

'And this will make your life less of a mess, will it?'

'Yes. No. No, of course it won't. Oh, I don't know. I just don't know what to do.'

'Does Janet know about this?'

'No. Of course not.'

'How do you think she would feel?'

'I don't know.' And this was true. Andrew had no idea how Janet might feel if she knew what was happening to him. There would be indignation, he was sure, for Janet's occupation of the moral high ground was second to none; hurt, perhaps; sadness, possibly. But would she mind? Would she really care if Andrew were to find someone else? It might even be a merciful release for her as much as for him. After all, she would emerge blameless, and he would be shown to be the weak-minded fool he felt she had always thought him to be.

'Is this girl – is Ophelia – beautiful?' The question was unexpected, and Andrew smiled.

'No. Oh, no. Attractive, yes. In her own way. She has a – freshness, a naturalness. But not really beautiful. Not in the conventional sense, anyway. Of course I find her attractive, but it's so much more than that. It's almost as though we – *match*, if that makes any sense.'

'Pity.'

'Why a pity?'

'It's so much easier to disentangle oneself from an attraction which is purely – or mainly – physical.'

Andrew wondered that an unmarried man – a celibate who had, he knew, chosen to live his life alone so that he could better serve his God and his church – should show such understanding. Prior to his retirement, Father Matthew had for many years presided over an Anglo-Catholic parish, hence his preferred title, but there had been no need for him to choose the single life. He

189

could have married, had he so wished.

'You're wondering what I know about it, aren't you?' Father Matthew looked amused.

Andrew blushed.

'Well, no. Or rather, if I am, I have no right to. And I certainly have no right to make assumptions.'

'You can make assumptions. Of course you can. You can assume that I've spent a blamelessly pure life, untouched by human passion. And of course you'd be wrong. I have loved, and I have lost, and like you, I have had to make painful decisions. Because whatever decision you make, there will be pain. For you, and for others. There always is.' He took a sip of the cooling cup of coffee at his side. 'Does she know? Does Ophelia know how you feel? And does she feel the same?'

'I don't know. We've never spoken about it. We've hardly ever been alone together. But there's something very strong between us; I know there is. Something I've certainly never felt before. In many ways I wish she were not so young. It's such a cliché, an older man falling for a young girl. But I think I would feel like this about Ophelia whatever age she might be. It's got nothing to do with age. It's something so much – so much *more*.'

'If nothing's been done or said, no one need ever know.'

'No.'

'But your mind is made up.' It was a statement rather than a question.

'Not really. No, of course not. I wouldn't have come to you if I'd already decided what to do.'

'Wouldn't you?' Father Matthew pushed his

coffee cup away, 'I think you might. Maybe you just needed someone to talk to. Someone to tell. Sometimes when one has a shocking secret – and this has the potential to shock a great many people – it helps to, as it were, get it out in the open. I believe that's why you've come here today. I've known you some time, Andrew. I like to think we know each other quite well. Whatever you may say, I don't believe that any words of mine will make you change your mind. I think you've already decided what you're going to do.'

'Am I that obstinate?'

'Not obstinate. No. But you've been very unhappy for a long time, and you think you may have found the answer. You've made this assumption on what sounds to me to be pretty fragile evidence, but there it is.'

There followed a lengthy silence in which Andrew pondered Father Matthew's words. Had he really made his mind up? It hadn't occurred to him before he came here today that this was the case; he'd come to talk, certainly, but also for guidance, for help, for advice. Or so he had thought. But now he had to admit that Father Matthew was right. After all, what could he say to Andrew that he hadn't already said to himself a hundred times over? They were both priests. They both knew right from wrong, and from a moral standpoint, this was a perfectly clear-cut case. A married priest, a young girl – the potential damage to his calling, his marriage, his reputation and perhaps to Ophelia herself didn't need to be spelt out. And yet nothing in the world seemed more important than that he should see her again.

'I can't stop seeing her grandmother,' he said now. 'She really does need me. And with Ophelia now living with her, I can't avoid her. It would look very suspicious if I were to check that she was out of the house every time I visited.'

But even as he spoke, he realised how feeble his words sounded. Whatever he might say, it was quite clear where his duty lay. Since any special relationship between himself and Ophelia was as yet unacknowledged, there was no need to go out of his way to avoid her. All he had to do was ensure that the two of them spent as little time as possible in each other's company. It would be perfectly possible to do this. He knew it was what he ought to do. Otherwise he was risking everything he had for a possibility – and that was all it was – of a happiness he didn't deserve and which would hurt people who didn't deserve to be hurt.

Father Matthew looked at him quizzically, but made no comment. 'I shall be here,' he said. 'If you need me. And now, would you like to pray?'

'Please.'

But while Father Matthew prayed – the familiar words of the Lord's Prayer, followed by prayers for Andrew: for guidance, for help, for strength and the courage to make the right decision – Andrew barely heard the words. The sun filtering through the leaves of some shrub outside the window threw bright coins of sunlight onto the patterned carpet; in the garden, a blackbird was singing; the clock ticked steadily on: Ophelia, Ophelia, Ophelia.

Father Matthew was right. Andrew had already made his decision.

CHAPTER TWENTY-EIGHT

Annie

Annie always said she could tell when it was Billy on the phone. Ophelia told her that this was probably because hardly anyone else ever phoned her, but Annie privately thought that the sound the telephone made was that bit more demanding when Billy was on the other end of the line.

'Mother.' Billy always came straight to the point. 'Where's Ophelia?'

'Well, she's here, of course.'

'No, I mean when is she coming home? She's been with you for nearly two weeks and her mother—'

'Needs the car,' Annie finished for him helpfully, thinking that it was rather sad that Sheila appeared to think more of her car than she did of her daughter. For no one seemed to be missing Ophelia.

'Yes. It's very thoughtless of Ophelia to take off like that in Sheila's car. Very inconvenient all round.'

'She didn't take off like anything. She came to stay with me,' Annie said. 'You told her to,' she added.

'Well, it's high time she came back and found herself a job,' Billy said.

'Oh it's all right. She's going to stay with me and

find a job here. And I'm giving her Dad's old car, so Sheila can have hers back. It's all arranged.'

'She's *what?*'

'She's staying with me and getting a job here and–'

'Yes, yes. I heard you.'

'Then why ask me to say it all over again?'

'Mother, please allow me to get to the point.'

'What is the point?'

'The point,' Billy said, 'is that Ophelia hasn't bothered to let us know any of this. That it's quite out of the question her staying with you. It would be utterly impractical. As for the car, Ophelia can't possibly afford to run a car of her own. It's absurd, when she hasn't even got a job.'

'Who does the car belong to?' Annie asked.

'Well, I suppose it belongs to you now. Yes, of course it does. Dad left everything to you.'

'Well then. I can give it to whoever I like, can't I? I'll pay for the petrol and Ophelia can drive it.'

'Ah, but it's not just the petrol, is it? I don't suppose either of you has thought about the insurance and the tax and–'

'Yes we have,' Annie said. 'We've thought of everything, and Andrew's been very helpful, and–'

'Who's Andrew?' Billy interrupted.

'I keep telling you. He's the nice vicar you sent round.'

'Oh, him.'

'Yes. And we can use it for shopping and the hairdresser, and Ophelia will have it for when she gets a job. And we're going to redecorate her room. I suggested some nice wallpaper, but Ophelia doesn't want wallpaper. She says it's too difficult to–'

'Mother, I haven't the time to discuss all these cosy little domestic arrangements you and Ophelia seem to have made. It simply won't work, the two of you living together like that. Let me speak to her.'

Annie covered the mouthpiece and turned to Ophelia. 'He wants to speak to you,' she said.

'I'm out,' Ophelia mouthed. 'I'll ring him back later.'

'She's out. I'll get her to phone you later.'

'Are you sure she's out?'

'Quite sure.'

'What's she doing?'

'She's – well, I think she's–'

'Looking for a job,' Ophelia whispered.

'That's right. She's looking for a job.'

'What sort of job?' Billy wanted to know.

'Oh, I'm not sure.' Annie wished Ophelia wouldn't leave her to answer all these questions. She wasn't able to think as quickly these days as she used to. 'She's down the job centre,' she said, with sudden inspiration. 'Yes. They'll give her the right sort of advice there. They'll soon sort her out.'

'Well, just you make sure she rings me the minute she gets back,' Billy said. 'I'll be in my office until four, but then I'll be in a meeting.'

'Well done, Gran,' said Ophelia admiringly, when Annie had put down the receiver. 'You're getting quite good at this, aren't you?'

'That's as maybe, but you're going to have to speak to him yourself next time,' Annie said. 'You can't keep hiding from him like this.'

'No. But it gives me time to concoct a good story.'

'Aren't you going to tell him the truth?' Annie asked.

'Up to a point. But it's always easier to tell Dad what he wants to hear. It saves a lot of hassle.'

Why had Billy turned out so – *difficult*, Annie wondered, as she sliced carrots for their evening meal while Ophelia scanned the local paper for job vacancies. She hadn't noticed it so much when Ernest was alive, but that could be because Ernest was even more awkward than Billy. But now it seemed that Billy had taken upon himself the mantle of the patriarch, and was making it his business to organise everyone else's lives.

'It's very tiresome,' she said aloud, putting the carrots in a saucepan.

'What is?' Ophelia asked.

'Your father. He's getting so bossy,'

Ophelia laughed. 'Dad's always been bossy. It's just that you probably haven't noticed before.' She turned back to the paper. 'They need sheet metal workers and tyre-fitters. D'you think they'd have me?'

'Would you want them to?'

'Probably not. What about a bus driver? I've always fancied driving a bus. Full training given. Imagine what Dad would say to that!'

'You're probably too young,' Annie said. 'I've never seen a very young bus driver.'

Ophelia had to admit that she hadn't either.

'Teaching assistant, evening cleaner (that always sounds so odd, doesn't it?), pig person.' Ophelia pealed with laughter. 'A pig person!

What do you suppose that means?'

'Anyone can tell you weren't brought up in the country,' Annie said. 'They're not allowed to say pig man like they used to because of the sex discrimination thingy, so it's pig person. Looking after pigs. That's what it means. I used to like pigs,' she added, 'but I don't think you'd be much good at it. Isn't there anything else?'

'Small boutique requires sales assistant,' Ophelia read. 'That sounds quite fun, and I'd probably get a discount. You might, too, being family.'

Annie tried to imagine herself wearing the kind of clothes she had seen in small boutiques, but failed.

'Don't worry, Gran. They probably sell cardigans and pinnies as well as your haute couture. Designer cardigans and pinnies, of course. You know, I think I might go for that. I've always fancied serving in a shop.'

'It seems to me there's a lot of things you've always fancied,' remarked Annie. 'How come you never did any of them?'

Ophelia ignored the question. 'I can tell Dad I'm working for a fashion house, which will be true in a way. Fashion house, house of fashion. Same sort of thing.'

'How do you know they'll have you?' Annie asked.

'You're right. They'll probably say I'm over-qualified.'

'Are you?'

'No. Of course I'm not. Joke,' explained Ophelia. 'I'm not really qualified for anything,' she added wistfully,

'Neither am I,' said Annie. 'Never did me any harm.'

But of course, it had, she thought now. If there hadn't been a war, if she'd been able to stay on at school, if she'd had qualifications... So many ifs. With the right job, and then the right husband, and – although she hardly dared even to think it, for it seemed so disloyal to Billy – the right children, life might have turned out so very differently,

'You must think I've wasted my opportunities,' Ophelia said, for Annie had told her something of her girlhood and the war. 'You'd have made a lot more of yourself than I have if you'd had all that money spent on you.'

'I might have,' Annie said, 'but I could be pretty obstinate, too. I don't suppose I'd have done what I was told any more than you have. But I wouldn't have minded the chance.'

'Have you ever – been in love?' Ophelia asked.

Annie eyed her sharply. 'What makes you think I wasn't in love with your grandad?' she asked.

'Well, were you?' Ophelia asked. 'Of course, you don't have to say. It's a bit impertinent of me to ask, really.'

Annie sighed. 'Well, no,' she said, sitting down at the table. 'I wasn't in love with Ernest. I – had to marry him.'

'Oh, Gran! You are a dark horse!' Ophelia said admiringly. 'I never knew that. Does Dad know?'

'Well your grandad didn't want him to know. Didn't want anyone else to know, either, so you're not to go spreading it around. But you can't hide that sort of thing for ever, what with marriage certificates and birth certificates and things like that. Especially from someone like Billy. He was a bit shocked when he found out,' she added.

'I bet he was.' Ophelia reached out and gave Annie's hand a squeeze. 'Poor Gran. You've not had it easy, have you?'

'No worse than a lot of folks,' Annie said briskly. 'Anyway, what's all this about love? Are you in love? Is that it?'

Ophelia blushed, hesitating. 'Perhaps,' she said. 'Well, not quite. Not yet. But there is someone. Sort of.'

'No good chasing after a married man, especially that married man,' Annie said. 'It'll lead to all sorts of trouble.'

'What do you mean?' Ophelia looked startled.

'I wasn't born yesterday, young lady. I've seen the way you are with Andrew. All those cups of tea, and walking him out to the car every time, and running downstairs whenever he calls. In fact I'm beginning to wonder whether your staying here is such a good idea after all. It'll only give you more ideas.'

'Oh, no. Oh, please, Gran! Don't make me go home. I really like it here with you.'

Annie noticed with surprise that there were tears in Ophelia's eyes. 'You don't deny it, then,' she said. 'About Andrew.'

Ophelia shrugged. 'No. There's no point, and in any case, it's nice to have someone to talk to about it. I know it's silly, Gran. You probably think it's just a childish crush. But being with Andrew is like – like coming *home*. I can't explain it, I don't know why it's like this, but that's how I feel.'

'Your trouble is, you're lonely, like me,' Annie

said, after a moment. 'Maybe that's why we get on so well.'

Ophelia nodded, wiping away a tear with the back of her hand. 'I can't remember a time when I wasn't lonely,' she said. 'I've had friends – some – and of course Mum and Dad, but we're not that close. You know, I don't think I've ever really felt understood. I always seemed to be fighting a battle against someone or something. And yet I don't think I'm that difficult. I certainly don't mean to be.'

Annie looked at Ophelia and her heart ached for her granddaughter. How could Billy and Sheila be so stupid? They had hoped that Ophelia would be beautiful and clever; that she would turn heads and win prizes; even Annie knew that. Instead, they had something so much better; a daughter who was genuine, who longed to love and be loved, and above all, who was *kind*. Yet it would seem that they utterly failed to see it. And now, here was Ophelia imagining herself to be in love with someone who was not only married but probably hadn't even noticed her.

'I'd like you to stay on here. Of course I would,' she said now. 'But if having Andrew around is going to be too hard for you, then you'll have to go home, because I can't stop him from coming here. He's been my lifeline these last few months. In any case, what would he think if I told him not to come any more? It would seem so rude. So ungrateful.'

'I'll try to be good,' Ophelia said. 'If you let me stay, I really will try to keep out of his way,'

'That's all right then,' Annie said. But she had

200

her doubts. It was true that she had never been in love herself, but if the opportunity had ever arisen, she knew she would have grasped it with both hands.

Could she trust her granddaughter not to do the same?

CHAPTER TWENTY-NINE

Annie's Story

When Billy was six months old, Ernest told Annie that he wished to sleep with her.

'But you do sleep with me, Ernest,' Annie said, hoping beyond hope that he didn't mean what she thought he meant.

'You know what I mean, Annie. *Sleep together*. Properly. Like husband and wife. I've given you time. Many men wouldn't have left it as long. But it's only right, with us being married. It's time we – got together again.' He spoke almost shyly, but there was no doubting the tone of his voice, and Annie's heart sank.

It was the moment she had been dreading. Sometimes, in her more optimistic moods, she had thought that maybe Ernest had forgotten about sex altogether. He hadn't mentioned it since their wedding night, and there had been virtually no physical contact between them since. Or it could be that he had gone off the idea as much as she had, for certainly Annie could think of few things less pleasurable than their antics in the cornfield.

She could imagine – just – wanting to have a sexual encounter with someone she loved; someone who was tender and caring, who would hold her and be gentle with her. She could even imagine that it might be possible to enjoy it. But with Ernest? She thought of Ernest's moustache, Ernest's white hairy legs, Ernest's clammy fumbling fingers, and worst of all, Ernest's Thing (she could only think of it as a Thing. She had never actually seen it, of course, but she certainly hadn't forgotten its startling size and even more startling effect).

'When?' she whispered. 'When do you want to – do it?'

'I think tonight,' Ernest said, folding his newspaper. 'No time like the present,' he added, as though they were about to embark on a household chore rather than what was supposed to be an act of love. 'I've got to be up in good time in the morning, so we'd better get to bed early,'

With trembling hands Annie washed and brushed her teeth, and put on her best nightdress. Frightened as she was, she wanted to please Ernest if it was possible, and the nightdress was a birthday gift from her mother and nearly new.

'You won't be needing that,' Ernest said, coming into the bedroom.

'Needing what?'

'The nightdress. You won't be needing it. Please take it off. I want to look at you.'

'Oh, please, Ernest! Let me keep it on. Please.

202

Just this time.' Annie was appalled. No one had seen her naked since she was a small child, and besides, while she had always been slim, she was aware that childbirth hadn't done her figure any favours. What if Ernest didn't like what he saw? What if it made him angry? Annie would go to considerable lengths to avoid Ernest's anger.

'I've allowed you your – modesty, Annie, up until now. But I'm entitled to see you. I'm your husband.' He undid his tie and started to take off his shirt. 'You should be flattered that I want to look at you.'

Was Ernest entitled to see her naked? Annie was sure her parents had never seen each other's bodies. They had always been very modest around the house, and she knew for a fact that her father always undressed in the bathroom before joining her mother at night.

'Must I? Oh Ernest, please. I really don't want to.'

Ernest took off his shoes. 'I haven't asked much of you, Annie. I want you to do this now. I want to look at you.'

Slowly, her heart full of dread, Annie began to undo her buttons. She could feel the blood flooding her face and neck, and her legs shook. How was she going to bear this humiliation? If the prospect of sex had been bad, the idea of standing in front of Ernest without a stitch was almost worse. She undid the final button and hesitated.

'Come on.' Ernest was staring at her, a half-smile on his lips. 'Get it off properly. Hurry up, Annie.'

There were tears in her eyes as Annie finally let

the nightdress slip to the floor. Too embarrassed to look down at her body and too ashamed to meet Ernest's eye, she fixed her gaze on a point above his head. And waited.

'Well.' Ernest was smiling now. 'That's nice, Annie. You've got a nice body. Very – attractive, I must say, Come here.'

Annie walked towards him, biting her lip. She wouldn't cry. She mustn't cry. Crying always irritated Ernest, and whatever happened, she mustn't do anything to upset him.

Ernest reached out and touched one of her nipples. 'Very nice,' he repeated, as though her breast were a cake she had just baked rather than part of her body, 'Very nice, Annie.'

Although she didn't dare look, Annie was aware of movement below Ernest's belt, and suspected that the Thing had awoken and was preparing to join in the proceedings. She swallowed.

'You can get into bed now, Annie. I won't be a minute.'

Gratefully, Annie threw herself under the covers, and drawing the blankets up to her chin, turned her face away. She heard Ernest going into the bathroom, flushing the lavatory, running a tap. He appeared to be humming to himself. Annie prayed that the baby might wake up; he represented her only chance of a reprieve. But for once, Billy, usually a light sleeper, slept on in the tiny bedroom next door.

She heard Ernest come back into the bedroom, close the door and walk over to the bed. The mattress dipped as he got into bed, and she heard him place his glasses on the bedside table, just as he always did, and switch off the bedside light. Annie waited.

What would happen now? Annie's memories of her sexual initiation, unpleasant as they undoubtedly were, had been blurred by the effects of cider, and now, with no such assistance, she wasn't at all sure what to expect. Was she supposed to do something to initiate the process, or should she leave everything to Ernest? Despite the bedclothes, her nakedness made her feel horribly vulnerable. She wondered whether Ernest too was naked, but there was no delicate way of finding out.

Ernest reached across and put a hand on her breast. Annie tried not to shudder. The hand smelled strongly of the carbolic soap Ernest favoured, and felt damp. She could feel Ernest turning towards her in the darkness. The hand moved downwards, touching her belly and thigh. Annie froze.

And then suddenly Ernest was on top of her, his breath hot in her face, his body pinning her down, his free hand roughly exploring between her legs. And Annie screamed.

Long afterwards, Annie wondered whether her life might have turned out differently had she managed to contain her fear. After all, she knew Ernest; she knew, more or less, what was involved. Ernest had never tried to hurt her before, and so she most likely had nothing to fear. But the suddenness of Ernest's approach, the roughness, the feeling of helplessness compounded by humiliation overwhelmed her totally. Hers was a cry not only of fear, but of desperation and hopelessness, for in that moment she realised as never before that this was what she was condemned to endure quite possibly for the rest of her life: sex without affection, desire without any consideration for how she might be feeling.

Annie's scream enraged Ernest, as she might have known it would. He hissed at her to be quiet, while the pawing and the thrusting became increasingly violent, and when he entered her body the pain was worse than it had been before. Annie bit her lip and braced herself, praying for it all to be over. Whatever happened, she mustn't scream again. If she kept quiet, she might be able to redeem herself just a little. But let it be over, she kept thinking. Please let it be over.

Abruptly, Ernest finished, and for a moment his body seemed to collapse onto hers. He sounded out of breath, and she could feel his heart pounding against her own. She turned her head towards the window. Some people passed in the street outside, talking and laughing. Annie had no idea who they were, but she wished she could have changed places with them; at this moment, she would gladly have changed places with anyone who wasn't married to Ernest.

'Well, Annie,' Ernest said, after he had regained his side of the bed. 'You've displeased me, I have to say.'

'I'm sorry,' Annie whispered.

'And so you should be. Making that disgraceful noise. Supposing someone had heard. What then, eh?'

'I don't know.'

'No. I don't suppose you do. That's your

trouble, Annie. You don't think. And you never gave a thought to my feelings, either. It's not as though you haven't done this before. More than once, I shouldn't wonder.'

'*What?*'

'That's what I said. I thought that first time, I wonder whether she's done this before. You certainly didn't make much fuss at the time.'

'But I never – I've never – I never even had a boyfriend before you, Ernest! You were the first. I swear to you, you were the first.' Did Ernest really mean what he was saying, or were his words simply designed to hurt her? Annie had upset Ernest, and she was genuinely sorry that she had, but surely she didn't deserve this?

'I only have your word for it,' Ernest said now. 'And after tonight's performance, I'm not sure I can trust you, Annie.' He turned on his side away from her. 'And now I'm going to sleep. I've got work in the morning.'

Within minutes, Ernest was snoring, leaving Annie feeling perhaps lonelier than she had ever felt in her life before. Very quietly, she slipped out of bed and retrieved her nightdress. Not until she had done up the last button did she feel safe enough to get back into bed, and it was some time before her heartbeats subsided and she was able to breathe normally.

Tonight, Annie knew, would almost certainly mark a change in her relationship with Ernest, and she feared it was not going to be a change for the better.

CHAPTER THIRTY

Ophelia

'No one wears hats to church any more, Gran.'

'We always wore a hat to church.'

'How long ago was that?'

'Doesn't matter how long. That's not the point. Anyway, what do you know about it? When did you last go to church?'

'When did you last wear a hat? Some time ago, I should think, considering the state of this lot. This one's got little holes in it.' Ophelia held up an ancient fawn beret.

'Moths,' said Annie, selecting a straw hat with a rather tired ribbon and trying it on in front of the mirror. 'Do you think this is too young?'

'It looks too old to me,' Ophelia said.

'No. You know what I mean. Mutton dressed as lamb.'

'It might look quite good on a sheep.'

'I wish you'd be serious, Ophelia. We're going to be late.'

'This then. Wear this.' Ophelia picked up a navy felt hat and gave it a shake. 'It's quite respectable.'

Annie put on the hat. 'I suppose it'll do. I'll have to get a new one, though.'

'Are you making this a habit, then?' Ophelia's spirits rose. Annie had taken up her suggestion of church with some reluctance, and had only agreed on the condition that they didn't 'hang about afterwards'.

'Don't you trust me, Gran?' Ophelia had asked.

'No,' had been the terse reply.

And rightly, Ophelia thought now, as Annie secured the hat with a vicious-looking pin. For while she had meant it when she said that she would try to avoid speaking to Andrew, she also knew that if the opportunity presented itself she would find it very hard to resist.

Ophelia herself hadn't been too sure what to wear to church. She had been with Annie now for three weeks, and was still wearing the clothes she had brought to last her four days. The gypsy skirt would have to do. Annie had said that jeans were out of the question for church, and Ophelia was anxious to keep on the right side of her grandmother.

In the event, they arrived at the church in plenty of time, and chose a pew near the back. This, it transpired, was hardly necessary since the church was large and the congregation sparse.

'What a lot of grey heads,' whispered Ophelia, as they sank respectfully to their knees. She omitted to say that only one other sported a hat.

'Mind who you're saying that to,' retorted Annie.

'Sorry, Gran. But everyone is rather old.'

'Probably preparing themselves for the life to come,' said Annie piously. 'Memento mori and all that.'

'Memento what?'

'Memento mori. A reminder of death I think it means. I read it somewhere.'

'How useful,' Ophelia murmured, regaining her

seat and looking around her with interest. She wondered whether Andrew's wife would be here – Janet, wasn't it? – and whether she would know her if she saw her. She would probably be about Andrew's age and sit by herself near the front. Ophelia had vague and rather traditional ideas about churchgoing, and imagined people sticking jealously to their own seats, with the village squire (or equivalent) and his family taking up the front pew. Today the front pews were empty, with everyone huddled in the middle or towards the back; a bit like school, with no one wanting to be too near the teacher. Ophelia would dearly have loved to be near the front, but hadn't dared suggest it to Annie.

'Here he comes,' whispered Annie. 'Now, you behave yourself.'

What on earth did Annie think Ophelia was going to do? Was she afraid she might rush down the aisle and fling herself into Andrew's arms? Ophelia had a brief and heavenly vision of herself doing just that, but perhaps more slowly, wearing a breathtaking white dress and carrying a bouquet of lilies, leaning on the arm of a very proud father (the proud father was almost as unlikely a part of the scenario as the waiting bridegroom, but a girl could dream, couldn't she?).

The service passed in a haze for Ophelia, as she struggled with emotions ranging from joy to despair. Andrew looked quite different in his vestments, but undeniably handsome, Ophelia thought, noting how well white suited him and wondering whether he kept his trousers on underneath. His voice was commanding but gentle, and the sermon (something about St Paul) delivered with authority, although Ophelia had difficulty in concentrating on the words. During the course of the service she dropped both her hymnbook and her collection money, earning herself a nudge in the ribs from Annie, and was too flustered to join in any of the hymns (although years of school assemblies had insured that she knew them all well).

Andrew greeted them at the door as they left, kissing Annie's cheek and shaking Ophelia by the hand. Ophelia wished it could have been the other way round, but contented herself with taking in as much of Andrew as she possibly could in so short a time. Make the most of this, she told herself, gazing at his lightly-tanned skin, his eyes (they looked almost blue today) with those attractive crinkles at the corners, that flop of hair over his forehead, the tiny bloodstain on his chin where he must have cut himself shaving (no electric shaver? Perhaps he couldn't afford one. Ophelia wondered whether she could get away with giving him one as a sort of thank you present – thank you for what, exactly? – but decided regretfully that it might look a bit obvious).

'You're still here then, Ophelia.' Andrew smiled.

'Yes. I told you. I'm staying on with Gran.'

'That's nice. For both of you.'

'Yes.'

Once again, for a few precious moments everything and everyone else ceased to matter except the two of them. She was vaguely aware of a child crying, of the thump-thump-thump of pop music sounding from the open window of a passing car; an aeroplane droned overhead, painting a vapour trail across the sky; but they were all part of a different world. The only world which mattered was the one in which Andrew and Ophelia were standing together outside the church. If only this moment could last for ever, she thought. If only...

'Ophelia. Ophelia! We must be getting back.' Annie's voice pulled her back to earth. 'I need the lavatory,' she added, in a loud stage-whisper.

'There are toilets in the church hall,' said a woman, overhearing her. 'Look, I'll show you, I'm going over there anyway.'

'Well...' Annie looked uncertain.

'I'll wait here for you,' Ophelia said.

'You won't move?'

'I won't move.' In fact nothing on earth would have induced Ophelia to move, for Andrew was still standing in the porch, chatting to the last stragglers as they left the church. Perhaps he would speak to her again. She wouldn't make the first move, of course, but if he were to approach her she could hardly ignore him.

She hovered in the churchyard, reading the inscriptions on some of the gravestones, which rose like ancient crooked teeth from the freshly-mown grass. Two little sisters aged one and three had 'fallen asleep in the Lord' in 1864, followed shortly afterwards by their mother, 'Mary Erskine, beloved wife of James'. Ophelia wondered what catastrophe could have befallen this unfortunate family, and how the bereaved James had coped with such a tragedy.

'I always wonder about the poor Erskines, too.'

212

Andrew had joined her. 'That sort of thing was quite common in those days, of course. People led very difficult lives. I often think we don't realise how lucky we are.'

'Do you feel lucky?' Ophelia asked.

'Well, I wasn't talking about myself. Just generally.'

'Antibiotics and washing machines and the NHS,' Ophelia said.

'That sort of thing,' Andrew agreed.

They stood together studying the gravestone of Mary Erskine. It was covered with lichen, and some of the words were difficult to read. Ophelia stared at the stone, her skin prickling with the awareness of Andrew standing beside her, hardly daring to move, not wanting to break the spell.

'Ophelia?'

'Yes?' Still she didn't turn round. There was birdlime on the 'M' of 'Mary', and someone had scratched their initials underneath.

'I need to see you.'

'Yes.'

'You mean – you'd like to see me?'

Slowly, Ophelia turned to face him. 'Yes,' she said simply. 'Of course.'

'I could take you up the top of the church tower tomorrow morning. There's an amazing view from up there. It's usually locked as the stairs are very worn, so most people don't get to see it.'

'That would be – great.'

'About ten-thirty, then?'

'Ten-thirty's fine.'

She had thought of this moment, dreamed of this moment, longed for this moment. And yet now that it had come, she felt not euphoria, not even excitement, but a deep sense of peace, and of acceptance of something which had always been inevitable. Because she and Andrew had to see each other, be with each other, talk to each other. It was almost as though she had no choice in the matter.

'What were you two plotting?' Annie asked as they drove home. 'What were you talking about?'

'Oh, this and that,' Ophelia said. 'Nothing special.'

'You're sure about that, are you?'

'Quite sure,' Ophelia said, surprised at how easily the lie had slipped off her tongue.

But then she was going to have to start getting used to telling lies. She suspected that lies were an inseparable part of the path upon which she was about to embark.

CHAPTER THIRTY-ONE

Andrew

They stood at the top of the tower like two shy strangers.

Even when Ophelia had nearly slipped on the worn stone of the stairs, Andrew had hesitated to put out a hand to help her in case it should be misconstrued. And yet, how could anything he said or did be taken amiss, when she seemed to understand so well how he felt?

'I ought to say something about the view,' Ophelia said now, still breathless from her climb. 'But everything I think of sounds so – un-original.'

'Well, you could say it's fantastic,' Andrew said. 'After all, isn't that the buzz word for everything nowadays?'

'This is so much more than fantastic, though.' Ophelia leaned on the parapet and gazed out across the town towards the countryside and the distant hills. 'Do you come up here often?'

Andrew laughed. 'Now that really is a cliché. No. Not really. We come up here for a short service on Ascension day, and occasionally I take someone up if they want to go and I happen to be about. But no. I suppose it's a bit like being in London and not going to the Tower or Bucking-ham Palace. You don't go, because you can do it any time. You take it for granted.'

'I don't think I could ever take this for granted,' Ophelia said. 'It's amazing. It's almost as good as a ride in a hot air balloon.'

'Have you ever been in a balloon?'

'No. I've always wanted to, but my parents think it's dangerous. It's funny, that. I'm not a very satisfactory daughter to them, but they'll do anything to protect me.'

'In what way unsatisfactory?'

'I think they wanted the sort of daughter they could *tell* people about. The sort that people write about in Christmas round-robins. Straight A's and first-class degrees followed by a star-studded career in rocket science or brain surgery. But I'm afraid I'm not that sort of person, even if

215

I had what it takes.'

'Are they round-robin people?'

'They were for a bit, but the whole point was to tell the world about their clever daughter, and they gave up when they discovered they didn't have one.' Ophelia laughed. 'They could hardly put "Ophelia came bottom in maths again and still hasn't managed to lose any weight".'

'Whatever do you want to lose weight for?' asked Andrew in genuine astonishment, for to him Ophelia was just perfect. Rounded in all the right places, curvy, feminine; just the way a woman ought to be.

'Oh, I don't particularly. But when it was obvious that degrees and prizes weren't on the agenda, they toyed with the idea of my being a model. That idea didn't last long, needless to say, but the losing weight thing lingered on. I'm afraid I still eat buns and chocolate, and I haven't shed a pound.'

'I'm so glad,' Andrew said. 'Those stick-thin concave women all look the same to me.' He hesitated. 'I think you're beautiful.' He watched as a deep flush crept up Ophelia's neck, and instantly regretted his words. 'I'm so sorry. I shouldn't have said that. It was too – soon.'

'I don't think it's ever too soon to say nice things to people,' Ophelia said, after a moment. 'It's just that no one's ever called me beautiful before. I suppose I'm not used to it.' She turned to him and smiled, and there were tears in her eyes. 'But thank you.'

They stood looking at each other, and Andrew felt suddenly panicky. What should he do now? It had been fine while they were both admiring the view, but now he no longer knew what to say. Of course, there were a hundred things he would like to say, but none of them seemed quite appropriate. That he loved Ophelia he had no, doubt, but this was the first time they had been truly on their own together, and surely he couldn't wade straight in and tell her that? Normally, there would be a gradual progression, from meeting to attraction to liking and then finally to loving, but this was almost the other way round. He seemed to have jumped straight into the emotional deep end, without even knowing how to swim.

'I'm not sure what to say,' he said at last.

Ophelia touched his arm. 'It's okay,' she said. 'You don't have to say anything at all. I understand.'

Hesitantly Andrew reached out a finger and very gently traced the line along Ophelia's jaw and down the side of her neck. He could see a tiny pulse beating in her temple and her skin felt soft and very slightly damp from her climb up the steps. She was still smiling, and he wondered at how relaxed she seemed. His hand came to rest on her shoulder.

'What are we going to do?' Ophelia asked, and she didn't have to explain what she meant, for Andrew knew only too well.

'I don't know,' he said. 'We have – problems.'

'Yes.'

'Can we perhaps be happy just for a while? Maybe leave the bridges to be crossed for later?'

'Yes.'

'May I kiss you?'

'Yes. Oh, yes.'

Andrew cupped Ophelia's face in his hands and kissed her very gently on the lips. It wasn't a passionate kiss in the conventional sense, and yet in it lay all the love and the longing and the tenderness which he felt he'd been saving up for years. A quotation came to him – 'To know the pain of too much tenderness' (Kahlil Gibran, wasn't it?) – and Andrew felt that he understood exactly what it meant. For although the kiss was so tender, so intimate and so absolutely right, with it came the enormous pain of loving too much a person who could almost certainly never truly be his.

Afterwards, they stood holding each other, Ophelia's cheek warm against his chest, his face half-buried in her hair, and Andrew knew that whatever happened, he would remember this moment for the rest of his life.

Within minutes, dark rain clouds over-shadowed the sun, and the first fat drops of rain began to splash the old stonework and dampen their hair and clothes.

'You'll get wet,' Andrew said, drawing away and stroking Ophelia's hair back from her face. 'I think perhaps it's time you were going. Where does Annie think you are?'

'I said I was having a little drive round, to get used to Grandad's car. But I think she knows. She keeps giving me looks.'

Andrew laughed. 'Oh, I know Annie's looks. I think I may be getting one or two of those myself. I'm seeing her this afternoon.'

'Will you tell her?'

'No. Will you?'

'Not yet. But I hate lying to her. She's been so kind to me. No one has ever been so kind.'

When they finally parted, it was without making any further arrangements, and yet with the full knowledge that such arrangements would certainly be made. It was as though the present was all that mattered; the future would look after itself.

After Ophelia had driven off, Andrew considered the strange, elusive emotion we call happiness. It can arrive out of the blue and unaccompanied by reason or rationality, entirely regardless of the price it may exact or the problems which may accompany it. Happiness such as he felt today was beyond any sort of examination or explanation. He was just happy – blissfully totally happy. How could he be so happy – how was it possible? – when he and Ophelia could never have a future together, and the gift of her love (for he was sure that she loved him) must some day be handed back?

I shall not analyse how I feel any further, he decided. Just for the moment, I shall enjoy this amazing sensation to the full.

'Good morning! Isn't it a lovely morning?' he greeted two women who were dusting the pews.

'I thought it was raining,' one said to the other, puzzled. Her companion agreed. It had certainly been raining when they arrived.

But Andrew didn't hear them.

CHAPTER THIRTY-TWO

Annie's Story

Annie's long slow punishment began.

Nothing much was said in the days following that traumatic night, although Ernest made no secret of the fact that she had seriously displeased him. Annie, dreading a repetition, did what she could to appease him, queuing for hours to buy the best cuts of meat (she herself sometimes ate bread and margarine so that Ernest had a decent-sized helping) and polishing their few bits of furniture until they shone. But when, a week later, Ernest instigated another 'early night', his treatment of her was little short of brutal. This time, there was no gazing, no words of appreciation, no preamble of any sort. Annie suffered a painful and humiliating ordeal in what appeared to be a frenzied combination of anger and sexual desire on Ernest's part, in the course of which she bit her lip until it bled to prevent herself from crying out.

'There,' he said, when he had finished. 'Perhaps that'll teach you a lesson, Annie. You're never shaming me again like you did last time, do you hear?'

'Yes,' Annie whispered, fighting back the tears. 'I'll try to do what you want.'

'That's better.' Ernest seemed calmer now. 'You

do what I want – what a wife ought to do – and we should get along all right.'

But while Annie endeavoured to be as cooperative as she could, Ernest's now twice-weekly lovemaking – if that's what it could be called – continued to be an uncomfortable, loveless process, and while Annie felt that she could get used to the physical discomfort, far harder to cope with was the deep sense of humiliation which accompanied it.

Often she thought of her parents, and wondered whether her mother had had to undergo similar ordeals in the marital bed. Was this sort of thing normal? Did other people's husbands behave like this? She suspected not, but it would have been of some comfort to know that she was not alone.

Outside the bedroom, things returned to something approaching normality. Although always critical and sometimes ill-tempered, Ernest was on the whole civil, occasionally even conversational, and Annie tried to count her blessings. At least he didn't hit her, he provided for them all, and he was a good father to Billy. Things could be worse. She soldiered on, and tried to avoid dwelling on her situation too much. After all, there was a war on. She wasn't the only person having a hard time.

Meanwhile, her relationship with Billy was gradually improving. While she still didn't have the strong maternal feelings she had expected and hoped for, she began to take a pride in her son and feel for him a degree of affection. Billy was by now a bonny baby – plump and smiling and, on the whole, very little trouble – and he often attracted compliments from strangers they met in the street. Annie, starved as she was of any form of approval, would glow with pleasure. She was a good mother; she must be a good mother. Billy was the living proof of it. She enjoyed making his little frocks and dressing him up, brushing his mop of fair curls and taking him out in his pram. If she had achieved nothing else, she had produced a baby who attracted attention and praise. She must be getting something right.

When Billy was nine months old, Ernest's mother came for a visit. Annie had never understood why she had hitherto shown no interest in meeting her new grandson (or, come to that, his mother) but she tried to be enthusiastic for Ernest's sake.

Ernest, on the other hand, reacted very strangely to the planned visit.

'I've found a nice clean room for her to stay in. I hope she'll like it,' he said anxiously. 'I hope she'll be comfortable.'

'Why shouldn't she be comfortable?' Annie asked. 'You're certainly paying enough for it.' (This last was a sore point. Money was short, and Annie saw no reason why her mother-in-law shouldn't pay for her own room.)

'And the flat,' Ernest continued. 'You'll give it a proper clean, won't you? I want everything to look nice when she comes.'

Annie was amazed. It was almost as though Ernest were pleading with her. Usually he didn't hesitate to issue orders as though she were little more than a servant.

'Of course the flat will be clean,' she said now.

'Isn't it always?'

'Yes, not bad,' Ernest conceded, 'but you don't know my mother.'

In the circumstances, Annie was beginning to feel that making this particular acquaintance was a pleasure she would happily forego, for anyone who could intimidate Ernest must indeed be a force to be reckoned with. But the train ticket had been booked and the arrangements made. She awaited the visit with trepidation.

Annie's forebodings proved to have been more than justified. Ernest's mother was a tall, stooping woman with darting critical eyes and a thin pursed mouth which looked as though it were more used to sucking lemons than smiling.

'So this is Annie,' she said, as Ernest led her into the flat.

'Hello,' Annie said, not sure whether she was expected to shake her mother-in-law's hand or kiss her. Fortunately it appeared that she was required to do neither.

'And William.' Their visitor turned to Billy, who was beaming obligingly on Annie's lap.

'We call him Billy,' Ernest ventured.

'William.' It was as though she hadn't heard him. 'He's quite a fat baby, isn't he? Are you over-feeding him?'

And so it continued. Her rented room – inevitably – was unsatisfactory the flat was described as 'pokey', the carpet was the wrong colour, the baby was behind with his milestones ('I should see the doctor about that child's teeth.' 'What teeth?' Annie asked. 'Exactly!'), and Annie's cooking 'bland'.

This last was almost more than Anne could bear, for Mrs Bentley senior had committed the cardinal wartime sin of failing to bring her ration book with her. Without additional food, Annie found it almost impossible to stretch what she had to feed them all, and then to be criticised yet again tested her to her limits.

'Has your mother always been – like this?' she asked Ernest, emboldened by anger.

'Well, she's never been easy,' Ernest admitted, to Annie's surprise. 'But then she's had a hard life.'

'Haven't we all?' Annie muttered, eking out some scraps of stewing lamb with a small mountain of wilting vegetables she had managed to obtain cheaply.

'What do you mean?'

'Oh, Ernest. You know what I mean. You and I – our life isn't exactly idyllic, is it?' She had never dared to speak like this before, and she wondered at her own boldness.

'Maybe not,' Ernest admitted. 'But Mother's been very brave. She's suffered a lot, but she never talks about it.'

Annie thought, but didn't dare say that Mrs Bentley didn't need to talk about it. One look at her shrewish, miserable face, or a few minutes of her carping and criticism spoke volumes about the state of her mind. Annie wondered about Ernest's father. How had he managed to live with such a woman? But of course, he hadn't. Ernest's father had wisely taken it upon himself to die relatively young. From what she had seen, Annie reckoned that he was well out of it.

Strangely despite the unpleasantness of their guest, those few days of Mrs Bentley's visit seemed to unite Annie and Ernest as though in the face of a common enemy. Annie had never seen Ernest cowed before, but this was the effect his mother seemed to have on him. Nothing she asked of him (and she asked a lot) was too much trouble, and he appeared to hang on her every word, agreeing with everything she said, however preposterous. He seemed to be in a permanent state of anxiety, and it was only when he and Annie were on their own that he was able to relax a little. Observing the strange relationship between the two of them, Annie wondered what kind of mother Mrs Bentley had been to the young Ernest, but she didn't like to ask him and risk jeopardising their present amnesty.

In fact, this peaceful state continued for several weeks. United in their discomfort during Mrs Bentley's stay and their relief at her departure (although Ernest was too loyal to say anything), Annie and Ernest got on better than they ever had before, and Annie began to hope that things might be taking a turn for the better. Perhaps Mrs Bentley and her calamitous visit had brought some benefit after all.

For a few days, Annie felt almost cheerful. She and Ernest had had an unfortunate start, but it was still early days. Maybe all that was needed was that they should get to understand each other better. It was possible that there might be life after marriage to Ernest after all.

If only it could have been that easy.

CHAPTER THIRTY-THREE

Annie

The shiny BMW which drew up outside Annie's house was as unwelcome as it was unexpected.

'You should have let me know you were coming,' Annie said, answering the front door. 'I might have been out.'

'You're rarely out,' Billy said, wiping his feet (it had been raining) and preceding Sheila into the house. 'Where's Ophelia?'

'She's at work.'

'At work? She never told us she had a job. What's she doing?'

Billy sat down in his father's chair, and for a moment it was almost as though Ernest had returned from the dead. Annie had forgotten how alike they were. Sheila stood by the window, casting a critical eye round the room.

'She's a – she's a...' what was it Ophelia had said she was? 'She's an assistant in a fashion house. Yes, that's it. A fashion house,' Annie repeated, pleased that she had remembered. She would have hated to let Ophelia down.

'That sounds – interesting,' Sheila said.

'You mean she's a shop assistant.' Billy said, ignoring her.

'Not exactly.' Oh dear. 'It's very exclusive.'

'That's what she told you, is it?'

226

'Well, yes, but–'

'Never mind that now. It's no more than I expected. I've given up hoping that Ophelia will make anything of herself. At least she's earning a living again, which I suppose is something. I hope she's giving you money for her keep?'

'Yes. Of course.' In fact money hadn't yet been discussed between them, but it was none of Billy's business.

'And how are you, Mother?'

'Fine. I'm fine.'

'What on earth's happened to your hair?'

'Ophelia did it. I rather like it.'

'Mmm.'

'Very nice,' Sheila murmured.

'We've actually come for Sheila's car,' Billy said. 'Ophelia's had it for over a month now. Very inconsiderate of her, I have to say. I had to come this way on business, and Sheila came with me to drive it back.'

'We've brought some of her things,' Sheila added. 'She must be running short of clothes by now. I'll just go and fetch them.'

'Would you like a cup of tea?' Annie asked, wondering whether there was any milk (Ophelia was going to buy some on her way home).

'No thanks. We can't stop. It's a long way back, and I've got a couple of calls to make,' Billy said. 'I just hope she's left some petrol in the car.'

'Don't you want to wait to see her? She should be home soon.'

'No time today. Another time perhaps.' Billy got up and started walking towards the door. 'I hope she's behaving herself,' he added.

227

'How's it working out for both of you? Is Ophelia well? Is she happy?' Sheila asked, depositing two large suitcases in the hallway.

'It's working out very well. We enjoy each other's company,' Annie said. 'And Ophelia seems very happy.'

Very happy indeed, Annie thought now, as the two cars disappeared round the bend in the lane. Too happy, if the truth be told.

Not that Ophelia had actually told her anything, but then she didn't have to. The odd little disappearances, the frequent use of her mobile phone, the evasion of any direct questions as to her whereabouts – they all added up. But above all, there was Ophelia's state of mind. It was odd, Annie reflected, as she put the kettle on (there was just enough milk for one cup, she noted with satisfaction), that she, who had had no experience of being in love, should so easily recognise the signs. Ophelia literally glowed, as though illuminated from within by some secret joy, a joy which was reflected in Andrew's eyes and smile every time he came to the house. Not so secret, though, for Annie knew only too well what was going on.

In many ways, she wished she didn't. If she had no idea of what was happening between Andrew and Ophelia, then there would be no dilemma, and things could carry on as they were. But knowing, as she did, placed her in a difficult position, for she couldn't approve of her young granddaughter having a relationship with a married priest, could she? Well, could she?

Annie paused, teapot in hand, and pondered her very ambivalent feelings about this – this

228

event which had happened between the two people to whom she perhaps felt closest. Morally, it couldn't be defended on any level, and yet from a purely human perspective, didn't they both deserve a little happiness? She knew from his occasional hints that Andrew was unhappy in his marriage, and she also knew that Ophelia craved love in a way that she herself had once craved it. She had done her best to warn Ophelia against this involvement, and had believed her when she'd said she would try to avoid Andrew, and yet how could she justify standing in her way now, even if she were in a position to do so?

Annie dunked a biscuit in her tea (a habit Ernest had abhorred) and considered her position. She could talk to Ophelia, but feared that it would make little difference. She could speak to Andrew, but doubted that she could tell him anything he hadn't already thought of. Besides, she didn't want to jeopardise her relationship with him. She had come a long way since he had started visiting her, and she had come to depend on him. Apart from valuing his friendship, she still had her story to tell – a difficult, painful story – and it would be very hard for her to have to stop now.

Ophelia burst through the front door.

'I missed them, didn't I?' she crowed.

'How did you know they were here?' Annie asked.

'I saw their cars. They didn't see me, though.' Ophelia helped herself to a biscuit. 'I bet they were annoyed with me.'

'They were. I do wish you didn't always leave

me to do your dirty work,' Annie said. 'You seem to have a knack of avoiding your parents.'

'Years of practice.' Ophelia started unpacking a bag of groceries. 'I sold five very expensive dresses today. I think I've finally found my vocation. I even managed to swap the labels on one because a customer was determined to fit into a size twelve.' She took a bite of her biscuit and grimaced. 'These biscuits are stale.'

'*Someone* must have left the packet open.'

'I love you when you try to be grumpy, Gran, but it won't work. I refuse to be put down today.' Ophelia topped up the teapot with boiling water and fetched herself a cup.

'You're very cheerful,' Annie said.

'Why not? Life is good.' Ophelia took another biscuit. 'Even soggy biscuits are good once you get used to them.'

'But this isn't just about life, or even soggy biscuits, is it?'

'What do you mean?'

'You know what I mean,' Annie said.

'Do I?'

'Ophelia, don't play games with me. This is too serious for games. I may be just a silly old woman, but I know what's going on.'

'Oh, Gran! I've never thought of you as a silly old woman. I think you're wonderful.'

'Don't change the subject.'

'You sound just like Dad.'

'Lucky for you that I'm not your dad.'

'Yes.'

'So – are you going to tell me about it? I think I have a right to know.'

'If you already know what's happening, why do I need to tell you?'

'I know about it, but I don't know *all* about it,' Annie said carefully, putting down her cup. 'I know you and Andrew are – seeing each other, but I don't know what you're up to.'

'Oh, Gran.' Ophelia sat down at the table. 'We're not up to anything. Not really. We've just seen each other a few times, and – talked.'

'Just talked?'

'Just talked.'

'Nothing else?'

'Not really. What opportunity would there be?' Ophelia's voice was bleak. 'As you must know, there's no future in it. There can't be. But I love him, Gran. I really do. And I'm sure he loves me.' She looked up and her eyes met Annie's. 'What am I going to do, Gran? I've never felt like this before about anyone. What would you do?'

'What would I do?' Annie pondered, dunking another biscuit and watching the crumbs float to the surface of her tea in sodden clumps. 'I suppose if I'm honest I'd probably do what you're doing, whatever that is. I just feel it's my job to warn you off.'

'You've done what you can, Gran, and I'm really grateful.' Ophelia squeezed Annie's hand. 'But I can't – I *can't* let this chance go. I might never get it again. I might never feel like this again. To know I'm loved, really loved, just for me. Not because I'm clever or useful or pretty. Just because I'm myself. Can't you see?'

'Oh yes.' Because of course Annie could see. Wouldn't she once have given everything she possessed to have what Ophelia had, if only for a short time? To know what it was to love and be loved; to experience that private little world exclusive to lovers? She could no more have turned her back on such an opportunity than could Ophelia.

'But you don't have to feel you're a part of it, Gran.' Ophelia seemed to read her thoughts. 'It's not your doing; not your responsibility. It's ours. Mine and Andrew's. And if there's a price to be paid – and I'm sure there will be – then we're the ones who'll have to pay it. Couldn't you – sort of turn a blind eye? Just for a bit?'

'Perhaps,' Annie said slowly 'But I think in that case it might be a good idea if you don't tell me any more than you already have. If I don't know, then I can't mind, can I?'

Ophelia got up and gave Annie a hug. 'Oh, I do love you, Gran!'

'Do you know, I don't think anyone's ever said that to me before,' Annie said.

'You and me both, Gran,' Ophelia said. 'You and me both.' She kissed Annie's cheek. 'Now, put away those horrible biscuits. I've bought something much nicer. Look!' She opened a paper bag and brought out two cream dough-nuts. 'Let's have these instead.'

'What about your diet?' Annie said.

'Bugger the diet.' Ophelia grinned and took a big bite from one of the doughnuts. 'I have it on the best authority that I'm okay just the way I am.'

CHAPTER THIRTY-FOUR

Annie's Story

At long last the war in Europe was over.

VE Day – May 8th 1945 – happened to fall on the day after Billy's first birthday so there should have been double cause for celebration. But Ernest seemed sunk in depression. The war – those devastating, cataclysmic years – had passed him by for he had taken no part in it. He had never had to don a uniform and march off into the unknown like so many other young men. There had been no emotional farewells or joyous reunions or military triumphs for Ernest. Excluded by the curse of his malformed leg, he had spent the war safely tucked away in his office, and he was deeply ashamed.

Annie couldn't understand it.

'But it wasn't your fault, Ernest,' she said. 'You would have gone if you could. And someone had to – work in the banks; keep things going.' She'd had no idea until now that Ernest had minded so much.

'I should have been there,' Ernest kept saying. 'I just should have been there.'

So it seemed there was to be no festivity in their household. Annie watched from their windows with envy as the streets outside erupted into joyous celebration; strangers embraced one another, tables were set out in the street and food appeared as if from nowhere. Everyone, it seemed, was contributing their precious rations for a day of sheer indulgence. Someone appeared with a piano accordion and was joined by a uniformed soldier with a violin. The sound was terrible, but nobody cared. They danced in the road and on the pavements, and they laughed. It was years since Annie had heard such laughter.

'Couldn't Billy and I join them?' she pleaded. 'Just for an hour? You don't have to come.'

Ernest grudgingly agreed, although he refused to go himself, and Annie took Billy out with her to join the party where they were swept along in a tide of rejoicing. Food was pressed upon them, although Annie hadn't dared to contribute anything, and Billy had his first taste of chocolate. The sun blazed down out of a cloudless sky and Annie, carried away by the atmosphere, waltzed Billy up and down the street, born along by a crowd made merry by a combination of joy and cider.

'And you? Your family? Is everyone all right?' a kindly neighbour inquired.

Annie nodded. Her family had been fortunate. Jack had come through the war with military honours, and Tom, who was progressing well, was engaged to marry one of the nurses who had cared for him during his illness. A distant cousin had been killed in the first week of the war, and another wounded, but she knew she was one of the lucky ones. She hadn't had to suffer the agony of bereavement. The war was over, and her family were safe.

But Annie wasn't to know that the all-encompassing danger of war was about to be replaced by another more personal and far more immediate threat, for a week after the war had ended, Ernest hit her for the first time.

Of course Annie knew that Ernest had a temper; she had lived with it for long enough. She had also had to endure his sexual attentions, which so often seemed powered by an anger whose source was a puzzle to her. But she had never thought that he would actually strike her.

It had all been so silly. Afterwards, Annie couldn't even remember what it had been about; a missing button, an un-ironed shirt; something trivial. But in that moment of irritation, perhaps fuelled by his fury at his own inability to rejoice with a nation in its well-earned victory, Ernest lashed out and struck Annie in the face.

There was a moment of stunned silence.

'Annie – I didn't mean – it was a mistake. I never meant to hurt you.' Ernest seemed as shocked as Annie at what had happened. 'I'm – I'm sorry.'

Annie raised a hand to her stinging cheek. 'You hit me,' she said. 'You hit me.' The tears sprang to her eyes, and she swallowed.

'Well, I haven't – I wouldn't – oh, Annie. It wasn't that hard. There's no point in getting worked up about it. I've apologised, haven't I? What more do you want?'

Annie shook her head. What could she say? That everything was all right? That Ernest was forgiven, and they should pretend it had never happened? What did he expect her to say?

'Well, Annie? Are you going to make a fuss, or shall we just forget all about it?'

'I can't forget about it, Ernest,' Annie said quietly. 'How can I forget about it? It – changes things.'

For Annie knew that after this, nothing would ever be quite the same again. Hitherto, she had feared Ernest's temper and had dreaded their 'early nights', but had come to feel that she could cope, provided she didn't have to deal with anything worse. But physical violence such as this was something different. Ernest was a big man; tall and well-built and heavy. Annie herself was small and relatively slight. She already knew that when Ernest exerted physical force upon her, she had no choice but to give in. If he set out actually to hurt her, she would be equally powerless. And Ernest enjoyed power.

From the day when Annie's parents had bribed him to marry her – from the moment when she had seen that glint of triumph in his eyes – Annie had known that Ernest would have all the control in their relationship, and while his triumph had all too soon given way to anger and disappointment, the power remained in Ernest's hands. From the furnishing of their house to the naming of their son, all the decisions had been Ernest's. It was as though all his frustrations at the events which fate had wished upon him – his non-participation in the war, Annie's unwelcome pregnancy, his less than satisfactory marriage – had been channelled into the things he could control, and most of these centred around his life with Annie.

Had the marriage been a happy one, Annie imagined that she wouldn't have minded too much. In a different kind of relationship it might have been rather pleasant to have someone else take the responsibility. It could have made her feel loved and protected; she would have felt *looked after*. But in Ernest's case, it had quite the opposite effect. The strength which in a loving marriage might have manifested itself in caring and tenderness had the potential to turn to brutality and force. Annie had already experienced something of this, but this was the first time that Ernest had deliberately hurt her in broad daylight and in front of their son. And if he could do it once, there was no reason why he shouldn't do it again.

Now Billy looking anxiously from one parent to the other, began to whimper, holding out his arms.

'You've upset him,' Annie said, making to pick him up.

'Upset him? What do you mean, upset him?' Ernest scooped Billy out of his highchair and swung him in the air. 'Who's upset now, eh?' he said, as Billy laughed and wriggled in his arms. 'Billy's fine, aren't you, son? Billy's just fine.'

'But what about me? I'm not fine.' Annie wondered at her own courage. 'How can I be fine, when you can do this?'

'Oh dear.' Ernest continued to address his remarks to Billy. 'Your mother's making a fuss again. It seems she makes rather a lot of fuss these days. We'll have to have a word with her, won't we?'

'Will you stop talking to Billy! Will you at least *look* at me. I'm trying to talk to you!' Annie had never spoken to Ernest like this before, and she trembled as she spoke. 'I know you're not happy. I'm not happy. But if we could at least talk to each other, maybe we could sort something out.'

'Sort something out? What exactly do you think we can sort out?' Ernest turned to face her at last. 'I've married a woman who can't control or discipline herself; a woman who is lazy in the house and puts herself about outside it; a woman who trapped me into marriage. How can we possibly be happy?'

'I don't know what you mean.' Annie sat down, shocked. 'I never trapped you into anything. I work hard – you know I do – and it wasn't my idea that we should marry.'

'Oh no?' Ernest sneered. 'And what would have happened to you if we hadn't? You tell me that.'

'That would have been none of your concern. I would have managed.'

'Oh, you'd have managed, would you? With no husband to make things – respectable, how would you ever have shown your face again? I did you a big favour, Annie, and don't you forget it.'

'And I suppose my parents didn't do you any favours, giving you their savings? They bought you, Ernest. *They bought you.*'

How easy it is, once the gloves are off, to say all the things you've longed to say but haven't dared. And how dangerous. For a moment, Annie's words hung in the air between them, as though waiting for something to happen. Annie shrank into her chair, gripping its arms, wondering what Ernest would do. She had been crazy to speak out as she had, and she feared there would be a price to pay.

Carefully Ernest restored Billy to his high chair. Then he walked over to Annie and bent over her, his face inches from hers.

'If you ever speak to me again like that, Annie – *if you ever dare to speak to me like that* – you'll regret it.' His words were so quiet they were almost a whisper, but the threat was real and quite unmistakable.

From now on, Annie was going to have to be very careful indeed.

CHAPTER THIRTY-FIVE

Ophelia

Happiness was something of which Ophelia had had little experience. She had long since learnt the art of being contented with her lot, whatever that might be, and had she been asked, she might have said that yes, she was reasonably happy. But any feelings she might have had in the past were as nothing compared with the way she felt now.

Happiness flowed from her like warm honey, colouring everything she saw or did. It lifted her out of the ordinary to the extraordinary; from the mediocre to the sublime. Ophelia had never had any illusions about herself. Long before her parents had come to terms with the fact that theirs was a run-of-the-mill daughter, Ophelia had resigned herself to being one. She had never expected anything else. And yet now it seemed that the simple fact of being loved and in love had changed her two-dimensional, monochrome world into one of glorious Technicolor.

Andrew had said that she was beautiful, and Ophelia had been grateful but disbelieving. And yet now, when she looked in the mirror, she saw someone who was, if not beautiful, then something very like it. Her hair shone, her eyes were bright, her complexion was clear and pleasantly flushed. Even her figure seemed to have improved.

This last could well have been because her new employer had insisted on kitting her out with a whole new wardrobe.

'You can't work here wearing any old thing,' Maria had said, dismissing the gypsy skirt and the jeans. 'It's important that you reflect the type of fashions we sell.'

So Ophelia was now in possession of several items of clothing with designer labels and price tags to match. It would take her months to pay Maria back, even allowing for the discount, but she felt she could get used to her new image.

As for the work, she was having a wonderful time. She knew nothing at all about fashion and cared even less, but she did care about people, and she spent happy hours advising and helping, encouraging and complimenting, allowing fat customers to squeeze into thin dresses and tree-trunk legs to hobble away in mini-skirts.

'You're certainly shifting the stock,' Maria remarked, not without admiration, 'but should you really have allowed that customer to buy the flowery dress?'

'Probably not,' Ophelia said. 'But she was desperate to have it and it made her feel good.

240

And when you think about it, that's what really matters, isn't it? After all, the only person who really cares what a dress looks like is the woman inside it, and if it makes that woman happy, then she's got her money's worth, hasn't she?'

Maria, who had the reputation of her establishment to consider, wasn't so sure, but she liked Ophelia, as did her clients. Ophelia was not at all the sort of young woman she normally employed, but she knew how to please the customers, and while her attitude to fashion was somewhat cavalier, it certainly wasn't harming business. Takings were up; the punters were happy. Maria decided to leave Ophelia to it. And if she was slightly puzzled by the visits of a man in a dog collar, who showed no intention of buying anything but engaged Ophelia in brief murmured consultations, then she wisely decided to leave well alone. What Ophelia got up to – if indeed she was up to anything – was her own affair. Maria was not one to pry.

Even though Ophelia's workplace was in a town some distance from his parish, Andrew's visits were indiscreet; Ophelia knew this. For what she was beginning to learn was that an illicit relationship poses more problems than the simply moral ones. For a start, where could they safely go together?

Andrew was well known in the area. Wherever he went, people would greet him and engage him in conversation, so local meetings in public places were out of the question. Trips out in the car were risky too, as Andrew's car – a battered Ford – was also well known, and he was reluctant to be seen in Ophelia's. Twice, they had driven separately to a more distant rendezvous, and on both occasions they had seen someone from Andrew's parish.

'It's like being on the run,' Ophelia said, after the second occasion, when Andrew had seen one of his church wardens sitting in the corner of a bar where they had planned to have a quiet drink together, necessitating a rapid retreat.

'We are on the run,' Andrew said. 'I think we'll always be on the run. It's the nature of the relationship.' He sighed. 'I sometimes think I should never have dragged you into this.'

'I didn't take much dragging,' Ophelia said.

'Maybe not. But it was up to me to put a stop to things before we got too involved.'

'Why up to you? Because you're older? Because you're a priest? Because you're a *man?*'

'Well, maybe a bit of all three, but–'

'No, Andrew. We're both responsible. If you deny me my responsibility, then you deny me the right to be an equal, and that isn't on. As for stopping things before we got too involved, we were always too involved. The involvement started the moment we first clapped eyes on each other.'

'Maybe. But I – we – didn't have to do anything about it, did we?'

'Didn't we? Do you regret it?'

'No. Oh no. How could I possibly regret it?'

'Well, then.'

They had just paid another visit to the church tower, the one place where they were unlikely to run into anyone else, and having been driven down once again by the rain, were sitting in the bell chamber halfway down.

'At least this is fairly safe,' Andrew said now.

'Who else has keys?' Ophelia asked.

'Just the church wardens, and the captain of bell-ringing. Bell-ringing practice is on Thursday evenings. Apart from that, people rarely come up here.'

'It's not exactly cosy,' Ophelia said, looking round the cold little room with its wooden benches, its neatly-looped bell ropes and the numerous plaques commemorating past bell-ringers.

'No,' Andrew took her hand. 'Better than nothing, though.'

Ophelia thought he looked tired. The joy they found in each other was still there, but the problems seemed increasingly insurmountable, especially for Andrew. And yet, anxious as she was, happiness would keep bubbling to the surface. One of the lessons she had learnt early was to appreciate the moment and not worry too much about what might happen next, and the moment – this particular moment, sitting here with Andrew – was all she could ever ask for.

But Andrew had Janet to think about, and of course God. Ophelia had still not met Janet and she wasn't at all sure how she stood with God, but Andrew could hardly avoid either of them.

'God and Janet,' she mused now.

'What?'

'God and Janet. They make all this very hard for you, and there's nothing I can do about that, is there?'

Andrew smiled. 'God will be all right. He's had

to cope with bigger problems than this, and I hope that one day I'll be able to make things all right with Him. Janet is another matter.'

It was an unspoken agreement between them that they shouldn't discuss Andrew's marriage to Janet. Andrew was too much of a gentleman to put any of the blame for what he was doing onto his marriage, and Ophelia was sufficiently sensitive not to ask. But there were inevitably times when she would dearly have loved to know how things stood between the two of them.

'We'll have to find somewhere a bit warmer than this in the winter,' Ophelia said now, giving a little shiver. The air in the room was cool and decidedly musty.

'The winter?' Andrew turned to Ophelia and took both her hands in his. 'Darling Ophelia, I don't know whether there will be any "us" by the winter; any meeting anywhere.'

'Don't say that!'

'All right. I won't say it, but our relationship has a – a–'

'Sell-by date?'

'If you put it like that, yes.'

'But can't we enjoy it until then?'

'Yes. Yes, of course. We already are, aren't we?'

'We are. Oh, we are.'

Ophelia put her arms round Andrew and rested her head against his shoulder. If I could stay like this forever, I would ask for nothing more, she thought. I wouldn't mind the draughts or the smells or the spiders (she was sure there must be spiders). Just to be alone together like this would be enough. They wouldn't even need to do anything; just hold each other and talk and be together. Although she was hardly experienced in the ways of men, Ophelia thought that the relatively chaste kisses they exchanged were intimate in a way nothing she had ever done before had been intimate. The way Andrew held her face between his hands and gazed at it; the way he stroked her hair or simply held her to him; the way he spoke to her, his voice caressing her in a way that was almost physical; the absolute tenderness and respect he showed her – all these made her feel not only feminine and beloved, but *precious*. His 'pearl beyond price' he had called her, and Ophelia had savoured the words, knowing that they came from the heart.

As for taking their relationship any further, they hadn't discussed it, although the passion and the desire were certainly there. Of course, Ophelia could imagine no greater bliss than to make love with Andrew, and to spend a night in his arms would be heaven indeed. But she didn't feel she could suggest it, and so far, he hadn't mentioned the possibility either. Although they had only met up together half a dozen times, she knew that time was not on their side. If the affair – for that was what this was, although she disliked the word – were to develop further, it would have to happen soon.

She looked up at Andrew.

'What are you thinking?' she asked.

'I was thinking,' Andrew said slowly, 'how much I would like to make love to you.'

'Mind-reader.'

Andrew smiled and placed a finger under her

chin. 'No. Just lover,' he said, kissing her. 'I'm not usually in the business of reading minds, but with you, I think I could be a good lover.'

'You don't sound very sure.'

'Oh, I am. I am sure. I've never been more sure of anything in my life. If you love someone as I love you, how can you not be a good lover?'

'But we can't, can we? Where would we – do it?'

'Not here. Certainly not here. Here would be – inappropriate. It would make everything – oh, I don't know – sordid, I suppose. And you deserve so much better.'

'Where, then?'

'Are you sure you want to?'

'I've never wanted anything so much.'

'Then we'll find a place. And a time.'

'Soon?'

'Soon. It will have to be soon. We don't have much time, my darling.' He stroked her hair back from her face and kissed her again. 'Dearest Ophelia, we have so little time.'

CHAPTER THIRTY-SIX

Annie's Story

After the initial celebrations, the weeks following VE day came as something of a disappointment to Annie. She wasn't sure what she had expected, but if she was honest, things appeared much the same. The rationing and the shortages remained;

life was still a struggle. Other people too seemed to be suffering from a sense of anticlimax, and some were even heard to say that they missed the feeling of camaraderie which the war had engendered. It was as though now that England was no longer under threat, they were almost reluctant to step back into the safe little lives they had left six years ago; nothing much had changed.

For Annie, of course, much had changed, but little of it could be seen as an improvement and none of it was connected to the war. Her life with Ernest continued to be humdrum and joyless, and while she was grateful that as yet there had been no repetition of his violence, she felt that this was more due to her own behaviour than Ernest's, for she had gone out of her way to ensure that nothing should happen to upset him.

The highlight of the year for Annie came that summer when Ernest agreed that she and Billy might go home for a week's holiday on the farm. She hadn't been back since before Billy's birth, and it was wonderful to revisit the changeless countryside and experience once again the sights and smells of her childhood. The warm welcome she received was as reassuring as the safe familiarity of her old bedroom and her mother's home-baked bread, and after a few days it was almost as though she had never been away.

'Couldn't I – stay?' she asked her father, emboldened by the unaccustomed affection she had been shown. They were standing together by the pig pens while Billy, who had never seen a pig before, bounced up and down in her arms with excitement.

'Stay? Why you are staying, aren't you?'

'No. I mean really stay. Live here with you all. Help on the farm, like I used to.'

'Without Ernest?'

'Well – yes.'

'What are you talking about, girl? Ernest's your husband. You can't just up sticks and leave him.'

'I'm not – I'm not happy,' Annie ventured.

'Not happy? After all everyone's done for you? Shame on you, our Annie. You've a nice home, your mother tells me, and a good husband. How can you think of taking this little babby away from his daddy? No. You made your bed a while ago, and you're going to have to lie on it. You don't know when you're lucky our Annie, and that's a fact.'

'But we're just making each other miserable, Dad. I'm sure Ernest would be happier without me, and you could do with another pair of hands on the farm. You said so yourself.'

'Not your pair of hands, our Annie. You said goodbye to farm life when you – when you married Ernest. You'll just have to make the most of it. Do you think anyone has a perfect marriage? Do you think your mother and I haven't had our problems? You have to work at it. Marriage isn't meant to be easy.'

Annie thought of the comfortable familiar relationship enjoyed by her parents; the small exchanges of words and looks which meant little to anyone else but which were all that was needed for one to convey a feeling or an idea to the other. She knew that her parents hadn't always had it easy – that her father could be stiff-necked and awkward and her mother was often silent and moody – but the marriage worked, and she had never heard them exchange a cross word. She couldn't imagine her father ever laying a finger on her mother in anger. She longed to tell him about Ernest's violent temper, but she didn't dare, and she could hardly tell him of what she had had to endure in bed.

'Come on, Billy,' she said now, setting him down and taking him by the hand. 'Let's go and see the cows, shall we?'

When the time came for them to leave, Annie wept.

'You will come and see us again, won't you, Mum?' she said, as she loaded her suitcase into her father's car for the journey to the station. 'You won't leave it so long again.'

'I'll do what I can.' Her mother kissed Billy and handed him back to Annie. 'But you know how it is. We haven't got Mavis any more, and the new men are still learning the ropes. I don't like to leave your father for too long. He needs me here.'

After Annie's return home, things went relatively smoothly for a while. Ernest seemed genuinely glad to have her home, and although never demonstrative, he did at least show her a degree of kindness. He seemed to have recovered from the depression he had suffered after VE day, and was hoping once more for promotion at work. Annie prayed that this time he might get what he wanted; she always felt safer when Ernest was content.

But once more, the promotion was not to be, and yet again Ernest was passed over in favour of a younger man.

'I don't know how they dare,' he stormed, when he came home with the news. 'After all I've done for that place. I've never been late, never made any mistakes. When they asked me to move up here, did I complain? All that upheaval – moving house – and I did it without a murmur, and this is how they repay me!'

'But I thought you were quite pleased to move,' Annie said. 'You said a change would be a new start for us. You were quite enthusiastic.'

'*Enthusiastic?* That's what you call it, is it? No. Duty. That's what it was. Duty. They don't know the meaning of the word.'

'But you like it here, don't you? The flat and everything. You said so yourself.'

'Don't you tell me what I like or don't like! You have no idea, Annie. *No idea.*'

'I try–'

'Oh, you try do you? Well, you could have fooled me, Annie, and that's the truth. A woman is supposed to support her husband, and what support have you been to me, eh? You tell me that.'

'I've done what I can.' Even as she spoke, Annie knew that she was treading on very dangerous ground. 'I didn't complain when we moved up here, and–'

'You didn't complain!' Ernest turned to face her. 'You've done nothing but complain, Annie. Nothing but complain. You're bored. You're lonely. You've got too much to do. Moan, moan, moan. That's all you ever do!'

'That's not fair!'

'Oh, so it's not fair. Well, try this for fair, then.

250

You just try this!'

The blow this time sent Annie reeling across the room, and she fell heavily banging her head against the wall. For a moment she lay slumped on the floor, her head spinning, unable to move and afraid to say anything that might provoke a further attack.

'There!' Ernest's voice seemed to come from a long way away 'Perhaps you'll mind what you say from now on. Perhaps that'll teach you a little respect.'

Painfully, Annie raised herself on one elbow. Out of the corner of her eye she could see Ernest silhouetted against the window. He had fallen suddenly quiet, but made no move to assist her. She tried to lever herself up with the help of a chair. If she could only stand, she would feel safer. Lying here on the floor she was completely at Ernest's mercy.

'I suppose you want me to help you up?'

Annie nodded, and Ernest pulled her roughly to her feet.

'There. You're all right now, aren't you?'

'You had no right – no right to hit me,' Annie whispered. 'Whatever I said, you had no right to do that.'

'Hit you? I didn't hit you! A little shove perhaps, and you banged your head on the wall. That's all. Of course I didn't hit you, and don't you go telling anyone that I did. If you hadn't wound me up, Annie, none of this would have happened. You brought it on yourself.'

So that was it. She might have guessed that it would be like this. Ernest was going to deny that he had done anything to harm her, and would make out that anything he did to her was her own fault.

Annie sat down in a chair. She felt dizzy and her head was throbbing, but beyond any physical discomfort, and far worse, was the fear which crawled like a snake in the pit of her stomach. Ernest had hit her once before, and she had hoped that that would be an end of it. But now he had done it again, and had managed to convince himself that it was all her fault. From Billy's conception to his own furious outbursts, Ernest had managed to distort everything that had ever happened between them and place the responsibility on her shoulders. Where would it all end?

'And don't go turning on the waterworks, either,' Ernest said now, standing over her. 'You know it gets on my nerves.'

But Annie was beyond crying. She was overcome by a sense of utter hopelessness, for never before had she felt so keenly the trap which was her marriage. She had nowhere to go, since her parents wouldn't have her back, and without Ernest she had no money. Once, she might simply have run away, and would even have been prepared to leave Billy with his father if she could be freed from her present existence. But not any more, for now she was tied to Ernest as never before.

Annie had just missed a second period. This time she didn't need a doctor to tell her that she was pregnant.

CHAPTER THIRTY-SEVEN

Andrew

The kitten was small and fluffy and sneering, with a tiny flat face and round expressionless eyes. Andrew disliked it on sight.

'What's this?' he asked, stepping carefully round it. 'Where did it come from?'

'It's – a present.' Janet seemed uneasy.

'A present? Who from?'

'Me. It's from me. To you. To – to replace Tobias.'

To replace Tobias. Andrew wondered whether Janet could ever understand that Tobias was, quite simply, irreplaceable; that the years of companionship and memories were what had made Tobias special; that in fact he had never particularly liked cats, and had Tobias not been as it were inflicted upon him, he would never have considered having one at all.

'I was wrong,' Janet continued, looking down. 'I should never have – well, never have done what I did. I still think it was right – kindest – to have him put down, but I shouldn't have done it without asking you. I suppose I was – jealous.'

'*Jealous?* Jealous of a *cat?*'

'Yes. The time you spent with him; the way you talked to him.'

'But Janet! He more or less lived in my study,

and that's where I do a lot of my work. Of course I spent time with him (or rather, he spent time with me). It was more his choice than mine. Tobias had a mind of his own.'

'Yes, well. I thought you might like a new one. He's Persian. He was – he was very expensive.'

I bet he was, thought Andrew now, as tiny pedigree paws stepped daintily round the kitchen as though their owner were wondering whether the place was good enough for him. This – this *animal* must have cost Janet a very great deal of money and she didn't have much. Andrew summoned up a smile.

'Well, thank you, Janet. It was very thoughtful of you.' He paused, wondering whether he was expected to pick his new friend up. The kitten challenged him with a cool blue stare. Perhaps not. 'What's his name?'

'He's got a very long one.' (Of course.) 'Blenheim something-or-other. I've got his papers. But I think it's customary to choose a less formal one for everyday use.'

Andrew thought it best not to ask when the posh name might appropriately be called into service, and concentrated on the job of feeling grateful.

'Well, I'm sure we'll think of a name. Shall we give him a few days and see what suits him?' (Alphonse, perhaps, or Sebastian?)

'I'm glad you like him.' Janet looked relieved.

'Of course I like him. He's – beautiful.' This at least was true, for although the kitten was not to Andrew's taste (and Tobias would almost certainly have had it for breakfast), it was undoubtedly very fine in a chocolate-box kind of way.

'He can live in your study, like Tobias.'

Andrew recalled the escapades of the infant Tobias, and opened his mouth to say that a small kitten climbing up his curtains and playing with his shoelaces was not what he needed when he was working. But Janet had swallowed her pride and made what was undoubtedly a very generous gesture. The least he could do was to accept it graciously. He noted the pricey little tins of 'Kittyfeed' ('Everything your precious pet needs in one tasty dish') on the kitchen worktop, and the gleaming new litter-tray with its hygienic gravelly contents. Janet had certainly done the job thoroughly. The kitten was here to stay.

Later, in the confines of his study, Andrew contemplated the day's events. What had moved Janet, after all these weeks, to hold out such an unlikely olive branch? And could it be true that she really had been jealous of Tobias? Certainly she had always disliked him, but she had never seemed to resent the time Andrew spent with him, and in any case, she was hardly the jealous sort. Andrew recalled the many occasions when he had sought her company only to be rejected because she was too busy to spend time with him. Surely – *surely* – Janet had never been jealous?

Or could it be that she suspected that there was a more recent and far more threatening focus for any jealous feelings she might harbour?

Could she know? Could she have guessed? Andrew sat down at his desk and put his head in his hands. That Janet should find out about Ophelia was the thing he dreaded above all else. He was not a vain man, and he had never been ambitious. He could probably have coped with a damaged reputation and even a ruined career. He knew that he was weak, and it would be no more than he deserved if that weakness should become public knowledge. But whatever he might feel about Janet, she didn't deserve the hurt and the disgrace which would accompany any revelation of infidelity on his part. He thought of the gossip and the pitying looks she might have to endure, and knew that he would do everything he could to protect her from them.

And yet the one thing – the only thing – which would ensure that she never did have to suffer in this way was the one thing he couldn't do, for Andrew couldn't find it in himself to give up Ophelia. He knew he was being selfish; he knew he was being irresponsible; he knew that he was putting everything he had at risk. He also knew that this relationship couldn't last, and that already there were intimations of its ending. Ophelia, as aware as he was that time was not on their side, would sometimes cling to him with a desperation which was heartbreaking, the more so because Andrew himself was the cause of her pain. And yet she brought to his life a peace and a fulfilment that he had never sought or expected from another human being, and the happiness she gave him seemed little short of God-given.

Nowadays, when he presided at church services, his awareness of his own hypocrisy was almost unbearable. Sometimes he could hardly look his parishioners in the eye, especially when they came to him with their problems. For how could he advise people on how to lead their lives when his own was careering towards a crisis which was entirely of his own making? He missed the serenity and the wisdom of Father Matthew, the only person to whom he could confide his problems, but had avoided him since their last meeting. While he knew that he would be neither reprimanded nor judged, he still felt he had let his mentor down.

And Annie. Hadn't he let her down too? He had become enormously fond of her over the past months, and had come to value her friendship. Had Annie known this, she would probably have been surprised, for most of the time they spent together was taken up with the unfolding saga of her past. Andrew had spoken little of himself. And yet there had developed between them a mutual respect and a shared sense of humour. Annie had a sense of fun which Andrew suspected had lain dormant for many years, but now that she was beginning to come out of herself, she made entertaining company. But recently she had been more withdrawn and thoughtful, and Andrew had on several occasions been the object of one of Annie's famous Looks.

'What's the matter, Annie? What are you thinking about?' he had asked.

But Annie had pursed her lips and shaken her head, and he had known the answer to his question. There was a lot more to Annie than the vague other-world eccentricity she displayed, and she was nobody's fool. She knew what was going on between himself and Ophelia, and was keeping her own counsel. Andrew would have given a lot to know what she really felt (although he might not like it were he to find out) but it was a matter he could never discuss with her. Drawing her into the situation would be as unfair as it was inappropriate. They must just go on as they were, both of them pretending, without actually deceiving each other.

Andrew's thoughts returned to Ophelia, and he wondered, not for the first time why it was that she, like him, had from the outset accepted the finite nature of their relationship. Her unselfishness was one of the things he loved most about her, and he knew that she would never pursue her own ends if it involved hurt to others. It would have been so easy for the two of them at least to fantasise about a future together, and yet they both carefully avoided the subject. When he did allow himself to think about it, Andrew felt that there could be no greater bliss than to be married to Ophelia. He imagined a rambling house, comfortably untidy filled with the noise of children, and presided over by Ophelia herself, wearing the gypsy skirt (of course), with the latest plump infant on her hip.

Of course, in theory his dream was perfectly possible. He could divorce Janet, and he was sure that if he were free, Ophelia could be persuaded to marry him. He wouldn't feel able to continue in the priesthood, but he could possibly retrain as a teacher, and would probably enjoy it. But the happiness he imagined would be tarnished by the hurt it had caused to others; he wouldn't be able to live with himself, let alone Ophelia, under a shadow which was unlikely to go away and which might eventually spoil what they had together.

But he had promised her the consummation of his love for her, and although he knew how dangerous, let alone foolish, this would be, he felt helpless in the face of a temptation and a longing which were overwhelming. For he felt that if in years to come he were to look back on his time with Ophelia and know that he had passed this opportunity by, he wouldn't have properly *lived*. To make love to someone who really loved him; to lie in her arms afterwards and hold her and feel at one with her; he might never have this chance again.

But how was this to be managed, and where? So far, Andrew had managed to get by without telling Janet any outright lies, and while he knew that this was more to salve what was left of his conscience than to benefit anyone else, he wanted to try to keep it that way. However, there was soon to be a midweek three-day conference to which he had been invited. He could go for the first two days, and then perhaps leave early and spend the last night with Ophelia. One night. Just one night. Was it so very much to ask, just one night?

He gazed out of the window at the pale green sky of a late summer evening. In another part of the house, Janet was talking on the telephone, and in the distance, a police car wailed its warning. Ordinary everyday sounds.

Andrew sighed. He had an uneasy feeling that life would never be quite so ordinary again.

CHAPTER THIRTY-EIGHT

Annie's Story

Annie dreaded telling Ernest her news. Obsessed as he was with order and control, how would he react to this surprise intervention in his life? Annie knew little about contraception, and on the one occasion when she had mentioned it to Ernest, had been told firmly that he was 'taking care of all that'. The taking care appeared to take the form of mysterious fumblings and rustlings in the dark before their sexual encounters, and while Annie had no idea what Ernest was doing, and certainly didn't dare to ask, she felt sure that if he considered the matter to be under control, then that must be the case. She had hardly given the matter another thought. She herself didn't particularly want more children, and Ernest had said that one child was more than enough, so that, as far as she was concerned, was the end of the matter.

And now this. Apart from Ernest's feelings on the subject, how would they cope? Financially, things were still tight, and the flat was too small to accommodate an additional child with any degree of comfort. As for Annie herself, she found life quite exhausting enough without the sickness and discomfort of pregnancy. And then there was Billy. No doubt due to the over-indulgence of his adoring father, he had become spoilt and demanding, given to tantrums whose sheer volume was astonishing in one so small. He was a strong sturdy child, and when he put his mind to it he could put up a great deal of resistance. Ernest seemed proud of what he seemed to regard as strength of character, but then it never fell to him to try to persuade Billy to eat anything other than mashed potato, or to have to lift him, shrieking, from the pavement and bend his rigid body into his pushchair, to the accompaniment of disapproving tuts and stares from strangers. Annie found him hard enough to manage now; how would she cope with the demands of a baby as well?

Better informed than she had been the first time around, Annie had by now heard of the miraculous effects of gin and hot baths, and decided to put them to the test. But while the gin (a contribution from a sympathetic neighbour) made her sick and the baths almost took her skin off, the baby remained firmly in place. It was time to tell Ernest.

To her surprise, he took the news quite well.

'Another baby eh?' he mused. 'Well, it could be worse, I suppose. And Billy could do with a little brother. Yes. A little brother might be the making of our Billy.'

Annie resisted the temptation to remind Ernest that there were no guarantees that the baby would be a boy, and breathed a sigh of relief. Perhaps another child might not be so bad after all, and if – as soon appeared to be the case – she were to be spared Ernest's more intimate attentions during her pregnancy, an extra child seemed a small price to pay. As time went on and the sickness passed, she actually found herself looking forward to the new arrival. This time around, she would try to be a better mother, and – who knows? – Ernest might even agree to let her breastfeed her baby. Annie secretly hoped for a girl. A girl could belong to her in a way that Billy never had. A girl could grow to be a friend. She would call her Amelia, after her mother. 'My daughter.' Annie tried the words out, and smiled to herself. She could be a good mother to a girl.

That November, Ernest received a telegram informing him that his mother had died. While this was unexpected, neither was it a total surprise. Mrs Bentley's health had never been good, and it would appear that she had succumbed to pneumonia following a bout of influenza.

'Well,' Ernest said, pacing the small living-room, the telegram still in his hands. 'Well!'

Annie waited, not sure how she should react. Ernest was always unpredictable, and this must surely mark a watershed if not a crisis in his life.

'I'm sorry,' she ventured, after a few minutes. 'It must be a shock for you.'

'A shock? Yes. Yes, I suppose it's a bit of a shock,' Ernest said, folding and refolding the sheet of yellow paper. 'Well, now. Who would have thought it? Mother never seemed the sort to – well, to die.'

While this was a strange observation, Annie knew what he meant. Notwithstanding the frailty of her health, there had been something indestructible about Mrs Bentley. Annie couldn't imagine her allowing something as mundane as death to get the better of her. She would surely have given the grim reaper short shrift if he'd had the audacity to knock on her door.

'I shall have to go up, of course,' Ernest said now.

'Of course,' Annie agreed.

'You needn't come, though, Annie. No one would expect you to come in your condition. Not our Billy, either. It wouldn't be right for a child to go to a funeral.'

Annie was both relieved and grateful. The journey up to Yorkshire was long, involving several changes of trains, and while she would certainly have gone with Ernest had he wanted her to, the reprieve was welcome.

When Ernest returned, he brought good news. As the sole beneficiary of his mother's will, he was to inherit her house and whatever money she might have put by. The house was small and in need of attention, and unlikely to fetch much, but together with Mrs Bentley's savings it should enable them to move into something larger in time for the new baby.

'A house this time, I think,' Ernest said. 'A proper house, with a garden. We won't be able to afford anything big, mind you, but a house will be a lot better than this flat. Somewhere in the country perhaps. The fresh air will do Billy good.'

The bank readily lent Ernest money on the strength of his impending legacy and when Annie was six months pregnant, the family moved out of town into the terraced house which was to be their home for the rest of Ernest's lifetime. The countryside was pleasant, and the village sported two shops, a post office and a school. The house itself was small and unpretentious, but the garden was big enough for Billy to play in, and compared with the flat, it was a little palace.

'Well, you are a lucky girl.' Annie's mother, who had come to help with the move, gave her approval. 'You've landed on your feet, our Annie, and no mistake.'

Annie nodded. Away from the town she felt that she could breathe again. From her bedroom window she could see open fields and trees which were already tinged with the misty green of early spring; she awoke to the sound of birdsong and heard the lowing of cattle as they were herded home for milking. If she half-closed her eyes, she could almost imagine that she was back home on the farm, and if she missed the few friends she had made in town, they were only a short bus ride away. Hope, once a thing of the past, began to stir again. If she could just keep Ernest happy, she wouldn't ask for anything more. She would be content.

And indeed Ernest did seem more cheerful, and while he continued to have bouts of ill temper, he didn't touch Annie. Once or twice in the course of an outburst, he made as though to strike her, and then seemed to think better of it. Annie prayed that this wasn't simply due to her pregnancy, and that perhaps Ernest was at last learning to control his temper. Gradually, the fear which had been her constant companion for so many months began to lift. People could change; why not Ernest?

But fate had another blow in store for Annie. Six weeks after they moved house, her tiny daughter was born. She lived for just two hours.

Annie wept. Rocking back and forth in her chair, she wept as she hadn't wept for more than fifty years.

'I never saw her,' she sobbed, her words muffled by her sodden handkerchief. 'I never saw my baby. I never knew how much I wanted her until I lost her. Until it was too late.'

Andrew, bewildered in the face of this violent outburst of grief, put his arm round her.

'I never cried at the time,' Annie said, wiping her streaming eyes. 'And I haven't cried since. I never cried at all. Can you believe that?'

'I – don't know.' Andrew shook his head. 'You'll have to tell me about it.'

'They took her away. My little girl. They took her away,' Annie continued. 'They did in those days. Just took her away, like a bit of rubbish. Ernest said not to worry. He said we'd got Billy, and must be happy with him. Ernest never wanted a girl.' She blew her nose. 'I didn't dare cry. Ernest didn't like me crying. And the nurses said to go home and try again, just like that. Can you imagine?'

'I've heard that people do say that sometimes, when someone loses a child. It always seemed to me to be a dreadful thing to say.' Andrew found a clean handkerchief in his own pocket and handed it to Annie.

'So I had nowhere to go,' Annie said, taking the handkerchief. 'Nowhere to go to remember her. No grave. Nowhere to put flowers. Nowhere. It was as though she had never existed. Except here,' she put her hand over her chest. 'Here. In my heart. If I'd seen her, if I'd just seen her, I could at least have imagined her, but in a way it was as though I was grieving for someone I didn't know. Someone I'd never met. Nowadays they let you see the baby, don't they? They let you hold it, and take photographs.'

'Yes. I believe they do.' Andrew took Annie's hands in his. 'How did you cope?'

'I just got on with it. I had to. I'd got Billy to look after, hadn't I, and Ernest. I just got on with it.' She sighed. 'And it was then that I started to have my dreams.'

'Dreams? Do you mean nightmares?'

'Oh, no. Just dreams. Happy dreams. Day-dreams I suppose you'd call them. To keep myself from going mad.' She looked up and gave Andrew a half-smile. 'They worked, too. I'm not mad, am I?'

'Not at all,' Andrew assured her.

'But I would have been if I hadn't had my dreams,' Annie continued. 'Without my dreams I'd never have survived at all.'

CHAPTER THIRTY-NINE

Annie's Story

She dreamed of life on a farm – a farm like the one at home – and of the shadowy figure of a man who loved her. She couldn't see his face clearly but he was tall and smiling and she dreamed of standing on the doorstep waiting for him to come in for the meal she had prepared for him, and of the roughness of his coat as he hugged her to him, and of the big safe double bed where she would learn to enjoy his love. She dreamed of a warm kitchen and a dresser with blue and white willow-patterned china and a cool dairy where she skimmed the fresh milk for its cream. But most of all, she dreamed of a little girl in a pink gingham frock, whose name was Amelia.

Amelia never grew older; she was always about five years old, with her mother's strawberry blonde hair and blue eyes, and she danced in and out of Annie's dreams, carefree and laughing, always happy. She was not unlike the imaginary sister Annie had invented for herself when she was a child. As the only girl, she had longed for a sister, and when it was apparent that none was to be forthcoming, she had made up her own. But while Annie had never allowed this sister to be either as pretty or as clever as she herself was, Amelia was allowed to be beautiful, obedient and gifted; far too good to be true, of course, but then that is the advantage of dreams.

Annie no longer permitted herself to think about the tiny baby she had lost. She put aside all thoughts of the little garments she had been making, the half-decorated nursery, her own empty arms and aching breasts. It was as though this older Amelia, this dream-child, was a kind of replacement. If she concentrated on her imaginary daughter, she could bear the pain of losing the real one, for somewhere at the back of her mind was the knowledge that if she ever allowed herself to think too much about her loss, she would quite simply drown in her grief. And she couldn't afford to do that, not least because, as far as Ernest was concerned, the death of their baby was not a matter for discussion. It had happened, it was sad, but they had to put it behind them. Had the child been a boy he might have felt differently, but a girl was of little consequence to Ernest.

'What are you thinking about?' he used to ask, irritated by Annie's air of preoccupation.

'Nothing much,' she would tell him. 'Nothing that would interest you.'

For Ernest would certainly think she was crazy if she were to tell him about this new world she inhabited, and would more than likely punish her for it. Besides, Annie's dreams were private. The peace they granted her would be destroyed if she were to share them with anyone else; the bubble would burst, and pain might leak back in to disturb her thoughts. It was best all round that she should keep her secret life to herself.

Fortunately, Annie was kept busy. Billy continued to be demanding, and there was plenty to do in the house. She had her routine: Monday was wash day, on Tuesdays and Thursdays she cleaned the house, on Wednesday she did the ironing (provided the washing was dry enough), Friday was for catching up and doing the weekend shopping. And so it went on. Busy, busy. She knew she must keep herself busy. She gradually redecorated the house, made curtains and tidied up the small garden. There wasn't room to grow much, and in any case, Annie was never much of a gardener, but Ernest managed to find himself a small allotment, where he began to grow fruit and vegetables with some success. He purchased his first half-dozen pullets and constructed a run for them at the bottom of the garden, and the first small brown eggs were a welcome addition to the larder. On the surface, the household functioned well, and neighbours admired the industrious housewife and her hardworking husband.

Some of these neighbours became friends, and Annie enjoyed having a cup of tea and a chat while the children played together. But while she longed for a close friend – someone she could really talk to – she knew that that could never be. For Ernest was jealous and distrusted confidences, and her fear of Ernest was greater than her need for a confidante.

'It wouldn't do for you to let people know our business, Annie,' he used to say. 'You can't trust people not to gossip. I don't mind you making the odd visit,' he added. 'No harm in that. But don't you go giving things away, Annie. Remember, your first loyalty must be to me. We keep ourselves to ourselves. We don't need anyone else.'

Annie guessed what Ernest meant, for shortly after the birth of her baby, Ernest had returned to his old habits, and she suspected that he was afraid that she might divulge what went on in their bedroom. In fact, he needn't have worried on that score, for Annie herself was far too ashamed and humiliated to tell anyone about her ordeals.

And then there was the violence.

The fact that Ernest had managed to control himself during her pregnancy only made it worse, for it meant that he could prevent himself from striking her when he chose. His was not an ungovernable temper, after all, but one which he indulged when the occasion arose, and as time went on the occasion seemed to arise with increasing frequency. Usually the blows were slight: a slap on the arm, a push, or a shake; enough to frighten Annie if not to injure her. Occasionally he struck her more heavily, leaving purple bruises on her arms or thighs, although he was careful not to leave signs that might be open to interpretation by others, so he rarely hit her on the face or about the head.

Once, Annie threatened to go to the police, but Ernest merely laughed at her.

'Do you think they would take any notice of you?' he asked. 'Why should they believe you? It's your word against mine, Annie. Your word against mine. You just behave yourself, and you'll be all right.'

But try as she might, Annie continued to displease Ernest, and she came to realise that her very existence was an irritation to him. She annoyed and infuriated him simply by being herself, and there wasn't much she could do about that. The way she ate her food, the clothes she wore, the way she cared for Billy, even the manner in which she spoke – everything she did seemed to get on Ernest's nerves. Annie had enough insight to know that it was the situation rather than she herself which infuriated Ernest; that he resented their marriage as much as she did, and was taking his frustration out on her. But to be allocated the sole blame for that marriage, and to have to endure almost daily reminders of what Ernest seemed to consider his personal sacrifice in marrying her, were very hard to bear.

Billy remained a problem for her. Annie still took a pride in her son, and had come to love him in her way. He was a bright child and could be both affectionate and entertaining, but as he grew from a wayward toddler into a temperamental and obstinate little boy, she often despaired. Over-indulged by Ernest, he could at times be a little tyrant, safe in the knowledge that even if he thoroughly displeased his mother, his father could be relied upon to take his part. Thus he learnt early on that he could usually get what he wanted by playing one parent off against the other.

'Can't you see what he's doing?' Annie asked on one occasion, when she had put Billy to bed three times. 'He doesn't want a drink, or his potty. He's not having nightmares. He just wants to stay up with us.'

'And why not?' Ernest said, setting the child on his knee and giving him a forkful of his own dinner. 'It's all right for you, Annie. You see him all day. I've hardly set eyes on the lad today.'

'But that's the whole *point!* I've had him all day, and now I want a bit of peace. I can get much more done when Billy's in bed.'

Ernest, too, often wanted peace, and on those occasions he conveniently overlooked the fact that he was missing the opportunity to spend time with his son.

'Can't you keep that child quiet, Annie?' he would say turning up the wireless or taking refuge behind his newspaper. 'I've had a busy week. I need time to relax.'

271

And so it was established that Billy was a welcome part of Ernest's life provided it was on Ernest's terms. The rest of the time his care was Annie's responsibility. Occasionally Ernest would take Billy for a walk, but he soon found that there was little entertainment to be had from walking at a snail's pace, examining every stone or beetle or puddle they happened to pass. Billy's interest and chatter gave him little pleasure. Once or twice, he took Billy with him to play in the allotment while he worked, but this, too, soon palled, and he would return complaining that he had got nothing done, while Billy, who had spent a happy time making mud pies, was covered from head to foot with the fruits of his labours. On balance, Annie was relieved when these little expeditions were abandoned.

And so life continued with all its pain and its difficulties, and Annie increasingly retreated into her dream world of a phantom farm and an imagined embrace, and the ghost of a little girl in a pink frock.

CHAPTER FORTY

Ophelia

'Are you okay, Gran?' Ophelia dumped a collection of carrier bags on the kitchen table, and sat down beside Annie. 'You look as though you've been crying.'

'I have.'

'Oh, Gran! What happened? Have you hurt yourself?'

'No. I lost a baby.'

'You *lost a baby?*'

'Yes.'

'But – but that must have been a long time ago,' Ophelia said carefully.

'It was. But I was telling Andrew about it. She died soon after she was born, and I never saw her.'

'Oh, Gran. I'm so sorry. A girl, too. I bet you really wanted a daughter.' Ophelia squeezed Annie's arm. 'She would have been my aunt,' she mused. 'I always fancied having an aunt.'

'Your Aunt Amelia.'

'A pretty name.'

'Yes. I thought so.'

'So why now? You never cry, Gran. You aren't the crying sort.'

'Perhaps I am now. Talking to Andrew brought it all back, and suddenly it was as though it had only just happened,' Annie said, getting up to put the kettle on. 'I couldn't cry before. I wasn't allowed.'

'Grandad?'

'Yes. Grandad.'

'Was he so awful?'

'Not really awful,' Annie said. 'I think I thought he was pretty awful at the time, but I'm beginning to understand a bit more about him. He wasn't *nice*, though. I'd never describe him as nice.'

Ophelia thought of the fierce, intolerant man she had known, and had to agree. She had been in awe of Ernest, and in a funny way she had

273

respected him, but she hadn't really liked him and she certainly hadn't loved him.

'Where is he now?' she asked suddenly.

'Where is he?' Annie turned, teapot in hand. 'In Heaven, I hope. Not that he believed in that sort of thing, of course, but he'd have been awfully annoyed if they hadn't let him in. Your grandad hated being left out of things.'

'No. I mean where is *he?* His body? His – ashes? Dad was asking the other day. I think he knew you wouldn't tell him, so he wanted me to ask you.' Ophelia grinned. 'But I'm asking for me, not him. I promise I won't tell Dad if you don't want me to.'

'I don't want you to.' Annie handed Ophelia a cup of tea and sat down again. 'But I will tell you. He's in the larder.'

'In the *larder?*'

'Yes. I think Andrew was surprised, too, but it's quite a good place. To be getting on with.'

'I never noticed him!'

'Exactly! He's in a jar behind the pickled onions.'

'But Gran, why?'

'Why the larder or why the pickled onions?'

'No. Why haven't you done something with him? Something more permanent? You can't keep him in the larder for ever.'

'I'm waiting to decide. And I have done lots of things with him. We've been to bingo and to Tesco's, and we've watched *Coronation Street* together. He hated *Coronation Street*. I even kept him in the shed for a while. But the larder seemed best.'

'Oh.'

'Yes. And ashes have to be scattered. I don't know why they can't be put or thrown, but they have to be scattered. It sounds such a messy untidy sort of business, doesn't it?'

'I suppose it does.' Ophelia had a vivid mental picture of scattering someone and having them blow straight back in one's face. It would be most discomfiting to find on your return home that small particles of the deceased were still clinging to your hair and clothes. 'You'd have to make sure the wind was in the right direction.'

'That's what I thought.'

'I could come with you,' Ophelia said.

'Would you?'

'Of course I would. Dad might be a bit miffed, though.'

'I don't want him there. Nothing against your dad, of course, but this is between me and Ernest. I don't mind you coming, though.'

'Mmm.' Ophelia could see that Annie had unfinished business with Ernest, and that it had to be up to Annie to finish that business herself and in her own way. 'What sort of place would he have liked?'

'I don't know. He never said. Andrew suggested burying him in the churchyard, but he wasn't religious. Abroad might be nice.'

'*Abroad?*'

'Yes. Your grandad never went abroad. Always said he'd like to but never got round to it.'

'So you've never been abroad, either?'

'Never really wanted to.'

'But you would? To – to scatter Grandad?'

'I might.'

'Where would you go?'

'I don't know. Your grandad didn't like the sea, but he was fond of mountains. I might find a nice mountain. With a bit of snow on top, even. When I'm ready.'

'You haven't really forgiven him yet, have you?' Ophelia said, after a moment.

'I'm not sure,' Annie said. 'It takes so much time. I want to forgive him, but it's not easy. Of course, you don't know the half of it. Andrew does. I've told him most of it, and I don't mind if he tells you, but I don't think I've got the energy to go through it all again. It brings it all back.'

'Of course.'

'And you see quite a lot of Andrew, don't you?' Annie gave Ophelia a shrewd glance.

Ophelia looked down. 'You know I do. But you didn't want me to talk to you about it.'

'No. But I worry about you, Ophelia. I can't see where it will lead.'

'Neither can I,' Ophelia said. 'But when I'm with him, it doesn't seem to matter. It's all about now, and about him and me, and about loving and being loved.'

'Have you and he–? I mean have you, well, *you know?*'

'Not yet.'

'Not *yet?*'

'There are practicalities, Gran, as well as – oh, I don't know. Conscience, I suppose.' How odd, Ophelia thought, that she was quite happy to discuss with her grandmother things which she wouldn't have dreamt of telling Sheila, although her mother was so anxious to be taken into her confidence. Maybe that was it. Annie's interest was just that. Interest. She didn't *need* to be Ophelia's confidante, and that of course made her the perfect person to talk to. 'I think that maybe I'm a more moral person than I thought I was. I've never met Janet, and I don't want to, but I wouldn't want to hurt her, either.' She cradled her teacup in both hands. 'What would you do, Gran?'

'That's a difficult one,' said Annie. 'The trouble is, there'd be no going back.'

'I know that. But there wouldn't be any going forward, either. I know I can't ever be with Andrew. Not properly. Even if he wanted me. I couldn't cope with the responsibility of it all. His marriage, the church, you–'

'Oh, you don't have to worry about me.'

'Yes, Gran. I do. You have to live here. In this village. And I care a lot for you. Apart from Andrew, I think you're the only person who's ever really wanted to understand me. I love being here with you. I can be myself, with no one nagging me about untidiness or crumbs on the carpet or when am I going to get a Proper Job.'

'Yes, well. It's not my job to boss you around, is it? Or bring you up, come to that. I didn't make a very good job of your father, so I don't suppose I'm in a position to bring anyone up.'

'What do you mean?'

'He's spoilt,' Annie said.

Ophelia laughed. 'How can someone of sixty be spoilt?'

'Well, isn't he?'

Ophelia considered for a moment. She thought of the way her mother ran around after Billy, of the fact that everything had to be done his way, of his strict adherence to routine and his total lack of flexibility, and decided her grandmother had a point.

'I suppose he is. I'd never really thought about it. Is he like Grandad, do you suppose?'

'In some ways. Not unkind, though. I don't think Billy ever means to be unkind, although sometimes it can seem like it.'

Ophelia thought of the many times she had been put down or criticised by her father, and wasn't so sure. How could anyone say the kinds of things Billy had said to her without realising how hurtful they might be?

'If I could just make him proud of me,' she said, 'or at least reasonably pleased with the person I am, I think I'd be happy. But I'm certainly not going to achieve that by having an affair with Andrew, am I?'

'He doesn't have to know,' Annie said.

'True.' Ophelia swirled the tea leaves round the bottom of her cup. 'He – Andrew – wants me to go away with him next week. Just for one night.' She paused. 'Why don't you use teabags like everyone else, Gran? They're so much easier.'

'Don't change the subject. And I've told you before. Your grandad wouldn't have tea made from teabags. Said he could taste the difference with his eyes shut. Are you going?

'Yes. Yes, I think I probably am.'

'Well, then.' Annie got up from the table and took their cups over to the sink.

'What do you mean, "well then"?'

'I mean,' said Annie, picking up a tea towel (Blackpool Tower, circa 1980), 'why've we been having this conversation if your mind's already made up? And I think – oh, I just want you both to be happy. But please be careful.'

'Oh, I do love you, Gran!' Ophelia got up and gave Annie a hug.

'That's the second time you've said that,' Annie said.

But Ophelia could tell that she was pleased.

CHAPTER FORTY-ONE

Annie's Story

Annie's daydreams soon became a part of her daily life, and as time went on, they became increasingly elaborate. She arranged and re-arranged things in her dream house (for this was a home where she had a free rein to do whatever she wanted) and planted the garden with pink and yellow roses. A herd of sweet-faced Jersey cattle grazed in a nearby meadow, a goat and her kid fed on the windfall fruit in the orchard, and the little girl in the pink frock played on the swing which hung from the bough of an old apple tree. Annie could see her clearly, with her blonde pig-tails and her speedwell-blue eyes. She held a crisp rosy apple in her hand, and laughed at the puppy which gambolled at her feet. Annie had

279

provided the dog as a companion for Amelia. A dog would keep the child safe.

The shadowy figure in the rough tweed coat came and went. Annie could never quite make out his face, but she could feel the warmth of his embrace, and breathe in the imagined smells of fresh milk and hay and good clean earth. Often, they would lie together in the big soft double bed. Annie rarely introduced sex into her fantasies; sex reminded her too much of discomfort and power-lessness and shame. But sometimes she imagined lying with her dream lover after lovemaking, holding him and being held; being *loved*.

Sometimes, Annie wondered whether she was going a little mad. Was it normal to inhabit a dream world such as hers? There was no way of knowing, for presumably people didn't talk about such things. But there could be no harm in it, and surely what she was doing was no different from a writer telling a story, or an artist painting a picture. The fact that no one would ever read her story or see her pictures was immaterial. Some people created stories and pictures to entertain other people; Annie's creations were for herself.

Meanwhile, Ernest became increasingly irritated by her daydreaming, the more so because there was very little he could do about it.

'I can think, can't I?' Annie said once. 'You can't stop me from thinking. I look after the house and Billy, your meals are always on the table, you have clean clothes. I try to do what you want.'

'But when you have that – that *look* on our face, I know you can't be concentrating on what you're doing,' Ernest said. 'For a start, how can you care for a young child if your thoughts aren't on the job?'

'Easily,' Annie said. 'Remember, I have a lot of practice.'

'And what's that supposed to mean?'

'Just that. Looking after Billy is what I do. Every day. I could do it in my sleep.'

'That's exactly what it looks like,' Ernest said. 'You look as though you're doing it in your sleep. If something happens to that boy–'

'Nothing's going to happen to Billy,' Annie assured him, well aware that it wasn't her neglect of her duties that Ernest resented but rather his own exclusion from an area of her life which he knew was unreachable.

'Well, if that's the case, I suppose I'll just have to leave you to get on with it,' Ernest said grudgingly.

'You do that,' Annie said.

For she knew she now had something which was beyond Ernest's reach; a place to go where he couldn't follow her. Her private world was her refuge and her sanity. It was the only thing in her life which was hers and hers alone. Ernest might read her letters and go through her things; he might cross-question her about where she'd been and whom she'd seen and what they'd talked about. He could rage and he could threaten, and he could possess and abuse her in the bedroom and outside it. He could and did invade every part of her life. But her dream-world was entirely private; a place of peace and tranquillity; and the more time she spent in it, the better she was able to cope with her life with Ernest.

Annie began to tell stories to Billy; not her own dreams, of course, but stories she made up especially for him; tales of steam engines and animals and red buses and seaside holidays. Billy adored these stories, and would ask for them again and again, but Ernest disapproved.

'Why are you filling the child's head with that rubbish?' he demanded. 'Hasn't he enough books, without you making up all this stuff?'

'He enjoys it,' Annie said. 'He likes me inventing stories just for him. It makes them more special.'

'He needs pictures,' Ernest said. 'A young child needs pictures to look at.'

'He has pictures,' Annie said, wondering that Ernest suddenly seemed to consider himself an expert on the needs of small children. 'They're in his head. They're the best kind of pictures.'

'I don't know what you're talking about. Pictures in his head, indeed! He'll soon be as crazy as you are.'

Ernest bought Billy more picture books, and was infuriated when Billy preferred to listen to his mother's stories. Since Ernest had little imagination, this was one area in which he couldn't compete, and in the matter of his son's affections, Ernest was very competitive.

In her better moments, Annie reflected that part of the trouble was that Billy was quite probably the only person Ernest had ever truly loved. He had hardly known his father, and had feared rather than loved his mother. He had few friends, and those he did have were more acquaintances than anything else. He might once have loved her, but that love had died the day he allowed himself to be trapped into this marriage. But Billy was his; *his son*. He didn't have to compete with Billy. He could celebrate Billy's small achievements as an extension of his own. Billy wasn't a threat.

And Billy adored his father, following him round like a small shadow. He seemed to accept that his own childish games tried Ernest's patience, and was content simply to be with his father when he did odd jobs around the house and garden. Thus, when Ernest tinkered with his car, Billy would fiddle with his own toy cars. When Ernest mowed the grass, Billy would push a little trolley up and down the lawn beside him. When Ernest fed the chickens, Billy accompanied him with his own little pail of corn.

Once, Annie had felt excluded, and had had her own moments of jealousy, but now she was glad that Ernest and Billy had each other. She didn't love Ernest, and knew she would never be able to love Billy in the way that Ernest did. If she had done nothing else for them, she had given Ernest a son to love, and Billy a father who loved him.

Life wasn't all bad for Annie. Sometimes, things would go smoothly for two or three weeks at a time. There were periods when Ernest seemed fairly content, and at times he was quite companionable. But Annie learnt to take nothing for granted, and to remain watchful, for beneath the surface there was always the threat of Ernest's anger.

Sex was less frequent, and Ernest no longer seemed to be punishing her. While never gentle, these days he rarely actually hurt her, and it was always over quickly. For Annie, it had become more of a chore than an ordeal, and she was well used to chores. Ernest's mysterious fumblings still occurred beforehand, and Annie was glad, for on one matter they were in complete agreement: there were to be no more babies. Ernest had his son, and as for Annie, there could never be a replacement for the baby she had lost. Besides, she daren't risk going through a similar ordeal. She had survived the loss of one child; she wasn't sure she had the emotional strength to risk losing another.

Ernest's violence was another matter. His outbursts were unpredictable, and were often precipitated by something relatively trivial, while on other occasions, when something might have been expected to arouse his anger, he would let the matter pass.

The unpredictability was the hardest thing for Annie to cope with, for it meant that even when things were relatively calm, she lived in a state of almost constant apprehension. If she could have pre-empted Ernest's fury, she would have done so, and occasionally this was the case. But as often as not, his rage would appear to come out of the blue, with little warning and no opportunity for her to prevent it.

She no longer dreamed of escape. She was too weary, and by now too entrenched in the life she and Ernest had made for themselves. Billy, the house, the village, her few friends, her routine; they were not only extensions of the trap which was her marriage, they also formed a framework for her existence. Without that framework, what would happen to her? At least it held her life together; within its boundaries she had a function and a purpose. If she kept her head down and worked hard, she would survive.

Whatever else might happen, Annie was determined to survive.

CHAPTER FORTY-TWO

Andrew

They met in a lay-by off the motorway.

'What if there aren't any lay-bys?' Ophelia had asked fearfully. 'What if we can't find each other?'

'There are always lay-bys,' Andrew had reassured her. 'And we have our mobiles. Of course we'll find each other. Trust me.'

They found a village cul-de-sac where they could leave Ophelia's car, and travelled the rest of the way together. It was already dusk, and a sharp drizzle was spitting against the windscreen. Andrew turned on the windscreen wipers.

'They always remind me of summer holidays,' Ophelia said. 'Sitting in the car waiting for the rain to stop, so that we could have a picnic. Dad drumming his fingers on the steering wheel (he hates weather because he has no control over it) and Mum with her perfect little picnic hamper. Knives and forks and napkins and proper coffee cups. They even had a little table and chairs. I longed to sit on the grass and eat sandwiches out of a paper bag, like other people.'

Ophelia's voice prattled on, nervous and staccato, and Andrew ached for her. It's because she doesn't know what else to say, he thought. Like me. Neither of us dares to talk about what's about to happen. It's as though we're both embarrassed. Suddenly, we're strangers once more, as though the past few weeks had never happened.

'You're not listening!' Ophelia said. 'I don't believe you've heard a word I've been saying.'

'I have. You were talking about sandwiches and paper bags.'

'That was about two topics ago.' He could see the pale oval of her face turned towards him. 'This feels so – so odd, doesn't it?'

'Yes,' Andrew agreed. 'But I'm sure it'll be fine when we get there. It's just that we've never done anything like this before.'

'It's a bit like seeing someone off on a train, and saying all the things you want to say, and then the train's delayed and you find you've run out of words,' Ophelia said. 'Which is odd, because no one's going anywhere, and I never run out of words. Mum always said I could talk for England, and she's probably right. Oh dear. I'm doing it again, aren't I?'

'Sweetheart, relax. It's okay to be quiet, you know,' Andrew said, trying to consult a map in the half-light. 'We should be able to be quiet with each other and still be comfortable. You can have a nap if you want. We've still about half an hour to go.'

'I don't think I could sleep.'

'No. I understand.'

'Do you feel the same?' Ophelia asked.

'I think I probably do,' Andrew said. He had expected to feel so happy, so excited, and all he felt was a dull nausea and something akin to fear. 'Shall we put on some music?'

'No. Not yet. I know! Tell me about Gran. She said she didn't mind me knowing some of the things she's been talking to you about. She's not up to going through it all again, but she doesn't mind you telling me. It's not that I'm nosy,' she added. 'It's just that I really love Gran, and I know so little about her.'

'It's a long story,' Andrew said, turning on the headlights.

'I'm listening.'

So Andrew told her. He told her about the lively girl on the farm, and about the war and the tragedies which had overtaken the young Annie. He told of the untimely pregnancy and the hurried wedding and the difficult abusive marriage which had followed. He omitted the sexual abuse and Annie's feeling about the infant Billy as he suspected that when Anne had had time to think about it, she might prefer that Ophelia should be spared certain things, but otherwise he told Ophelia everything he knew.

When he had finished, there was complete silence, and for a moment he wondered whether Ophelia had gone to sleep after all. Then he realised that she was crying.

'Darling! Whatever's the matter?'

'It's Gran. Poor, poor little Gran. I'd no idea.

No idea at all. I knew Grandad was difficult, but not that he was so cruel. How could he? How could he be so cruel?'

'Well, there are always two sides to any story,' Andrew said carefully. 'Try not to judge him too harshly. He didn't have it easy, either. I think he must have had a pretty hard time as a child, and maybe he found it difficult to love.'

'He loved Dad.'

'Yes. It seems that he did. But doesn't that redeem him a little? It shows he was capable of love. He just married the wrong person. Like Annie. In a way, they were both victims. Victims of circumstances, and of the times they lived in. Nowadays, they would never have had to get married. They might have found happiness with other people. We'll never know.'

'Does Dad know?'

'I don't know. He certainly knows Annie was pregnant when she married, but I'm not sure about the rest. He must have been aware that they didn't get on, but I think Annie protected him as much as she could. Ernest, too. I'm sure neither of them wanted him to suffer for something which wasn't his fault.'

'I suppose so.' Ophelia blew her nose. 'How did Gran survive all those years?'

'She's a strong woman. Much stronger than she looks. And she had that dream world of hers. I think that kept her going. And once she'd resigned herself to life with your grandad, I think she stopped expecting much; expecting happiness. She just got on with it.' Andrew pulled off the road. 'Look. I think this is it.'

'It' was a small country inn. They carried their cases through the cheerful smoky atmosphere of the public bar, where horse brasses gleamed along low oak beams and several bucolic-looking locals were already propping up the bar. Their bedroom, situated at the other end of the house, was simple and clean, with whitewashed walls and hunting prints and its own small bathroom.

'This is nice.' Ophelia sat down on the bed. 'Which – which side do you sleep?'

'I don't mind. What about you?'

'I don't really know. I'm not used to sleeping with someone. I'll stay on this side, shall I?'

'Fine.'

There followed a pause in which both of them seemed to be wondering what to do next. Andrew looked at his watch. Seven o'clock. A bit too early for dinner and not enough time for anything else. Usually when they were alone together, they couldn't keep their hands off each other, but now they both seemed overcome by shyness. Andrew had imagined this moment so many times; had envisaged the passionate kisses and the tangle of discarded clothes and the longed-for feeling of Ophelia's bare skin next to his own.

'It's not – not quite how we expected, is it?' Ophelia said, and her voice sounded forlorn.

'It will be.' Andrew touched her cheek. 'We just need to relax a bit and get used to being here together. Why don't you go and have a nice hot bath, and then we can both change for dinner? We don't have to rush things. We've got all night.'

The bath seemed to improve Ophelia's spirits,

and she emerged from the bathroom flushed and cheerful and wearing a very obviously new and expensive-looking dress in a soft floaty material. Andrew thought he had never seen her looking so beautiful.

Dinner was pleasant, and their tongues were loosened by the presence of other diners and the noise from the adjoining bar, but once again, Ophelia, perhaps anxious to avoid any awkward silences, began to chatter almost aimlessly. For a moment, Andrew wondered whether it was the wine, but when he looked at her, he saw in her eyes a kind of desperation he had never seen before.

'Darling, stop. Please stop.' He reached across the table for her hand.

'Oh dear.' Ophelia looked down. 'I'm still doing it, aren't I? I don't know what's got into me.'

'What is it? What's the matter?'

'I don't know. I just don't know how to behave, I suppose. I've never' – she lowered her voice – 'well, I've never committed adultery before.'

'That's what I love about you.'

'What? That I've never committed adultery?'

'No. Your directness. Your honesty. Your integrity, I suppose.'

'This is hardly the behaviour of someone with integrity,' Ophelia said. 'Oh, Andrew! I don't think I like myself very much at the moment.'

'Let's go. Let's go back to our room, and I'll try to make you like yourself a bit more,' Andrew said, with more humour than he was feeling.

Back in their room, he locked the door and took Ophelia in his arms.

'You do know that I love you?' he said.

'Of course.'

'Well then.' He drew her down beside him on the bed. 'There's nothing to be afraid of, is there?' He tipped her face up towards his and kissed her.

'No. I suppose not.' She returned his kiss. 'Just – hold me for a moment would you?'

They leaned back against the pillows and held each other, Andrew's face against the softness of Ophelia's cheek, her arms tightly round his body. I love her so much, he thought. So much, the pain is almost unbearable. As he felt her relax against him, he moved his hand down from her shoulder, allowing it to cup her breast through the thin material of her dress, and she turned towards him, kissing his face and neck.

'Better?' Andrew asked.

'Mm.' She began to unbutton his shirt, slipping her hand inside it and stroking his chest. 'We've known each other all this time, and I never knew you had a hairy chest!'

'Is that okay?'

'Everything about you is okay.' Her fingers felt cool against his skin.

As Andrew kissed Ophelia and felt her moving against him, he waited for the first stirrings of the passion he had been controlling for so long; for the urgent physical response which had so often almost overwhelmed him and which he had been saving up for this moment. But his body failed to respond. It was as though something within him had been severed; as though his mind and his body were no longer connected. He loved

291

Ophelia now as he had never loved her before, and yet in that moment, he knew with absolute certainty that he wasn't going to be able to do anything about it. That he would never be able to do anything about it.

Very gently, he put Ophelia away from him and laid her back against the pillow, then he swung his legs over the edge of the bed and put his head in his hands.

'Ophelia. Ophelia darling. I – I can't.'

For a moment, there was complete silence, then Ophelia reached out and touched his arm.

'I know.'

'You know?'

'Yes. I think in a way I've always known.'

'Oh, darling. Sweetheart. I'm so so sorry.'

'Don't be.' She was sitting beside him now, holding his hand, like a mother comforting a child. 'I don't think we're cut out for this sort of thing, you and I.'

'It's not that I don't love you. Not that I don't find you more beautiful than any woman I've ever met–'

'You don't have to explain.'

That alone would have been enough to make him love her, Andrew thought, as he sat miserably on the edge of the bed. She really did understand. And of course that made it the more painful; that having found someone who understood him as no one else ever had, to whom he owed so much, who he felt was so much a part of himself, he was unable to consummate his love for her. The unwanted censor which was his body had denied him the ultimate joy of being entirely at one with Ophelia.

They sat together for a long time, hand in hand on the edge of the bed. At one stage, Andrew turned off the light and drew aside the curtains, exposing a crescent moon dodging in and out between dark rags of cloud.

'So it stopped raining,' Ophelia said at last.

'Yes,' Andrew agreed.

'It'll be all right.'

'Yes,' he said again.

'I mean – this isn't the end of the world, is it?'

Andrew longed to cry out that yes, it was the end of the world; that he couldn't imagine that things could have turned out any worse; and that while he knew he probably deserved some kind of punishment, did he really deserve this? Did *Ophelia* deserve this? But he bit his lip and gave her hand a squeeze.

'No, my darling. It isn't the end of the world.'

They sat on, chatting about little things; silly superficial things; things about which neither of them cared in the least. Once or twice they even laughed; small, brittle, self-conscious laughs. Then they would lapse into sudden silence, as though afraid that a single word might spoil an evening which was already in ruins. After what seemed a very long time, they finally fell asleep, fully dressed, in each other's arms.

They slipped away early the next morning. Neither of them felt like facing the promised full English breakfast, and besides, Ophelia had to be back in time for work.

'Will you be all right?' Andrew asked, as he dropped her off to pick up her car.

Ophelia nodded.

'I love you,' Andrew said. 'If you remember nothing else, always remember that I love you.'

'Me too.' Ophelia's voice was shaky. 'Will you be in touch?'

'Of course. I'll be in touch as soon as I can.' He kissed her cheek. 'Drive carefully.'

Sitting in his car, Andrew watched Ophelia drive off down the road, and felt that she was taking with her all his hopes and dreams; everything he had ever wanted.

Leaning on the steering wheel, he rested his head against his arms and wept.

CHAPTER FORTY-THREE

Annie

'Well? How was it?' Annie had been waiting anxiously for Ophelia's return from work, unsure what sort of state her granddaughter would be in after her night away. 'I made a cake,' she added, gesturing towards a rather lopsided sponge bleeding pale pink jam onto a doily. 'I thought it might help.'

'Oh Gran. It was a disaster.' Ophelia dropped her case on the kitchen floor and sat down at the table.

'Why? Didn't you get on?'

'Oh, we got on. We always get on. It just – it didn't work, that's all.'

294

'Ah.' Annie wasn't entirely sure what it was that hadn't worked but she did know that further questions might seem intrusive.

'We – well, we couldn't. That's all there was to it. We couldn't. And now we never shall.' Tears began to pour down Ophelia's face. 'Oh, Gran! You've no idea how much I've been longing to come home. All day, my face has been aching with wanting to cry. I thought I'd never hold out. Maria kept asking me what was the matter, and I just said I was under the weather. But Gran, what shall I do? Whatever am I going to do? I can't bear it. I simply can't bear it. I never knew it would hurt this much.' Ophelia wrapped her arms round her body and rocked to and fro, her sobs coming in great gulps.

Annie was at a loss as to what to do or say. She would like to have taken Ophelia in her arms, but being unaccustomed to demonstrations of affection – it was a very long time since she had hugged anyone, and she felt that she had almost forgotten how – she contented herself with stroking and patting Ophelia's hand. She longed to do something to ease Ophelia's pain, but she knew that this haemorrhage of grief had to run its course; that there could be no short cuts. Should she offer tea? Annie was a great believer in the healing properties of tea. Perhaps not the cake, though; not yet, anyway. Cake didn't seem the right antidote to heartbreak. She gave Ophelia's hand a final pat, and went to put the kettle on.

'I always knew it couldn't last,' Ophelia said, between sobs, 'but I never thought it would be like this. I thought it would be worth it – that everything would make it worthwhile – but nothing's worth this, Gran. *Nothing.*'

Annie put a cup of tea in front of Ophelia and poured herself one, feeling that perhaps she had been spared a lot of heartache after all. She'd always regretted that she had never been in love, but if this was what it did to people, then perhaps she'd had a lucky escape.

'Will you see him again?' she asked.

'Oh, yes. Probably. But it's over. It has to be. We can't hack it; either of us. We haven't actually finished it, but I think we both know. There's so much in the way of us being together, I suppose we're lucky to have had any time at all.'

Annie wished she could think of something helpful to say but didn't feel she had either the experience or the wisdom to make a contribution which would be of any comfort to Ophelia at the moment. She had never really encountered heartbreak, either personally or on the part of someone else. Billy had probably had his share – he had married late, and there had been many girls before Sheila – but he had never spoken to her about them. She suspected that sons didn't talk about such things.

'I'm sorry, Gran,' Ophelia said now. 'I'm so sorry.'

'Whatever for?'

'All this hassle. It's not fair on you, all this happening on your doorstep. You don't need it, after the year you've had.'

It took a moment for Annie to realise that Ophelia was referring to the death of Ernest.

'That's all right,' she said, patting Ophelia's hand again. 'It's not been such a bad year, you know.'

'Do you miss him?' Ophelia asked, after a moment.

'Miss who?'

'Grandad.'

'Not really. I suppose I ought to, but life's been much – well, easier, I suppose, since he died. Awful, isn't it? I'd never have said that a few months ago, and there aren't many people I can say it to now. People expect me to be sad still, so I have to pretend. I meet them in shops, and their faces go all serious and they say "How *are* you?" in that special voice, and I have to pretend I'm miserable, when sometimes I'm feeling quite cheerful.'

'You're much braver than I am, Gran,' Ophelia said. 'Andrew was telling me what you went through all those years. I don't know how you survived.'

'Not brave. More sort of numb. That's how I got through it. I think I stopped feeling things a long time ago. After the baby died.'

It was later on, when Ophelia had had a lie down and Annie had persuaded her to try some scrambled eggs, that Ophelia had her idea.

'Shall we go away?' she said suddenly. 'You and I? We could just – go, couldn't we? What's there to stop us?'

'What do you mean, go?' Annie said, alarmed. She had hardly ever 'just gone' anywhere in her life, and certainly not like this, on the spur of the moment.

'I mean just take off, travel, see a bit of the world.'

'Oh.' The bits of the world Annie knew were limited, but they were safe and familiar; everyone spoke English, and you could get a decent cup of tea when you wanted one. Ophelia's idea sounded altogether too adventurous. 'Which – bit were you thinking of? Would it mean planes and things?'

'It might mean planes, but it's up to you, Gran. You choose.'

'Goodness.' The idea of travel and just taking off was so alien to Annie that it was going to take some getting used to.

'I know! We could take Grandad!' Ophelia said.

'And scatter him?'

'Why not? You've got to do it some time, and I said I'd come with you. He can't stay in the larder for ever.'

Annie was used to having Ernest in the larder, and she wasn't sure whether she was ready to let him go yet. She'd enjoyed moving him about, taking him on little outings, having control over him. (She had once – secretly, guiltily – mixed a teaspoon of him into her tea, but he had floated to the top and she'd had to throw the tea away.) How would she feel if he wasn't there any more?

'You said he liked mountains,' Ophelia continued. 'We could find him a nice mountain.'

'With snow?'

'Definitely snow.'

'Would we have to go up it too?' Annie asked fearfully.

'Probably,' Ophelia said, 'but you'll be fine. I'll

look after you.'

'Your grandad didn't like heights. Said they made him dizzy.'

'Then we could scatter him at the bottom of the mountain, but with nice views.'

'Nice views,' Annie repeated, thoughtfully. 'Ernest liked a nice view.'

'There we are, then.'

'Are *you* ready for this?' Annie asked. 'After – what's happened?'

'Probably not,' Ophelia said. 'But if I wait until – until this doesn't hurt so much, I may have to wait for ever. And I'd love to go away with you, Gran.'

'Whatever will your father say?'

'He'll say "And what are you going to use for money, Ophelia?"' Ophelia said, in a passable imitation of Billy. 'And I suppose he'll have a point.'

'I'll pay,' Annie said. 'Your grandad had a building society account. I never knew what was in it, but he had seventeen thousand pounds. Imagine that, Ophelia! *Seventeen thousand pounds*, and it's all mine.'

'But don't you need it?' Ophelia said.

'No,' Annie said firmly. 'I want to fritter it away. That's what Ernest always said. He said if I got hold of any money, I'd just fritter it away, so he never gave me any. Well, we can fritter it together, can't we? Some of it, anyway.'

'I wonder how we'll get him through customs,' Ophelia mused. 'There are probably regulations.'

'We could divide him up into little bags,' Annie suggested. She knew nothing at all about customs, but had heard that they could be awkward.

'No. They might think he was drugs. I'll make enquiries. Someone's bound to know. Let's look for a suitable mountain.'

Annie fetched Ernest's atlas, and together they examined it. There seemed to be a great many mountains, and Ophelia's (failed) GCSE geography and Annie's limited knowledge of the world didn't amount to much, but they agreed that Austria looked manageable.

'I've always fancied Austria,' Ophelia said. 'Edelweiss and gentians, and those pretty wooden houses with balconies and geraniums.'

'And those funny little leather trousers?' Annie asked.

'Lederhosen. Yes, I expect so.'

'They wouldn't have suited your grandad,' Annie said.

'Quite possibly not.' They both laughed.

The knock at the front door made them both jump.

'Who can that be, at this time of night?' Annie said.

But Ophelia knew exactly who it was. She got up slowly.

'I'll go and let him in,' she said.

CHAPTER FORTY-FOUR

Andrew

Andrew sat on in his car for some time, and was eventually disturbed by two policemen, who pulled up beside him in a panda car. He wound down his window.

'Is everything all right, sir?'

'Yes thank you, officer.' Andrew wished he was wearing his dog collar.

'It's just that you looked – distressed.'

'No. I'm fine.'

'Then you won't mind if I breathalyse you, sir?'

Did he really look drunk? He may have appeared a bit dishevelled, but he was respectably dressed, legally parked, and it was 7.15 in the morning. Had the police nothing better to do?

Andrew duly obliged.

'That's fine. Thank you, sir. Have a good day.' The police car roared off down the road, officious, businesslike, purposeful.

Unlike me, Andrew thought; because for once he had nothing particular to do. The conference wasn't due to finish until lunchtime, and he didn't want to arouse suspicion by arriving home too early. He longed to talk to Ophelia – to make sure she was all right, to hear the sound of her voice – but she didn't finish work until 5.30 and he didn't want to phone her and risk causing her further upset.

I have no one, Andrew thought, in a rare moment of self-pity. There is no one I can talk to; no one who will listen and understand. Once, he would have prayed, secure in the belief that God at least would be there for him; would hear him and guide him. But his recent relationship with God had become increasingly fragile, and he was aware that guilt and self-doubt could be bigger barriers than a mere dwindling of faith.

Then he remembered Father Matthew, and the words which were almost the last he had spoken to him: 'I shall be here, if you need me.' In his unassuming way, Father Matthew had of course known that sooner or later Andrew would have need of him; that he was the only person to whom Andrew could turn when his life reached the crisis which had become inevitable. At the time, Andrew had wondered whether he would ever see his spiritual adviser again; after all, what he was doing was so incompatible with his calling, that involving Father Matthew seemed an indulgence he didn't deserve. And yet now he knew that that gentle, wise man was precisely the person he needed.

He looked at his watch. It was still only half past seven, but he knew that Father Matthew was an early riser, and it would take him some time to get there. He switched on the ignition.

An hour later, Father Matthew, not looking in the least surprised at this early and unscheduled visit, was holding the door open for him.

'Ah. Andrew. You're just in time for breakfast.'

'Thanks. No breakfast, thank you, but coffee

would be nice.'

'Coffee it is, then.'

Andrew had never been in the kitchen before, and was reassured by its state of mild bachelor chaos. There were books and papers strewn on work tops, unwashed cups and plates on the draining board, and a pile of crumpled laundry on a chair.

'I would ask you to excuse the mess, but I always think it's such a ridiculous thing to say.' Father Matthew, having hunted down the coffee, was spooning it into mugs. 'All it really means, is "I acknowledge the untidiness, but have better things to do than deal with it."' He put the mugs on a tray, together with a plate of buttered toast ('I'm hungry even if you are not') and led the way to the study.

'You've been expecting me, haven't you?' Andrew said, as he sat down.

'Not exactly expecting you. More waiting for you.' Father Matthew took a bite of toast. 'I suppose I hoped you would come. You could say that I needed you to come. I felt that we had unfinished business.'

'We?'

'Don't look so surprised. When you told me – well, when you told me what was happening in your life, I was unable to offer much in the way of comfort. Maybe now I shall be able to do more.'

'I'm not sure anyone can offer comfort now,' Andrew said.

'Try me.'

So Andrew told Father Matthew everything. He talked of his love and his fears, of his guilt and his doubts, and of the enormous joy and the utter despair of loving Ophelia.

'I was greedy,' he said, as he reached the end of his story. 'Just for a while I thought I could have it all. I managed to persuade myself that I owed it to Ophelia. I even managed to convince myself that I deserved it. But all I've done is hurt Ophelia, and probably Annie too, and put everything else in my life at risk. I've done so much damage. How can I begin to put it right?'

For a few moments, there was silence. Father Matthew sat peaceably, his hands folded in his lap, his eyes on Andrew's face.

'But have you really done that much damage? Think about it. You've given love to Ophelia, and that is never bad. And you have received love yourself. Annie sounds to me as though she's had a lot worse to contend with than this. And you say you don't think that Janet knows, so your marriage may well survive. As for God, well, He's always had a soft spot for sinners.'

'I feel I've lost my grip on God,' Andrew said.

'Ah, but has He lost His grip on you? That's what matters.'

'I suppose I hadn't thought of it that way.'

'Well, perhaps you should.'

'Yes. Perhaps I should. For a long time, I've felt that my faith's been dwindling, and yet when it comes to it, I can't let it go, either.' Andrew stirred his coffee. It was almost cold. 'But what shall I do now? What's the best thing to do?'

'Well, I can't answer that. It depends on what you come to feel is right. If you want to remain in the priesthood – and I hope you will – it's

304

possible you may need a break of some sort. Perhaps a retreat. And then maybe you might consider a change of parish.'

'Would it be right to run away from Ophelia?'

'A great deal better than leaving her to run away from you. A new parish might be a challenge, for you and for Janet. A fresh start for both of you.'

'Janet and I aren't happy. We haven't been happy for years.'

'I know that. But when did the two of you last really talk to each other?'

'Oh, ages ago. Janet won't.'

'*Janet* won't?'

Andrew thought for a moment. It was certainly a long time since he had tried to talk to Janet, and recently there had been indications that perhaps she was ready to make a move towards him. The purchase of the kitten had been a big step for Janet, and yet he hadn't been especially gracious.

'Perhaps I haven't tried hard enough,' he admitted.

'Then try. What have you to lose? At least find out what she feels; what she wants. *Communicate* with her.' Father Matthew got up and opened the window to release a fly which was buzzing against the window pane. 'It will be difficult,' he continued, as he sat down again, 'because you want Ophelia, and wanting Ophelia will get in the way of trying to make things work with Janet. Also, at the moment you are heartbroken, and heartbreak's like an illness. It takes time. But believe me, Andrew. One day, you will be happy again. It may not be for some time, but there will come a day when happiness will surprise you. Whether or not you stay with Janet; whether or not you remain in the church. The human spirit – your human spirit – will find something to rejoice about, and you will know that you have turned a corner. That you are *alive* again.'

For the second time that day, Andrew found that tears were running down his cheeks, and he buried his face in his hands.

'Have hope, Andrew.' Father Matthew put his arm around Andrew's shoulders. 'It will be hard, but have hope. Thank God for Ophelia's love, and then let her go, as I believe you already have.'

'How will I bear it?' Andrew asked. 'How does anyone bear the pain of parting from someone whom they love so much?'

'You will bear it because you have to; because in a way you have never given yourself any other choice. And because it's the right thing to do. It's sometimes easier to live with this kind of pain than to live with the knowledge that you have paid for what you want with the happiness of others. Believe me. I know.'

'It's happened to you?'

'Oh yes. As I believe I mentioned. And I thought I should never get over it. But I did. I have never forgotten – one never does forget – but I have – healed.'

'May I see her again?' Andrew asked, after a moment.

'That's not up to me. But yes. I think you owe it to her to see her again and say goodbye. And I shall be here. If you need me.'

When Andrew got back to the vicarage, he

found it in a state of mild pandemonium.

'Oh, Vicar! Thank goodness you're home.' Josephine met him at the door. 'Janet's mother's been taken ill, the heating's broken down in the church, and that dratted kitten's gone missing.' Josephine felt much the same as Andrew did about the kitten, and made no attempt to disguise her feelings.

'Goodness.' Andrew hung up his coat. 'Where's Janet now?'

'She had to go. Her mother's in hospital in Birmingham. She tried to get hold of you, but your mobile was switched off. The heating engineers can't get here till next week. As for the kitten, it's probably been run over by now.'

'Josephine!'

'Well. Nasty little thing, with its snooty little face. You don't like it either, Vicar. You know you don't.'

'No, but I try.'

'I don't have to try,' Josephine said loftily. 'It's nothing to do with me.'

'Janet will be upset if anything happens to it,' Andrew said. 'She's become quite fond of it. And Josephine, please put that duster away.'

'What did you say?' Josephine was becoming forgetful, and often neglected to wear her hearing aid.

'The duster. Don't bother with that.'

'Your study's a disgrace. What will people think?'

'People will think what they've always thought. It's always been like this. Just sort out those agendas for next week, there's a dear.'

'I've done them.'

'Then do go home. Before it starts raining again.'

After Josephine had gone, Andrew sat on in his study for a long time. The phone rang several times, but he ignored it. The clock struck three and then four o'clock. Someone came to the door to ask about a wedding. Eventually, Janet rang him on his mobile to tell him her mother wasn't expected to live, and she would be staying on.

'Do you want me to come and join you?' Andrew asked. 'I could get away for twenty-four hours. If it would help.'

'No. I'll be fine.' Janet's voice sounded unsteady. 'You've got enough to do without this.'

'Well, keep me in touch, won't you?'

'Of course.'

Poor Janet, Andrew thought, as he went to make himself some tea. She was close to her mother, and would take her loss badly. Whatever had happened between himself and Janet, he cared about her, and hated the idea of her being alone and distressed in Birmingham. They were still a couple; she was still his wife. And if their marriage was a disappointment to him, it must be just as disappointing for her. We're both trapped, he thought; like Annie and Ernest. What was it Annie had said, when he last saw her? That she had been determined to survive. Whatever fate threw at her, Annie was going to survive it, and she had done just that.

But Annie was made of sterner stuff than he was, and Andrew wanted more than mere survival. If he couldn't be happy – and at the moment, happiness didn't appear to be an option – then perhaps the answer lay in change. A change of direction for his ministry, and perhaps even for his marriage. If he and Janet could involve themselves in a new parish with new demands and new challenges, they might at least become more of a team. Father Matthew had been right. They needed to talk, and he was the one who would have to instigate it. Andrew had never been particularly assertive. Perhaps now was the time to start.

There was a knock at the front door. Andrew went to answer it.

'I think this is yours.' A small boy was standing on the doorstep holding a very bedraggled-looking and not very white kitten.

'Thank you. Yes, it is.' Andrew fumbled in his pocket for some change. Whatever he might think of his pet, its safe return was certainly deserving of a reward.

The kitten seemed humbled by its experience (whatever that had been) and pathetically pleased with the saucer of milk Andrew offered it. Maybe it, too, was not beyond redemption.

Andrew must have dozed off in his chair, for the next thing he knew, it was dark outside and the clock was striking seven. He awoke to a feeling of doom, without fully remembering its cause, but within seconds the events of the day and of the previous night came back to him, and he was filled with a dull despair.

It was raining again, the bright drops caught in the lamplight as they splashed against the uncurtained window. The room had grown chilly, and Andrew shivered. He got up and went into the hallway for his coat and car-keys.

He had a visit to make.

CHAPTER FORTY-FIVE

Annie

The murmur of voices in the hallway continued for some time, and Annie wondered what she should do. She didn't like to go through to the living-room as that might disturb them, so she decided to stay where she was. She was glad that Ophelia had closed the kitchen door, for while a part of her longed to know what was going on, she disliked the idea of eavesdropping at a time like this.

She went to the sink and washed up the tea things, wondering what she should do with the cake, which was sitting reproachfully in its moat of sticky pink jam. She herself was quite hungry, for neither she nor Ophelia had eaten much supper, but to sit on her own in the kitchen eating cake while Ophelia and Andrew had their talk seemed heartless, so she put the cake in the larder and buttered herself a piece of bread instead. Bread was serious stuff. No one could be considered thoughtless for eating a piece of bread.

The hands of the electric clock jerked towards nine, and she turned on the radio to listen to the news. A blizzard was forecast, and someone famous had fallen off a cliff. Annie wasn't interested in the blizzard, since there was little she could do about it, and she'd never heard of the dead person. There seemed to be an awful lot of people she hadn't heard of these days. She sometimes read about them in magazines at the hairdresser's. They seemed to spend much of their time getting their noses and bosoms rearranged and having posh weddings and then getting divorced.

After what seemed an eternity, the kitchen door opened and Andrew and Ophelia came in. They both looked drained, and Ophelia had been crying again.

'Hello, Annie.' Andrew kissed her on the cheek. 'I'm so sorry to descend on you like this. Ophelia and I needed to talk.'

'Would you like me to go?' Annie asked, making to get up from her chair.

'No. No, of course not. But I'll sit down for a moment if I may.'

'Tea, anyone?' Ophelia took the kettle over to the sink.

'There's some wine in the cupboard,' Annie said, thinking that perhaps something stronger than tea might be helpful and recalling Ernest's secret cache. The whisky had of course long gone, but Annie had never cared much for wine.

'Wine?' Ophelia looked doubtful.

'Yes. It was your grandad's. I think he won it in a raffle.' Perhaps wine wasn't such a good idea after all.

'Oh, why not?' Andrew said. 'Thank you,

Annie. Wine would be very nice.'

Annie found the wine while Ophelia dusted three glasses. There didn't appear to be a corkscrew, but Annie remembered Ernest's Swiss army knife, which had all manner of exciting gadgets, so they used that.

It was a long time since the three of them had sat together round the kitchen table, and Annie thought with a pang that it might well be the last. She took a sip of her wine. It tasted sour, not nearly as nice as whisky, but the other two didn't seem to mind. For several minutes, nobody spoke. Ophelia looked dangerously near to tears again.

'I gather you two might be going abroad,' Andrew finally said. 'It sounds quite exciting.'

'To scatter Ernest,' Annie said. She looked down into her wine glass. Bits of cork were floating in it. They were uncomfortably reminiscent of the fragments of Ernest floating in her teacup. She fished them out with her finger.

'It's probably time,' Andrew said.

'That's what we thought.'

'When are you thinking of going?'

'As soon as possible,' Ophelia said.

'Are we?' Annie asked, surprised.

'It might be best,' Ophelia said, 'though I'm not sure about the weather. Austria in November doesn't sound very inviting.'

'Unless you ski,' Andrew said.

Annie had a brief, terrifying image of herself and Ophelia tearing down a snowy mountainside, with little clouds of Ernest billowing in their wake. 'Perhaps we should wait until spring,' she said. 'Your whatsits will probably be out in the spring.'

'Edelweiss and gentians,' Ophelia said forlornly.

'Yes, those.'

'But what shall I do until spring?' Tears began to spill down Ophelia's cheeks once more. 'Oh, what shall I do?'

'I'll look after you,' Annie said.

'Will you?'

'Of course I will. And you'll sell lots of those posh frocks and we'll have a nice Christmas.'

'Mum and Dad will expect me,' Ophelia said.

'Then we'll go together,' said Annie rashly. After all, Billy and Sheila could hardly expect her to spend a solitary Christmas in her newly-bereaved state.

'You don't know what you'd be letting yourself in for,' Ophelia said. 'Mum always gets in a state, and then there's an atmosphere. It's awful.'

Annie remembered both the state and the atmosphere from the last time she had spent Christmas with the family, but reckoned she could cope pretty well with both. Right now, she felt she could cope with anything if it would help Ophelia.

'I'd better be going,' Andrew said, getting to his feet.

'Oh!' Ophelia gave a little cry.

'I've got to go some time, sweetheart.' He put a hand on her shoulder. 'Better get it over with.'

'But – won't I see you again?'

'No. We agreed, didn't we? And I'd rather we parted here, with Annie to look after you.'

'But you'll be seeing Gran again, won't you? She needs you. It's not fair on her if you don't come back. And I could keep out of the way, couldn't I?'

'Could you?' Andrew asked.

Ophelia shook her head helplessly. 'I suppose not. But what *about* Gran?'

'I'm all right,' Annie said. 'I think I'll be all right now.'

'Are you sure? Are you quite sure?' Andrew asked.

'Yes. I'm sure,' Annie said, surprising herself.

For now she had a job to do. She had someone to look after; someone who loved and needed her; someone to whom she could make a real difference. For the first time in years, Annie had a purpose. She would see Ophelia through the weeks and months to come, and she would help to make her whole again. Of course, eventually, she would have to let her go, but she knew that from now on she would always play a part in the life of her granddaughter.

Long after Andrew had gone, Annie lay in bed unable to sleep for the thoughts tumbling around in her head. It was a cold, clear night, and a pale fuzz of moonlight glimmered through the thin material of the curtains, outlining the heavy oak wardrobe and dressing table. A car sped past, its tyres swishing in the puddles left by the last of the day's rain, and somewhere a dog barked.

Annie wondered whether she should get a dog. She'd always wanted one, but Ernest had been against the idea. A dog might be just the thing to cheer Ophelia up.

She heard Ophelia's bedroom door open, and there was a soft tap at her door.

'Can I come in, Gran?'

'Yes. Of course.'

Ophelia came in and sat down on the bed. 'You weren't asleep, were you?'

'No. I was just thinking, we could get a dog.'

'A *dog*?'

'Yes. Why not?'

'A dog would be rather nice,' Ophelia mused, pulling the corner of the eiderdown round her shoulders. 'I always wanted a dog, but Mum said it would leave hairs all over the place.'

'So did your grandad.'

'You're going to miss Andrew too, aren't you?' Ophelia said after a moment.

'Yes. Of course.'

'Did you – have you told him everything you wanted to tell him?'

'Almost,' Annie said. 'I think I've told him all I *needed* to tell him.'

For she had told him the worst; she had broken the seal of the pain and the secrecy of the past sixty years, and it was as though she had gradually drained her mind of the poison which had filled it for so long. That she hadn't actually brought her story up to date didn't seem to matter very much, for the years which followed Billy's infancy had been little different from the early years. Ernest had continued to be ill-tempered and abusive, and she had continued to fear him, but as she grew older she had become more resigned, and eventually she had ceased to hope for anything more. In fact it wasn't until

315

that first occasion when Andrew had asked her if she was happy that she had fully realised how miserable much of her life had been.

'Andrew told me about it,' Ophelia said now.

'Yes. You said.' Annie hoped Andrew had omitted some of the more intimate parts of her narrative.

'You had a pretty dreadful time, didn't you?'

'Yes and no,' Annie said carefully. 'I think I sort of got used to it. You can get used to most things if you have to.'

'Was Grandad very violent?'

'Yes. Sometimes. I suppose he got a bit mellower as he grew older, but he still used to hit me. He used to lash out with that walking stick of his.'

'Goodness!'

'I got quite good at dodging, though.'

They both laughed. It was good to hear Ophelia laugh again.

'What happened to your dreams?' Ophelia asked. 'Andrew said you had this dream world to escape into. Do you still – go there?'

'Not any more. Not since your grandad died. And the dreams were becoming vaguer; not so real. Just little bits of dreams really. And the little girl–'

'Amelia?'

'Yes. Amelia. She faded away over the years. I suppose I couldn't imagine her growing older, and I grew out of having a little girl.'

'Do you think Grandad was unhappy too?'

'I'm sure he was. But he got his promotion in the end, and he had his allotment and his committees. Your grandad loved committees. I think they made him feel important.'

Over the years, Ernest had been on so many committees that Annie had lost count. The allotment committee, the village hall committee, the bowls club committee (Annie suspected that Ernest had only taken up bowls because it offered the possibility of another committee for him to sit on) – the list had been various and at times astonishing. But she had never raised any objections because the more Ernest had to do, the less time he spent at home.

'Why did you stay with him, Gran?' Ophelia asked.

'I didn't have any choice. I had no money, and no way of earning any. And in those days people did stay together. They just got on with it. I wasn't the only one. And I had a child to bring up.'

'You and Dad aren't – close, are you?'

'Not really. I'm proud of him. Of course I am. He's done very well for himself.' That could hardly be denied, although privately Annie attached more importance to kindness and patience than she did to posh houses and shiny cars. 'He was very close to your grandad, but I think I've always irritated him. I expect I can be pretty annoying. Your grandad certainly thought so.'

'Dad finds me irritating too. I can't seem to please him, whatever I do.'

'Do you want to please him?'

'I used to. But I suppose I've got used to things the way they are.' Ophelia paused, winding a loose thread from the eiderdown round her finger. 'You and I – we're quite alike, aren't we, Gran?'

317

'Yes. I suppose we are. Sometimes I like to think that Amelia would have grown into a girl like you.'

'Do you really? I think that's one of the nicest things anyone's ever said to me.'

'Well, it's true.'

'Gran?' Ophelia said, after a pause.

'Yes?'

'Will I – will I get over this one day?'

'Yes. I think so.'

'But not yet.'

'No. Not quite yet.'

'I can't imagine never seeing him again.' Ophelia wiped her eyes on the hem of her night-dress, and pulled the eiderdown more closely round her. 'But we did do the right thing, didn't we, Gran? Andrew and I?'

'Yes. I think you did. The right thing and the brave thing.'

'Like you staying with Grandad.'

'I told you. I didn't have much choice. It's much braver if you have a choice.'

'I don't feel very brave.' There was a catch in Ophelia's voice, and Annie, who hadn't embraced anyone in years, sat up and took her grand-daughter in her arms and rocked her like a baby.

'You'll be all right, my love. You'll be all right. You've got me to look after you now.'

'And in the spring, we'll go to Austria and scatter Grandad?' Ophelia's voice was muffled by Annie's shoulder.

'In the spring, we'll go to Austria and scatter Ernest.'

To her surprise, Annie found that she was already looking forward to the spring.

CHAPTER FORTY-SIX

Andrew

It was typical funeral weather. A raw December day with penetrating drizzle and an angry little wind tugging at the coats and scarves of the mourners as they gathered at the graveside.

It was a long time since Andrew had attended a funeral at which he was not officiating, and he felt ill at ease, although he would hardly have been the right person to conduct the funeral service of his mother-in-law. He and she had had a civilised if chilly relationship, and while he had respected her for her undoubted courage in the face of what had been more than her fair share of adversity, he would have been hard pressed to find any of the heart-warming little anecdotes usually favoured on these occasions. As it was, this role had been admirably filled by a distinguished archdeacon, a friend of the family, who had taken a most fitting service and who had deviated from the truth just enough to make everyone feel comfortable about the life and death of the deceased.

The service had been traditional and, as befitted the widow of a bishop, suitably splendid and well-attended. Janet's sister had read a poem and Janet herself a passage from Corinthians, and a small grandson had sung a solo. Everyone

319

said it had been a beautiful service.

Now, chilled and shivering after the comparative warmth of the church, the family watched as the coffin was lowered into the grave. Janet, looking small and vulnerable in her red coat ('Mother disliked black'), stood beside Andrew, and although she made no sound, Andrew knew that she was crying. When the undertaker handed her a small clod of earth, she looked for a moment as though she wasn't sure what to do with it.

'Just throw it in,' Andrew whispered. 'Drop it onto the coffin.'

The earth landed with a soft thud, fragments of soil and tiny pebbles slithering over the polished lid of the coffin and obscuring the shiny brass plaque. Janet's sister added her own contribution, and a granddaughter threw a single stem of freesias as the wind whipped the final words of the burial service from the frozen lips of the archdeacon.

Gradually, the atmosphere was broken and people began to drift away from the graveside, no doubt with thoughts of a warm room and tea and perhaps a glass of wine. In the end, Janet and Andrew were left on their own.

'I'll miss her,' Janet said.

'I know you will.'

'She wasn't easy, I know she wasn't easy. But she was brave, and she was – she was my mother.'

'Of course.'

'I know you and she never really got on.'

'I had a lot of respect for her.'

'Did you really?'

'You know I did.'

Janet took her hand out of her pocket and seemed to hesitate, then she slid it into Andrew's. The hand felt small and cold, like a tiny frightened animal. It was a very long time since Andrew had held Janet's hand. He gave it a squeeze.

'Shall we go back, now? You're frozen.'

'Yes. Yes, we'd better go. People will wonder where we've got to.'

Back at the hotel, where a room had been booked for refreshments, people milled around holding glasses and teacups, suddenly cheerful and talkative, relieved that the serious business of the day was over. Someone lit a cigarette, attracting disapproving glances, and Andrew wondered whether there was ever an occasion too solemn for the self-righteous to manifest their displeasure. He himself had never been a smoker, but tended to take a tolerant stand where others were concerned.

'I think I'd like a cigarette,' Janet said. She hadn't smoked for years.

'Then you shall have one.' Andrew silently applauded her, and went in search of one. 'There,' he said, when he returned a moment later. He handed Janet the cigarette and a borrowed lighter. She nodded her thanks and lit the cigarette gratefully.

'I shan't make a habit of this,' she said. 'I just needed one today.'

'I understand.'

Andrew himself had managed to obtain a glass of quite respectable claret, and a sausage roll. He had never much liked sausage rolls, and wondered why they always seemed to play such an important part in these occasions, but it had been a long day and he was hungry. He might even have another.

They were booked into a bed and breakfast for the night so as to avoid the long journey home, and as soon as they decently could, they made their excuses and left.

'I'm afraid I couldn't get separate rooms,' Andrew said, as they pulled up in the driveway. A sign outside the house pronounced the accommodation to have NO VACANCIES. 'There's a conference or something, and everywhere else was booked up.'

'That's all right.'

'But we've got twin beds.'

Janet nodded. It was difficult to know what she was thinking. Andrew himself felt uneasy about their spending a night in the same room; after all, it had been a long time. He thought of the night he had spent with Ophelia – the last time he had slept in the same room with another person – and felt the familiar ache of her loss. It was now nearly three weeks since he had last seen her, and his thoughts and dreams were still haunted by her smile, her voice, her bare freckled arms, the smell of her hair. He wondered what she was doing; how she was coping. Ophelia was resilient. She would be all right eventually. One day, there would be another man who would love her as she deserved to be loved, and while the thought inevitably caused him pain, Andrew loved Ophelia well enough to hope that she would not have too long to wait.

'Here we are,' he said, as he carried their cases upstairs into their small but adequate bedroom. 'It seems all right.'

'It's fine,' Janet said.

'Which bed would you like?' Andrew asked, remembering Ophelia asking a similar question.

'I don't mind. You have the one by the window.' Janet sat down on the other bed and took off her shoes. 'Shall we have some tea?'

The room was equipped with a tray with cups and a kettle and an array of little packets: tea, coffee, hot chocolate. Convenient, if somewhat clinical. Andrew switched on the kettle.

'The service went well, didn't it?' Janet said.

'Very well. She would have been happy with it.'

'It makes me feel – older. Not having a mother any more.'

'Yes. I think a lot of people feel like that.'

'My turn next. An uncomfortable thought.'

'Yes. But not for some time, I hope.' Andrew handed Janet a cup of tea.

They sat in silence for a while.

'I nearly lost you, too, didn't I?' Janet said at last.

'What do you mean?'

'You know what I mean.' Janet sighed. 'There was someone else for a while, wasn't there?'

'Well–'

'You don't have to say anything. Just please don't lie to me, Andrew. I don't know who she is. Or was. I don't think I even want to know. I'm not blaming you. I'm not even angry. In fact, I'm not surprised it happened. I haven't really been

323

the wife you wanted. I suppose you were bound to fall for someone else sooner or later.'

'I don't know what to say.'

'There's nothing to say, is there? You fell for someone else, and I believe it's over. Thank you for – for not leaving me.' Her tone was flat, but underneath there was a bleakness which touched Andrew.

'I'm sorry,' he said. 'I never – never looked for anything like that. It, well, it–'

'Just happened?'

'I suppose so. That's such a cliché, isn't it, but yes. It just happened.'

'Did you sleep with her?'

Andrew hesitated.

'Please, Andrew. That's something I do want to know.'

'Then no. Not in the accepted sense. We did spend one night together, but nothing happened. You must believe me.'

'I do believe you.' Janet put down her teacup, and Andrew noticed that her hand was shaking. 'Why did you stay? Why didn't you leave me?' she asked.

'I'm not entirely sure,' Andrew said. 'You asked me to be honest, and that's the truth.'

'Was it the Church?'

'Partly the Church, yes. But you too.'

'Me too,' Janet repeated, turning her wedding ring round and round on her finger.

'Yes. You. We made promises, you and I.'

'A long time ago.'

'Certainly, a long time ago. But still, promises.'

'I've been wrong, too,' Janet said. 'I've

neglected you. I don't think I ever really knew how to be a wife. I thought it was all about working hard and getting on with things. That's what my mother always said. But there's more to it than that, isn't there?'

'I think there should be.'

'Do you think there's any hope for us?' Janet asked, after a moment.

'I don't know. If we start talking to each other, maybe. But we have to talk, Janet.'

'Yes.'

It occurred to Andrew that already they had talked more than they had in months; years, even. With no other distractions, it was possible for them to talk.

'Apart from anything else, I'm considering a move,' he continued. 'To another parish. I can't do that without talking to you; without your wanting it too.'

'Another parish. To get away from – her?'

'Partly, but also because I thought a new start might help us both. We've been where we are for too long. I've become too comfortable. A nice country parish, helpful parishioners, efficient lay-readers to assist with the workload.'

'And Josephine.'

'Yes. Josephine. But I suspect that most parishes have their quota of Josephines.'

'I hope she's not forgotten the kitten.' Josephine had been left on kitten-duty during their absence.

'Josephine won't forget the kitten,' Andrew re-assured her. 'She may not be fond of him, but she's very conscientious.'

'It's true that I was jealous of Tobias, you know,' Janet said. 'Poor Tobias. I really hated him.'

'You needn't have. He was pretty harmless. You might even have liked him if you'd got to know him.'

'Possibly. But he seemed to be able to reach you in a way I couldn't.'

'Did you try?'

'I suppose not. I don't think I knew how to begin.'

'Perhaps we should both start trying to reach each other. Before it really is too late.'

Later on, after they had taken it in turns to wash and undress in the bathroom and had finally switched off the light, Andrew lay awake for some time. He wondered whether Janet was asleep. He could hear the sound of her breathing and the occasional rustle of the bedclothes, but didn't like to risk disturbing her by speaking. Besides, conversations in the dark were somehow more intimate than those conducted in daylight, and he suspected that neither of them was ready for that yet.

He tried to analyse how he was feeling. Tired, certainly. It had been a long day. Sad, of course. The grief which had become a part of him over the past weeks had to run its course, and he knew that would take time. How long, he wondered? For how long must he be haunted by the swirl of a gypsy skirt, a husky laugh, the warmth of a soft body pressed against his own? He had always known there would be a price to pay; he suspected that he had only just embarked on the first instalments of that debt.

But he also felt an unexpected sense of peace. After a period when he had felt spiritually barren, when prayer had seemed impossible and his God so distant, Andrew found himself able to pray once more. Now, when he stood at the altar of his own church, he was able to face the God upon whom he had turned his back all those months ago, and find a degree of tranquillity and perhaps of forgiveness. Maybe Father Matthew had been right, and Andrew had underestimated God.

Yet apart from the hurt caused to Janet, he had no regrets. How could he, when he and Ophelia had given each other so much? And perhaps the intensity of his feelings had been due in part to the fact that they had both known and accepted that the relationship couldn't last. All the passion and the joy had been concentrated into the short time they had together, making it all the more precious for that, and all the more painful in its ending.

There had been moments when Andrew had wondered whether perhaps he and Ophelia might have had a future together after all, but now he knew with absolute certainty that this could never have been the answer. It wouldn't have been right for Ophelia, it would have caused incalculable hurt to Janet, and besides, if he had caused his marriage to founder without any proper attempt to salvage it, he would never have been able to live with himself. In the end, it is being able to live with yourself that counts. For if you cannot live with yourself, with whom can you live?

As a nearby church clock struck two, Andrew's

last waking thoughts were of Ernest. Ernest, whom he had never known in life, had been the cause of his meeting Annie, and through her, Ophelia. Ernest had indirectly made a considerable impact on his life; an impact which might well change his life's direction as well as its substance. On balance, Andrew felt that he had cause to be grateful to Ernest.

Ernest. Dead Ernest. Andrew smiled to himself.

The clock struck the half hour, but Andrew was asleep.

CHAPTER FORTY-SEVEN

April 2005

'It seems such a funny place to have your photo taken, Woolworths. I hope no one sees me.'

'No one will see you, Gran.'

'That's all right, then. What do I do now?'

'Well, you draw the curtain, put your money in and sit down on that little stool, and when the light's on, you know it's about to take your picture, and then there's a flash–'

'Oh, I could never remember all that.'

'Of course you can, Gran. It's perfectly simple.'

'Can't you come in here with me?'

'No. Because then there'd be a picture of both of us. This is your passport, so it has to be a photo of you.'

328

'Do they want me to smile? I've never been much good at smiling. Not to order.'

'You don't have to smile. Just look straight ahead.'

'My hair's a bit messy. D'you think I should have had it done first?'

'No one's bothered about your hair, Gran. So long as it's you. That's all that matters.'

'I never did take a good photo. Your grandad said–'

'Just put your money in and sit down. Don't worry, Gran. You'll be fine. I'll be right outside waiting for you.'

'That suitcase looks as though it's about to fall to bits, Gran. When did it last see the light of day?'

'Oh, years ago. We didn't do a lot of travelling, your grandad and me.'

'I think you'll have to get a new one.'

'Won't that be very expensive?'

'Not necessarily. And you said you wanted to fritter Grandad's money, so why not fritter it on a decent suitcase?'

'I always fancied leather. Posh matching luggage, in leather.'

'Matching luggage in leather sounds great. A big suitcase, and a little one for your hand luggage.'

'Hand luggage?'

'Things you might need on the plane. Something to read perhaps, a spare cardigan in case it's chilly when we land. That sort of thing.'

'We could pop in a little bottle of whisky, couldn't we? To keep out the cold. I've always thought it must be very cold up there.'

'The plane will be heated, Gran. And they sell drinks, anyway.'

'Do they really?'

'They certainly do.'

'I think I'm quite looking forward to the aeroplane after all.'

'Good for you, Gran. So am I.'

'I'm not sure about this, Ophelia. I think I'd like to get out. It doesn't feel safe.'

'Too late to change your mind now, Gran. We're about to take off.'

'How does it stay up? I've always wondered how they stay up. All these people; all this luggage. It doesn't seem natural.'

'Something to do with lift and thrust, I think. I'm not sure what that means, though.'

'Lift and thrust! Fancy!'

'We're moving now, Gran. Isn't it exciting? Gran? *Gran?* What's the matter?'

'I was holding my breath.'

'Whatever for?'

'I don't know. I think I was helping the plane get off the ground. Sounds silly, doesn't it?'

'No. I understand. I used to do that when I started flying. Look! We're up and away! Can you see all those houses and cars? Don't they look tiny?'

'I daren't look.'

'Open your eyes, Gran. Come on. You might even enjoy it.'

'Oh yes! Gracious, these windows are grubby. Someone ought to give them a good clean.'

'Ophelia?'

'Yes?'

'That wing's moving. Do you think we ought to tell someone?'

'No. They do that sometimes. It'll be fine.'

'Are you sure?'

'Quite sure.'

'How does the pilot know how to get there? It's all cloudy up here. Supposing he gets lost?'

'He won't get lost, Gran. He's done it lots of times before. And he's got instruments and things to help him.'

'It's all very clever, isn't it?'

'Yes, it is.'

'I suppose they know what they're doing. Your grandad wouldn't have liked it, though. He was a bit of a backseat driver, your grandad. He'd have been up there telling them what to do.'

'Then it's probably a good thing that he stayed in England.'

'That lifejacket thing they showed us.'

'Yes?'

'I can't remember what you're supposed to do with it. All I can remember is the bit about the whistle to attract attention. I think I could manage the whistle. But I'll need the jacket. I can't swim, you know.'

'Don't worry, Gran. If it comes to it – and it's extremely unlikely – I'll help you.'

'That's kind of you, love.'

'Don't mention it.'

'Ooh, look, Ophelia! People are having drinks.

Shall we have a whisky?'

'Let's have champagne! After all, this is a special occasion.'

'Champagne! Fancy! And such dear little bottles. Can we take them home with us?'

'Of course we can. Cheers!'

'Cheers! I haven't had champagne for years. Isn't it funny how the bubbles all go up your nose? Do you know, I think your grandad might have enjoyed this after all.'

'Well, he is on the plane.'

'So he is. I'd completely forgotten.'

'He's why we're here, remember?'

'Of course. And we never toasted him. D'you think we ought to have another?'

Annie settles into the corner of her seat, drowsy with champagne, thoughts drifting through her head like the clouds outside the window. There are suitcases and aeroplanes, Ernest and Ophelia, Billy's latest shiny car and a small rescued dog (hers? Ophelia's?). The clouds themselves take on different shapes and hues; the bearded face of a man, which lengthens and dissolves as she watches it, a lopsided castle, a bird, a pink-tinged fluffy pillow. In the distance, a tiny aeroplane catches the sun like a sliver of silver, and above, the sky is a light clear blue.

As Annie's eyes begin to close, part of the shifting cloudscape seems to form itself into a human shape, and she imagines that she can make out the figure of a little girl; a little girl in a gingham dress, her bright hair caught in two pigtails, who turns her head to smile at Annie.

Annie makes as though to reach towards the child but the little girl shakes her head, laughing and blowing Annie a kiss. Not now, she seems to say. Not any more. That was all a long time ago. A long, long time ago.

Gradually, the figure begins to fade, until she is barely an outline; an outline of a little girl moving away, looking back over her shoulder, her hand raised in a gesture of farewell, before she melts away once more into the dissolving clouds.

Annie smiles and her head falls forward, and she sleeps.

Epilogue

Austria,
May 22nd

Dear Billy,

Everything in Austria is very clean, and the mountains are nice, but they don't know how to make tea. There don't seem to be any teapots in Austria. They don't have proper bedclothes, either, but I am getting used to one of those quilt things. The room is cleaned every day, and the food is interesting. The cows have bells round their necks, which make a pretty sound but must be very distracting for the cows. Ophelia says they're probably used to it. There's something delicious called gluwein, and we drink it every evening to keep out the cold.

Today, we scattered your father. First, we lit candles in a church with lots of curly cherubs on the ceiling. I don't think Ernest would have liked the cherubs very much, as he didn't hold with Catholics, but Ophelia thought it would be a good idea. She said it would make it more of an occasion.

There are lots of wildflowers, but we found a little patch of grass where there weren't any (because of Ernest's hay fever) with a nice view of the mountains, and we scattered him there. Scattering is a lot harder than you would think, as nothing lands quite where you want it to, but we did our best.

It feels funny not to have Ernest around any more, but I think it was time we let him out of his jar. Ophelia said that now that I'm free, it's only right that Ernest should be free, too, and she's probably right. That may sound odd to you, Billy, but I think you know that your dad and I didn't make each other very happy. Ophelia understands, and I hope you will one day, too.

We might come here again next year, but Ophelia quite fancies Egypt. She wants to learn to dive in the Red Sea. It doesn't sound very safe to me. I'm quite glad I can't swim.

Love from Mum

PS. Ophelia sends her love and says to tell you she's well and happy.
PPS. I think I am happy too.

This Large Print Book for the partially sighted, who cannot read normal print, is published under the auspices of

THE ULVERSCROFT FOUNDATION

THE ULVERSCROFT FOUNDATION

... we hope that you have enjoyed this Large Print Book. Please think for a moment about those people who have worse eyesight problems than you ... and are unable to even read or enjoy Large Print, without great difficulty.

You can help them by sending a donation, large or small to:

**The Ulverscroft Foundation,
1, The Green, Bradgate Road,
Anstey, Leicestershire, LE7 7FU,
England.**
or request a copy of our brochure for more details.

The Foundation will use all your help to assist those people who are handicapped by various sight problems and need special attention.

Thank you very much for your help.